IN TUJUNGA

GEORGE COMBE

Cover design by Danielle Stamper

Full Moon Publishing, LLC
Glade Spring, VA
Fullmoonpublishingllc.com

ISBN: 1946232033
ISBN-13: 978-1946232038

DEDICATION

For Mario Scala, Michael Vatovek and Demetrius Maroosis:
Outlaws to the Bone.

CONTENTS

CHAPTER ONE

Did my best to exhibit no surprise or concern when ordered out of morning chow at the medium security work camp in South Georgia referred to by the cognoscenti as the Valdosta Chain Gang. Kept my mouth shut and tried to appear indifferent as trustees began processing me for release. I expected they would realize their administrative blunder soon enough, but didn't intend to be the one to disturb their slumber.

A couple hours of paperwork, waiting, photo checks, waiting and print scans carried me through two remote controlled gates, leaving one set of yellow painted steel bars between my body and the free world.

Had begun considering ways to place the most real estate between myself and Valdosta before the hue and cry went up, when the deputy warden burst upon the scene, bearing down on me with clamped lips.

I struggled to retain an expression of remote disinterest, while inmate/clerks scrambled out of his path and hope died.

He was a natural clothes horse, whose movie star good looks conveyed no cautionary tell of the savage satisfactions he enjoyed as the warden's hatchet man, a legend within the state's penal system, due to the amount of permanent injury he could inflict on a prisoner without killing him, through virtuoso application of a leather and lead sap carried in his hip pocket.

He stalked to within a couple feet and paused to display his lofty disdain. I kept an eye on his hands, resolved to crush his larynx and damn the consequences if he reached for the sap. Nobody moved or spoke while he glared at me. After several lifetimes, he snorted, shoved a heavy manila envelope into my trembling hands, and turned on his heel, signaling the hack in the security cage to open freedom's gate as he swept away.

Walking outside in a daze, I stopped to look around, half expecting the nearest gun tower to start chucking lead. But the Ray-Banned sharp shooter fired only a grin and thumbs up, then turned his attention back to the work gangs lined up in the sally port.

A Department of Corrections station wagon entered the parking lot, the elderly black trustee behind the wheel waved. I nodded and walked over, the bulky manila in one hand, a giant clear zipper bag in the other, containing clothing and personal items I'd been relieved of on my arrival and a check for the twenty- four hundred dollars I had on the books. The trustee reached over the seat back and shoved the passenger side rear door open. I grunted thanks and got in.

Ripped open the manila envelope, and tipped out a bulky FedEx package addressed to me care of the warden, and a smaller buff envelope holding a single page parchment. It reeked of authority and instructed the warden to attend to my release from custody forthwith.

The FedEx package contained a handwritten note from The Law Offices of Levy and Fleece, explaining my early release had been arranged because my presence was required in Los Angeles. Anticipating I might have unfinished business in Atlanta, as well as property to ship or dispose of, travel arrangements were left to my discretion..

The enclosed cash should cover travel, lodging and ancillary expenses. The note's author looked forward to seeing me in his office at 10:00 am, one week hence, and signed himself, S. M. Levy. A business size envelope contained ten thousand dollars, in hundreds.

I've no love for lawyers, but admired S.M. Levy's style, and hoped it would keep me on my toes when we met.

The station wagon pulled to the curb at the Valdosta

Greyhound terminal, and the old trustee, who'd driven in silence, turned to me, "You about a lucky motherfucker, Hollywood."

"Better to be lucky than smart, Nathan," I said, and gave him a hundred.

"God's troof," Nate said, tucking the bill in his shirt. "An' I done got fucked outa bofe."

Time and temperature display on a bank building down the street said it was 8:55 and 88 degrees, didn't mention the 90 percent humidity. I took off the jacket of the cheap suit, donned as part of the release process, and buttoned the luggage-size transparent Ziploc holding my possessions into it, tying the sleeves together so I could sling it over a shoulder, and started walking back the direction I'd come, half a mile to a motorcycle dealership spotted on the drive in.

Business hours on the showroom door were 10:00 to 8:00. Went around to an alley behind the building, looking for shade. A detached garage sat at right angles to the main building, the first of its three roll up doors raised about four feet. I ducked under and stepped inside, eyes adapting to the interior light. A lanky youngster with abundant blond hair and a wispy Fu-Manchu mustache perched on the edge of a three legged stool next to an old 900F Honda, up on center stand before him with its innards exposed. I took a step closer and saw he was inserting a shim into one of the valves and had a 1% tattoo on his shoulder. I stayed silent. He finished what he was doing and threw an eyeball in my direction.

"He'p you?"

"Need some transpo."

"Sales people be here at ten."

"Holding any good used stuff?"

He rubbed his chin. "Got a six year old Sportster, about a grand overpriced, and an old Pan head with an oil leak. It's a goner."

"What about Jap crap?" He frowned. I spread my hands. "At the moment, I can't afford to be proud."

He grinned at that, nodded, "Been there. They took in a 900 Shadow you might like, and a couple low-mileage V-Maxes. Pair of sissies owned em', washed and waxed them on Saturdays, rode them through town real slow, and put them back in the garage." He told me the asking prices.

"Firm, or can I beat them down some?" .

"Depends," he said, "cough up a big down payment..."

"I'll pay cash."

He looked thoughtful. "President of my chapter's got a big Suzuki he's looking to unload, C90, 1400cc, pretty cherry. I believe he'd come about five hundred under one of those V-Maxes. Might could call him, if you're interested."

"I'm interested."

He got up and dragged his boot heels over to a pay phone on the rear wall, scuffed back a couple minutes later, reclaimed the stool and picked up a twelve millimeter combination wrench.

"Store owner catches me sending business out the door, he tells his daughter, she bitches at me and tightens up on the puss." I nodded. "My man will meet you at the Waffle House, couple blocks down, on the other side of the street, about a half hour."

"Good enough," I said. "We make a deal, I'll leave half a yard for you with him."

"Preciate it."

`Stabbing hunks of sausage patty and using them to wipe up the remains of a strawberry and whipped cream waffle, I watched a black and chrome Harley inspired Suzuki roll into the parking lot. The rider stopped over by the public phones and let the bike rest on its side stand. I gulped my coffee, picked up most of the change from a hundred and went outside.

President of the local one-percenters was in uniform, Levis had never been inside a washing machine, engineer boots, black leather vest unbuttoned and held open by a cannonball belly. Hair thick, going gray, tied with a piece of rawhide in back.

He stepped off the C90, hanging a yarmulke size helmet on the mirror.

"I used to see you on my way to work, on that gang draining Murphy's swamp, thought you were about my size, but up close you're a big fucker."

"Yeah, I'm out of proportion or something. You the Moto Guzzi?"

"That's me. Good eye." He stuck out his hand. "Outlaw, Gypsy."

I stuck out mine. "Good ear, you mean. Diablo, Mark."

4

"Meetcha."

"So," I said, "what's the skinny on this rice burner?"

Two hours later, in Florida, I traveled West on Interstate10 at a velocity that would have got me pulled over in half a tick had the bike been wearing tags from some Yankee state.

Pausing for my ritual swim in the Colorado River two and a half days later, I splashed around near the East bank long enough to wash the rest of the country off my hide, and felt confident I'd blasted the preponderance of jailhouse fragrance off my soul, on the night ride from El Paso to Tucson, across the badlands at speeds in excess of a hundred miles an hour.

Crossing into California with no urge to plunge at once into the L.A. cauldron, I made a three day rest stop at a sprawling motor lodge not far from the state line.

Did a little work on my tan (very little), which prison jumpsuits arrested at neck and elbow. Adhered to a regimen of thick t-bones and Wild Turkey 101.

My eighteen month wall of celibacy fell (again and again) under the onslaughts of a blond, barely legal, wide-eyed chubette, who delivered clean towels to my room with relentless frequency.

Arrived in Los Angeles nine hours before my appointment at Levy and Fleece, checking into a Van Nuys motel named for a conquistador, operated by a Mandarin, and illuminated with neon enticements in English and Spanish: Weekly Rates, Closed Circuit Adult TV(we have the grossest), Air Conditioned.

The Oriental proprietor came out to the office at the ring of a bell, sleep stunned, in a green and gold silk dragon robe, Glock 17 tucked behind the belt . I passed the weekly rate and key deposit through a curved slot, and a few minutes later swiped the card reader to a refurbished detached bungalow, last in a row of six, facing a standard two-story motel California across the pepper tree shaded double drive.

A narrow kitchen ran the length of the rear wall, an oak butcher block table and matching chairs flanked the archway to the bed/sitting room. The other end of the kitchen held the unit's water heater, earthquake strapped next to a door to the alley running behind the property. I covered the linoleum inside the kitchen door with a thick layer of L.A. Weakly from the dumpster, and parked the C90 on it. Three minutes later, naked except for my money belt, I tucked the queen size top sheet under one arm, told myself to wake at seven, and slept.

CHAPTER TWO

Elevator doors sighed open, and I strode across a short marble foyer onto a vast carpeted expanse, reception area to the Law Offices of Levy and Fleece.

My mother did a double take in my direction and dropped her tea. The white haired man in butler's livery, tipping a silver tea service over her cup, took a step back as the china bounced quietly on ankle deep wool. He drifted his handkerchief onto the spilled liquid and patted it with his shoe. Mom glided across a small fortune of prime commercial square footage into my arms.

I patted her back a little awkwardly. "I guess you didn't expect to see me here, hey Mom?"

"I should say not! How on Earth?" Her hand fell on my arm like a talon." Mark, you didn't!"

"I should say not! The very idea!"

Mom's lips disappeared. "Mark, I swear by Jesus Christ!"

Unable to maintain a poker face, I took out my wallet and showed her The Document. Mom's in laws, my fraternal relations pressed around us, trying to read over her shoulder. Mom scanned the parchment, handed it to my cousin, Glen, breathing down her neck, then looked up at me with a smile of relief. "You are such a turd."

I protested. "I was just as surprised to see you, but I didn't have anything to drop. Besides, I was going to head out to your place as soon as I finished here."

Mom looked mollified, but before she could respond Glen said in a loud, aggrieved voice, "Oh, give me a break!" He took a couple steps in my direction, the little cluster of relatives drifted apart. Glen shook the parchment in my face. "Are you trying to tell us you got a pardon?"

I took the parchment out of his hand and folded it back into my wallet, then looked at him. Glen has red hair and green eyes, but otherwise bears a strong physical likeness to actor, Paul

7

Newman, when he was in his forties. But the resemblance ends at the skin. Glen is dumber than a Texas Republican, but enjoys nice income from his father's multi-office real estate business, splitting listings his old man hands him with reluctant but resigned sales agents. "You still here?" I said.

"You expect us to believe that thing's real? You put it away fast enough."

I resisted the urge to grab him by the neck and slap him around a little. "It's what they gave me when they booted me off the work camp," I said. "But, for all I know, it could be phony as the Rolex you're wearing, not that I give a shit, at this point."

"Levy set it up," said Glen, as if by revelation, "that slimy toad."

Glen's mother, my Aunt June, stood near her elder brother (my father), framed by tinted glass, with the Santa Susanna Mountains showing faintly through the smog. June came over and led Glen a few paces away, speaking to him in muted tones. I looked at my father, trim and erect as when he'd flown bomber escort across much of the Pacific, over half a century before. He gave me a big smile of greeting, but to my astonished glance at Aunt June replied with a slight out turning of his palms, the physical equivalent of "beats me".

My father was bearing up well to the ravages of time, good genes, but also an ongoing act of will, he wasn't giving an inch. But Aunt June, the baby of her generation, eight years senior to me, the eldest of mine, looked better now than when she'd performed overtime duty in my pubescent romantic fantasies. She looked, not young, but so present and in sync with all her parts, through some strange alchemy, observing her in conversation with her retarded middle-aged son convinced me, despite a lifetime of evidence to the contrary, that older was better, finer, sexier. For the first time in twenty years I wished I was older.

"Quit staring at my little sister, you perv." Aunt May.

Turned to find her and Uncle Max grinning at me. "Don't be jealous, baby," I said. "You know I'm crazy about you."

She gave a hug, and said, "It's a good life if you don't weaken, Marky, and you're not weakening, that's for sure. So put the business of turning big rocks into little rocks right behind you."

"It was forest into meadow," I said, "and swamp into dry

ground. But I take your point. Anyway, it was an eye opening experience, and one I needed, because I was in a coma, or those fat-assed Gomers would have never got the drop on me. Speaking of which, where's Al? I figured he was behind it when they kicked me out of that dump. Now he has to put up with my slobbery gratitude."

May's husband, Max, looks like the studio budget department accountant he was prior to writing, producing and directing a ground breaking trio of horror films, in the nineteen seventies. They've recouped many times their negative costs every year since. He froze, hand half extended toward mine. The grin on his face stopped crinkling his eyes behind the horn rimmed glasses, then evaporated altogether.

My left ear heard Glen, "Damn it, Mother, can't you see what Levy's up to? He'll use that goddamn dope peddler to screw us all."

Aunt May, who'd been turning toward Max, froze with him, then swiveled just her head back at me. She mouthed the words. "You don't know?"

Realization hit, like a kick in the crotch. "Aw, hell, Max, Al's dead?"

Max nodded, and looked glum. "I'm sorry, Mark. We assumed you knew."

"When?"

"A week ago. Died in his sleep, Autopsy report says a blood clot lodged in his brain, disrupted the automatic nervous system. Heart stopped beating, lungs stopped breathing."

"I didn't figure he'd stick around too long after Aunt Ruth died." I said. "Especially with Leni jumping ship."

"And yet," said Max, "fear of losing him, too, may have propelled her into the arms of that crazy cult "

"I hear, they have too much money to be called crazy," I said.

"Eccentric, then," amended Max. "but I won't dignify them with the label church."

"Why? They short of pedophiles?"

"Oh, Mark, you're brutal!"

"Brutish, Max," I said, "there's a difference."

I'd been shooting glances around the room, taking inventory. Several seating groups were scattered across the carpeted sprawl, like oases on a gray plain, each loosely enfolded by broad leafed semi-tropical trees and bushes, spilling out of waist high ceramic vessels, and separated from its neighbors by enough top dollar commercial space to assure privacy.

It was a reception area conceived in the awareness that legal problems often go hand in hand with financial difficulties. Any prospective client of that stripe, brash enough to ride the private, high speed express elevator to Levy and Fleece's roof top suite, would shortly experience a sincere desire to ride back down in that glass walled conveyance, and catch one of the dozen pokey buffed aluminum-walled elevators to one of the TV law firms, with the rest of the great unwashed.

Uncle Bill, Glen's father, was at one of the seating groups, perched on a scantly upholstered straight back priced in the range of an economy car. He had his laptop and cell phone on a polished redwood burl, while he spoke over the available land line. An attractive youngish woman in a Westside power suit stood behind him, massaging his shoulders. A recent addition to the sales staff, I mused, unaware she's about a minute away from Aunt June ripping her lungs out. Then she looked at me. It was my cousin, Phoebe, daughter of Bill and June, sister of Numbnuts, but a distant relation to the green haired, army booted punk rocker Phoebe I'd last seen a decade before. I sent her a wink and a grin. She returned the wink and a lip curl Billy Idol would have envied..

Phoebe and Leni had been road dogs since their births, seven days apart. I was about to excuse myself from May and Max, to get the lowdown from Phoebe, when a drop dead gorgeous young woman walked into our midst and announced that Mr. Levy would see us now.

I followed along behind May and Max, down a hallway ending at imposing double doors. For the first time in years I found myself wondering just how big Al's money pile really was.

Family scuttlebutt regarding Al's deep pockets had always been respectfully vague. From the time I was old enough to know what money was I was given to understand that Al had a bunch of it, though he displayed none of the usual trappings of wealth. He and Aunt Ruth raised Leni in a slightly less prestigious housing development than the one we lived in, a few blocks away. Leni attended the same public schools my sisters and I went to, and was accorded the same deference and respect they enjoyed, sustained not by Al's bankroll but by common knowledge that to mess with them was to mess with me. She never cliqued with the Little Rich Girls, daughters of local land developers, currently popular media personalities and conscienceless medical men, and would have been perhaps more astonished than the snobettes to discover her daddy owned their daddies, or at least the corporate entities they served. Their daddies appeared to inhabit a completely different economic strata from Leni's dad, tooling around the Westside in their new Caddies, Lincolns and Mercedes, on shopping forays, then back to The Valley (South of Ventura) with the plunder. Leni's dad drove Buick Electras that looked like they'd never been washed (they hadn't), was rumored to have gone as long as two years between new car purchases, seldom went near the Westside.

During nickel ante poker games, held (in those pre-mosquito days) Friday nights in the gazebo beside our pool, Al employed a time consuming squeeze in spreading his cards for a peek after the draw, often prompting Aunt May to unleash a flurry of tiny, high velocity smoke rings in his direction, followed by, "Let's go, moneybags. You think long, you think wrong. It's fifteen cents to you. What you gonna do, sucker?"

During one holiday season, while still in feet pajamas, I saw achingly beautiful Aunt June (at 14) greet the long overdue arrival of my father (then pilot with Flying Tiger Airlines) and Al, with, "Well, well, well, if it isn't Captain Bonaroo and Mister Long Green. And where have we been?"

Such comments were all I had to support my unspoken belief that Al had more money than anybody else I knew, personally, until I strolled out of embrace of the State of Georgia Department of Corrections eight and a half years sooner than the judge intended, and despite my captors' extreme reluctance to see me go.

I had no notion what those eight and a half years cost. And a pardon? Not only was I free, I had no criminal record, no parole officer. A million? Two million? I would have paid in a heartbeat, if I'd had it. But I expected pardons, if they could be bought or traded for, demanded currency more potent than money. (Like, if you could offer somebody the presidency of the United States, you might be able to swing one.) Maybe Al had been pursuing my release for the entire time I was confined, and hadn't

11

communicated about it to spare me should he fail? Given the eerie juxtaposition of his death and my release, freeing me may have been his final move in life, and cost him plenty of something more weighty than money. I was finding his motivation a little harder to envision, while becoming more confident every minute it wasn't the prospect of my slobbery gratitude.

The edible looking female who guided us to Levy's office, held open one of the massive doors for us to enter, and spoke softly to each one entering. When May and Max went in just before me, I saw she was offering condolences. She began the same with me, but caught herself, and said, "I suppose congratulations would me more appropriate for you, Mister Brown."

"Don't start with the Misters," I said. "You can call me Honey." She looked at the floor, and I'd have let her twist, if she hadn't been blushing almost purple. I tossed her an ego preserver. "Or don't call me."

She betrayed the hint of a smile when she raised her eyes back to mine, and murmured, "I wouldn't dream of it, except at Mr. Levy's behest."

I walked into an office the size of a nine-hole golf course, and heard Glen quacking behind my ear. "Suave. Yes sir, very suave, indeed."

"Eat shit and die, dick face," I mumbled over my shoulder, and began my trek to the converging corner windows, where S. M. Levy sat at one end of a twelve-foot oval of transparent green glass.

Before I laid eyes on him it never crossed my mind that this lawyer, S. M. Levy, might be The Sid Levy, but he was.

Levy and I were contemporaries. He was a nationally recognized student activist and anti-war protester during the period I was the youngest E-7 in the United States Marine Corps. He had burned draft cards. I'd burned thatch villages and slaughtered the fleeing inhabitants. It sounds monstrous in retrospect, but I recall growing indignant when I heard about those draft cards.

He had a distinctive profile, recognizable because for three years it was everywhere, magazines, posters, TV news, like a rock star, but better. Half his groupies were rock stars.

When the war he'd fought to end ended, Levy's fifteen minutes was up. From the look of things he'd grown up and sold out, and not cheaply. His shoulder length hair, falling in heavy ringlets and driving female protest singers mad with desire, was gone along with the lean hungry look. The curls were short and tight now, trimmed close to the head, thinning at the crown. He sat very erect in a wrought iron and leather director's chair, Brooks Brothers clad, eyes framed by oval spectacles in fine gold rims.

I sat across from him, at the end of the emerald colored slab. He smiled a greeting in my direction, and stood to take Aunt June's hand as she settled into the director's chair at his left, then shook hands with Uncle Bill as he pulled the next one out.

When everyone was seated, Levy thanked us for coming, and said, "All of you here today are beneficiaries of Albert's will, with one exception," he nodded in my direction. Glen smirked, my mother gave me a sympathetic smile. "The two nieces who were unable to attend (my sisters) are also beneficiaries. Aside from the provisions of Albert's will, his estate reposes in a series of interlocking trusts under the proprietorship of the Albert Brown Family Trust. The trust will cover any tax liabilities applying to the bequests. These parting gifts were something Albert gave considerable thought, and he wished to present them personally. I'll let him take it from here."

Levy picked up a remote control unit off the table, and pointed it at a free standing partition separating the conference area from his office proper. Al appeared there, larger than life, in living color.

Aunt May gasped, muttered, "Jesus H. Christ, Albert," and lit a Camel. After that, except for Al's voice, there was silence.

CHAPTER THREE

It was past six when I crossed the reception area to the marbled vestibule, where the elevator stood open. The butler was at a seating group nearest the elaborate food trolley he presided over, tie undone, cocktail and a pack of Players at hand, on a cube of polished black marble serving as an end table. He brought a cigarette to his lips, leaving it to smolder while he turned a page of the racing form, then glanced up at my approach. "A very good evening to you, Mr. Brown."

"Thanks," I said. "And thanks for the sandwiches, best Ruebens I ever had."

"Very kind of you to say so, sir."

Levy's delectable assistant entered the elevator's foyer from a door serving the inner offices, and stepped into the open lift. She flipped through some papers in her hand, and wasn't cognizant of my approach until my boot heels hit the marble. She looked up from the papers, gasped and stabbed at the control panel with a perfectly manicured finger, then gave me a killer smile and licked her lips as the doors came together six inches in front of my outstretched hand.

"Mr. Brown." I looked back at the butler's smiling face. "A fellow could hurt himself on that."

"I'd sure like to try," I said, and took the fire stairs down one flight to the public elevators, thinking, you dog, she wants you bad.

When the doors spread open at the first basement parking level, I found myself confronting the mainly Mexican cleaning crew and their equipment, they parted in deference to my unsavory appearance, then swarmed into the elevator in my wake.

I retrieved the C90 from the area reserved for motorcycles, behind the attendant's kiosk. With three thousand miles of road grime, it looked out of place among the gleaming, low-mileage BMWs and HDs. A turbaned attendant took my validated parking stub and I shot up the ramp to an alley, down to Ventura Boulevard, where I darted into heavy Southbound traffic and cut a weaving swath through it at velocities some people might find alarming, especially those interested in surviving a motorcycle accident.

Giving control of the machine to my automatic self, I pondered the strange quality of my perceptions, beginning, near as I could figure, about the time I passed the Capitol Records building, speeding up the 101, upon my arrival.

During fifteen years I lived away from Los Angeles (four in Milwaukee, six in Boston, three and a half in Atlanta, one and a half at Valdosta), I had plenty of occasions to return on business or family matters. I came to regard those visits as necessary evils. So far as purposes of the trips were concerned I'd no cause for complaint, invariably got what I came for, frequently a good deal more. But being in Los Angeles was irritating in the extreme. Having grown up in its environs, I found few familiar features, though nothing changed all that much. The hustle and bustle of its freeway rhythms seemed bleak as a lunar landscape. Spent most of my time anxious to finish what I'd come for, so I could go home.

This time I'd arrived with no date of departure, no place to return, or thought of leaving anytime soon.

Los Angeles became real to me, again. Whatever my eye fell on seemed to occupy space more densely. Sounds were separate, distinct, like the first stirrings of a psychedelic drug in the brain. Possibilities seemed to jostle for prominence within the surface reality.

Whipping along Ventura Boulevard, through the Friday night expectancy of late afternoon traffic, ignoring sidelong glances from expensively maintained stovettes in German road machines, it hit me: Los Angeles hadn't seemed this real since I'd moved away, fifteen years before. I swerved into a left turn lane at Sepulveda and downshifted up to the red light, realizing with a sudden sense of loss no place else had, either.

Tooled up Sepulveda to a Fatburger stand. The place was packed but everybody was eating, and the counterman stood ready to take my order.

"Two double chili-cheeseburgers, to go please."

"Joo wan everytheeng?"

I nodded. "The whole cha cha."

"Chilies?" he said, looking a little too beady eyed.

"On the side," I said, "in a cup, or something."

He grinned through his disappointment, took my money and gave me a receipt.

A younger, thinner version of the counterman sold custom t-shirts and tank tops under a purple awning attached to a Windstar van parked beside the building. While my burgers cooked I looked over the merchandise, passing up such tired offerings as "Beam me up, Scotty, there's no intelligent life on this planet" "LAPD we treat you like a King" and "Jesus loves you. Everybody else thinks you're an asshole."

The counterman brought out my burgers in a paper bag, and I bought three black v-necks, extra-large, with yellow lettering, "Don't forget to think about your dead homey."

"Joo got a dead homey?" the vendor asked, bagging them.

"Bunch of them."

"I only got one," he said, "my homeboy, Cisco, got knifed by some niggers up in Soledad."

The kid looked thirteen, and seemed proud of having a dead homey, something to do with that machismo horseshit, I suppose. "Well," I said, taking the bag and waving away the change, "don't forget to think about him."

Housekeeping had been to my bungalow, tidied up, changed the bedding, removed a pair of singles I left on the toilet tank and departed, leaving the through the wall air conditioner and swivel arm mounted flat-screen pumping in the empty space. I flipped the a/c over to fan only, cranked open a couple windows behind the drapes, and got naked to address my burgers, placing a bath towel over the bedspread, keeping another close at hand. Fatburger is generous with their paper napkins, but for the Double Chili Cheeseburger, terry cloth is much to be preferred. If you can squeeze in a shower after eating, so much the better.

My attention split between catching gobs of chili with my tongue, as they tried to escape down my arm, and the television the maids had left tuned to the in house porn channel. I watched long enough to convince myself the neon sign had not misrepresented, they have the grossest. But watching my asshole cousin, Glen, inherit half ownership of a West Valley shopping mall had left me in the mood for something really filthy. I flipped over to the network offerings and found it right away.

Three heavily made up, immodestly dressed girls in their teens, were bending the attentive ear of a carefully coiffed talk show host with complaints about their own dear mothers, who had stolen their boyfriends. After letting the indignant junior misses tell their stories, applying sympathetic promptings as needed, the host turned to the studio audience and announced he would now bring in the mothers and boyfriends. And they strutted on-stage to a hearty blend of cheers and jeers. But the cheering men in the crowd carried the day, and rightly so, those mommies were smoking hot, the boyfriends pussy whipped to a man.

I was tempted to stick around for the carnage certain to follow commercials, but I had things to do, and more to think about.

After a quick shower I snagged the toilet brush and some complimentary shampoo packets, and went out front, wearing camo shorts and heavy soled flip flops, picked up at a thrift store in Needles. I put the big bike on its center stand and managed to clean every nook and cranny and get some Teflon lubricant inside all the cable housings before losing light.

One of my neighbors across the way, a muscular black man, living with a wanton overweight blond, leaned on the second floor railing in front of his room, while his girlfriend serviced a john inside. Wiping the bike down with handfuls of L.A. Weakly, I happened to glance up as he fingered a joint out of his shirt pocket. He noticed, and made a slight show of dragging it under his nose before firing it up, then extended it toward me in an offering gesture. I cupped my palm and he lobbed it down. Two tokes was more than enough, and I lobbed it back up, croaking, "Kick ass shit. Thanks."

While I coiled the hose next to the building and disposed of my damp wads of newsprint, he drummed a tattoo on the window of his room with the fingers of one hand, and said, "Hey, what the hang up, in there? He come yet?" I didn't hear the response, evidently not affirmative, because he said, "Well, lap his goddamn nuts, or something. That other trick gone be here in five, so snap it up."

Went inside, took another quick shower, then dressed in black cotton pants, tucking them into the tops of British Army combat boots picked up in a surplus store outside Pensacola, my first day out. It was warm outside, so one of the new dead homey v-necks rounded out my ensemble. Checked myself in the bathroom mirror.

My parents are good looking people, in their day they were knockouts and have the pictures to prove it. I look like a throwback to an earlier epoch of their gene pool. Those physical characteristics inherited from my father make the blood tie obvious to anyone seeing us together. The Brown bow legs, gray eyes, big toe, in his case nicely balanced, in mine ripe pickings for a caricature artist.

After all the happy beneficiaries departed Levy's office, shortly past noon, Levy looked at me across the long, green oval, just looked. After five seconds, I broke eye contact, being uninterested in either fucking him or killing him. .

He sent the remote control clicker spinning across the green glass to me. "My instructions are to leave you alone, to watch this next video file," he said. "It's in a flash drive and contains a virus that will corrupt the data beyond all retrieval, while it plays."

"I can only watch once?"

He smiled. "How's your memory?"

"I am memory," I said, stealing a line from Jeff Goldblum's Mr. Frost.

He stood. "Push play, when you're ready. I'll be back in twenty minutes. Can I bring you something to eat? Our butler makes a pretty mean Rueben."

"In that case, I'll take two," I said.

"Anything to drink?"

"Couple Steinlagers, if you have them."

"I'll get them," he said, and left.

Had signed a receipt for the keys to my new job, six color coded metallic items, vaguely key shaped, but defined by circuitry rather than teeth. Preparing to leave motel accommodations, I loaded two of the six onto the ring with my motorcycle key, and put the other four in an inside zipper pocket of a naugahyde gym bag used to carry my worldly goods from place to place. The keys were accompanied by a list of addresses and vehicles.

The address for Al's primary residence elicited an unguarded grunt, when I first looked at it in Levy's office.

"What's the matter?" he said at once.

"Didn't know Al lived in Tujunga,"

"You must have heard he was building the place," Levy said.

"Yeah," I said, "in the foothills. I assumed it was Calabasas, or maybe West Hills."

"Strange place," Levy said, "Tujunga."

I shrugged. "You can say the same about any of the canyon areas, Tujunga, Trabuco, Box, Kagel. Canyon people tend to weird. Any idea why Al decided to build there?"

"He said it was the most geologically stable place in L.A."

Saw no reason to tell Levy my grunt of surprise had been prompted by Al's street address in Tujunga. My last visit to Los Angeles, three years before, had been to a cemetery on the same remote, privately maintained road.

The cemetery caretaker, scion of a prominent local family greeted me warmly, my visit having been arranged by a mutual acquaintance of a certain stature.

He lived in an alpine looking A-frame, perched near the top of a long driveway running up from the gated entry to the crest of a low hill, and circling around a defunct fountain. I followed him to a Westward facing lawn that sloped away from one side of the A-frame, spotted with flush to the ground grave markers, small concrete plugs, with names and dates on brass insets.

A pair of redwood chaise lounges with thick, sun-faded pads sat at the top of the slope, in the shade of a lemon tree, overlooking the Northeast quadrant of the San Fernando Basin from a high remove.

Got settled into one of the chaise lounges, while my host went to an open top steel drum, with big chunks of ice floating in water. He plunged both arms in to his biceps, and pulled them out, a Modelo in one hand, Sam Adams in the other. He offered me the choice, Modelo.

We sprawled on the chaises exchanging business gossip in muted tones, playing catch up on mutual acquaintances and firming up our business arrangement, while Sun set on the Santa Monica Mountains and Earth rolled us toward shadow.

He stood, stretched, "I'll be baahk," then went in the front door of the A-frame, out the back moments later, pushing a Sportster, straddled it, thumbed the starter switch, gave me a nod and roared down the driveway. I went to the steel drum for another beer.

A layer of smog hung over The Valley, visible from the

lounge chair, perched on a ridge, partway up one of Mount Lukens' lower slopes. Within a distant V, formed by the convergence of two lower foothills, a remote piece of The Valley was framed, the geometric stamping of civilization more hinted at than seen. I stared at the hazy landscape, wondering how the faintly seen fragment was able to transmit the unseen mass of humanity extending out of sight around it. It was a sleep making thought.

I woke up cold and needing to pee, stepped behind the chaise to relieve myself, facing away from the grave markers, I thought. A pale metallic glimmer in the half-light led to the realization I was watering a grave stone. Damn. Hey, buddy, remember that guy who said he'd piss on your grave? He sent me, Take that, and that.

I got a jacket out of the car and sat back on the chaise, sipping Bohemia and watching The Valley light up like a carpet of jewels. I realized I'd been hearing a background buzz only when it upgraded to a sputter. A minute later the Sportster came rumbling up the drive. I followed the caretaker into the A-frame, commenting on the million dollar view he had at night. He walked into the living room, shrugging out of a small backpack, and laughed.

"View? You like the view?" He laughed again. "Lay an eyeball on this panorama." He lifted the bottom of the open pack off the smoked glass surface of the coffee table, and several fist sized pieces of what looked like quartz crystal skittered across the smooth surface.

I walked closer and looked down at the table top. "Appears to be the kind," I said.

"You want to do a blast?" he offered, eyes big as saucers. It was evident he had.

"I don't guess I'll need to," I said, handing him an envelope stuffed with cash.

While he counted money, I put the chunks of methamphetamine hydrochloride back in the pack. He walked me out to the car and, after a couple quick goodbye stops, I drove straight back to Atlanta, licking a little piece of crystal I broke off with a tire iron, whenever I felt sleepy.

Back in my Druid Hills bungalow, I pulverized the chunks of crystal with a single jack, tripled the weight of the resulting powder by mixing in water soluble B vitamins, and portioned it out to Emory University and Georgia Tech students at a mark-up best left to the reader's imagination.

The two electronic keys I loaded on the ring with my motorcycle key would grant me access to Al's property in Tujunga. My new job required I live on and maintain the property until I could turn control of Al's estate over to his daughter, Leni, without her donating any of it to her new church.

My pot smoking neighbor was still leaning on the guard rail in front of his room, when I came out and secured my bag to the C90's sissy bar with a couple bungee cords. I took my room keycard out of my pocket. "Hey, Sport." He looked my way, and I spun him the card. "It's got six days and a fifteen dollar deposit left on it. Use them wisely."

His demeanor brightened. "No bullshit? Hot damn! Thanks a lot, Bro."

"Don't mention it, Cuz."

CHAPTER FOUR

I cruised the big Suzuki down to Burbank Boulevard at a sedate pace, hit the Northbound 405 ramp and wound it out, allowing the speed limit plus twenty Valley studs to partake of my dust, up to Sherman Way, then glimpsed four aquamarine orbs over in the carpool lane, streaked past the CHP bikes, down shifting like hell, not wanting to flash brake lights, got down to seventy-five and in no mood to be polite to the police, exited at Roscoe Boulevard, heading East and staying with the traffic flow.

Cruising through Panorama City, it appeared to be girls' night out, five to ten year old Hondas, Toyotas and Nissans, packed with fourteen to eighteen year old Latinas, some of them fine enough to make your teeth ache. I did a little flirting at the red lights. Want some candy, little girl? All day sucker?

After passing Van Nuys Boulevard, traffic began to thin, and I made better time. Awhile later Roscoe became Tuxford St, and shortly after La Tuna Canyon Road. La Tuna lifted off the flat grid work of Valley streets, winding and rising along one canyon wall. Five miles later I roared up out of the canyon, where it ended, and where the Interstate 210 plowed through the foothills between The Valley and Pasadena.

I shot under the monolithic mass of freeway overpass, and the road made a hard right, running parallel to the Interstate, down a half mile slope to a signal controlled T intersection at La Tuna Canyon Road's terminus. The left side of the T is Tujunga Canyon Boulevard, the right, though it is the same street, is labeled Honolulu Ave. The good citizens of Montrose, a hop/skip down Honolulu Ave. probably share Sid Levy's opinion, that Tujunga is a strange place, and don't want a street so named running through the middle of their community.

Swung left through the green light, and a minute later put my feet down for a red light at the intersection of Tujunga Canyon and Foothill Boulevard, Foothill's highest elevation. Could have turned either right or left onto Foothill and coasted for several miles.

Instead, when the light changed, shot straight across, passing a bank building on my right, moving deeper into Tujunga..

Decided, before presenting myself to the rent-a-cops guarding Al's property, it would be prudent to check in with the Ayatollah of Tujunga.

His unprepossessing house looked the same as it had three years before. In fact, little about it had changed in the quarter century since I'd first seen it.

The house stood hard by the curb-less street, a covered porch extending across the whole front. A yellow bug light threw some weak shafts of illumination through wood lattice shielding the porch front, and reflected off the paint of a restored 1955 Chevy pick-up, parked tight to the porch.

A driveway ran up the left side of the dwelling, tall wooden gate closing it off a few feet past the porch, leaving an outer driveway long enough to accommodate a single vehicle. A late model Cadillac two-seater squatted there, on what I took to be a modified suspension, nose pointing down at the street. I pulled the C90 onto a short stretch of asphalt between the pick-up and the driveway, shut it down, and pulled it up on center stand.

Walking past the tricked out little Caddy to the porch steps, I resisted an urge to wave at a bird house on a ten foot pole at the top of the drive, housing a video pick up. One of my rules in life is, you don't front off your friends, even if you think nobody's watching.

The door, a stout slab of hardwood, was centered on the porch and adorned with a selection of knockers. I lifted a heavy brass ring hanging from a lion's mouth, and dropped it The sound of a heavy barrel bolt being thrown answered at once, and the door swung inward.

"What's happening, Troll?" I said.

Troll was a nickname he acquired during military service in Southeast Asia, where, during three consecutive tours of duty, he built an impressive reputation as a medevac corpsman. A persistent rumor had it that, even decades later, each Christmas(or his birthday, the day before) found him deluged with cards and gifts from men whose lives and limbs he'd retrieved from certain annihilation. I was present on one occasion somebody asked about the rumor, he answered, "Fuck all that. What are you getting me for Christmas?"

The nickname came as a result of his off duty exploits, when, scornful of exotic R&R locales, he'd get one of his First Cav buddies to let him ride along on missions into areas he'd noted attractive bridges while on duty. He'd take to the water upstream of his target, with mask, fins and a long breathing tube disguised as a clot of vegetation on its upper end. Arriving at the bridge near dusk, when mosquitoes swarmed and people were loathed to approach the water's edge, he'd wedge C-4 into the bridge's underpinnings. It didn't take a degree in civil engineering to mount the pressure switch where it wouldn't activate until a heavy load of arms and ammunition came across. By full dark he'd be a mile or so downstream, holding an underwater flashlight between his knees for the returning helicopters.

When stories began going around about trolls under Charlie's bridges, his First Cav buddies, who knew the truth, began addressing him as Troll. Soon, even the clueless were following suit...

Now he stood shirtless, in Levis, one hand on the open door. He jerked his head back to indicate surprise, regarding me from behind his full, unruly beard, combing it a few strokes from the underside with the fingers of his free hand.

"Hey, now," he said. "Double D. Long time." He stuck out his hand, and we shook for perhaps the third time in our twenty-five year association.

Double D was a nickname that attached to me during my second tour of duty in Vietnam, and hung on through my next three.

Brought my recon team back to base camp after a week in the bush, and was cleaning my M-16, when a couple jar-heads in the camp's perpetual poker game started ragging on me to join the game. I let them run their mouths until I had my weapon reassembled, then turned and stared at them. They shut up, and a huge, black corporal spoke around his cigarette while dealing a hand of five card draw.

"You leathernecks wasting your breath. Ain't gone get Sarge in no card game. Sarge a death dealer. Sarge's body count so high, he let his grunts take credit for half of them. You deal as much death as that jar-head, you ain't got time for fucking with no cards.

24

Ain't that right, Sarge?"

"Fuck you, nigger," I said, not unkindly, and walked away.

For the next day or two it was death dealer this and death dealer that and blah blah blah. Then, mercifully, the black corporal, who was the closest thing I had to a friend on that tour, shortened it to Double-D, and that stuck like a burr, even after time and attrition carried away everyone who knew what it signified.

Troll and I never crossed paths in Southeast Asia, though we knew of each other by reputation. About a year after I was evacuated back to the states (along with all the other U.S. personnel), I was introduced to Troll while trying to locate and purchase a large quantity of amphetamines. I'd grown accustomed to them in the war zone, where corpsmen passed them out like M&Ms, to offset the lassitude of the tropics. It wasn't an environment that fostered their abuse. Let them get out of hand and you'd be going home lickety-split. In a body bag.

Back at Pendleton, it was no more free bennies. The new party line was "speed kills". Corpsmen couldn't carry them, anymore, a thriving black market grew around the base.

It seemed to me a grateful government had arranged things just so, for my benefit. Instead of frittering away my accumulated combat pay on living expenses, I could invest it under the protection of strict new drug laws, have easy access to the CNS stimulants I'd grown accustomed to in the service of my country, and turn a tidy, tax-free profit on them.

When we were introduced, Troll and I recognized each other by type, at once. The nicknames we'd been known by was how we established our identities to one another. What began as a business relationship evolved over time into a solid if undemonstrative friendship. We never spoke about Vietnam at any length after our first meeting. He'd said it all that day, propping his chin on his hand, with a faraway look in his eye, and muttering, "It got to be too good."

Troll ushered me inside and re-secured the door. I followed him past pinball machines and arcade video games into the bedroom, where a redhead about half his age and weight, dressed in a tank top and panties, sat near the edge of the room's king size water bed, one shapely foot propped on the bed's wooden frame while she applied nail polish, a position that left no doubt.

She held the brush away from her foot, as Troll rolled onto the bed setting off serious tidal activity.

He waved me into an armchair not far from the bed, saying, "Lori, Double-D. Double-D, Lori."

She looked at me, then at Troll. "The Double-D?"

Troll snorted. "No, a different one. Now, be a good girl and go fix us something to eat."

She capped the nail polish and got off the bed, stepping past me to the bathroom door, pushed it open and stepped through. As she was swinging it closed, she shot me a glance, and said, "Heard a lot about you."

I threw a questioning look at Troll. "Don't look at me," he said, "I don't motor mouth. Anyway, fuck all that. Where the hell you been?"

"Chain gang," I said, "swinging a bush ax."

Troll was Sicilian. Now middle aged, he'd developed the stomach of a man of respect. He sat there, bare-chested, bobbing gently on the water filled mattress, A tattoo of The Grim Reaper, scythe pointing back over its robed shoulder, covered one upper arm. He nodded sagely, fingering his bearded chin, a satanic version of Santa Clause. "I figured you caught a beef," he said. "Why didn't you drop me a note?"

"Too embarrassed," I said. "Plus, I couldn't see passing out your name and address."

He gave me a slow look I couldn't read, and said, "I'll be go to hell. What kind of weight they catch you holding?"

"About a hundred fifteen pounds."

He looked aghast. "Holy fucking.."

"Of slightly underage female," I finished.

"Oh, joy," Troll said, looking pained.

"Her mother was one of my customers," I said. "Moved half a pound a week, in one of those hick Alabama towns, about half an hour from Benning."

"What?" said Troll, "you couldn't move enough product in the big city?"

"Wasn't that," I said. "One day I got a call on my beeper, broad just moved back to Alabama from SoCal, said Angel Dave gave her my number."

"Valley Angel Dave, or Riverside Angel Dave?" Troll

inquired.

"Riverside. Her sister's Dave's old lady."

"Jesus." Troll pinched the bridge of his nose and closed his eyes. "Her name, Gina? Tina? Something like that."

"Rita," I said.

At this point, Troll's redhead, having gone to the kitchen through the bathroom, which was double-doored, came back around into the bedroom through the living room, balancing a platter of sandwich halves on one hand, a couple bottles of Michelob dangling from the other. I noticed a folded TV tray leaning against the chest of drawers beside my chair, and pulled it out, snapping it open between Troll and myself. She put the sandwich platter on it, and placed a beer bottle at either end.

"Good girl. Thanks," Troll said, scooping up half a sandwich and a beer, gesturing for me to help myself.

The redhead picked up a pair of designer jeans from the foot of the bed and put them on. I chewed a bite of sandwich, thin sliced roast beef on soft sour dough, lots of mayo and pepper, and watched her get into the jeans. The girl knew how to put on some pants. She smoothed the tank top over the waist of the jeans, and stepped into a pair of backless pumps, adding a little more tilt to an ass that didn't need any help. She stepped over to a tall oak dresser and fished a ring of keys from among the handguns and broke open boxes of ammunition littering its top.

She said, "I have to go put my bratty girls to bed." Troll slid off the water mattress. She gave me an arch look.

"Great sandwiches," I said.

"Your friend seems to be all that I've heard," she told Troll as they moved toward the front door. "Semi-conscious, even."

"His trance is fairly light," Troll said.

"I still think he ought to be punished."

"Don't expect any help from me," said Troll.

"I'll come by in the morning, after I drop the girls at school," she said. "I may be a little pressed for time, try to have your pants off when I get here."

"I'll see what I can do," said Troll. "Shouldn't be a problem." He closed the door behind her, threw the barrel bolt, then came back into the room, saying, "Look here, douche bag, I ain't near to being done with that girl, so how about you find your own trim?"

"Ud I oo?" I said around a wad of roast beef.

"You had her making a career out of putting her pants on!"

I swallowed, and said, "Maybe that's how she plans to punish me. What's up with that?"

"Oh," Troll waved it away, "Lori's Annette's cousin."

"So what?" I said. "I'm good with Annette. You gave her the ozee I left for her, didn't you?"

"Course. She got all weepy-eyed when I gave it to her."

"The fuck?" I said.

"I had her moping around here like a broke dick dog for a week after you split back to Atlanta."

"I see," I said. "And, did we find it necessary to issue a little tune up?"

"And your fault I had to do it," Troll said with a righteous look.

"I'll buy that," I said. "Mister Compassion, Mister Mercy fuck. And while we're at it, throw in a few acres of Florida swamp land, and I'll buy that, too. Face it, man, you're a hog!"

"Hey, now," Troll looked hurt, "it's my job."

We polished off the rest of the sandwiches in comfortable silence, leaving the beers untouched, the sandwiches were that good.

Ever the gracious host, Troll caught himself while reaching for the last sandwich half and offered it to me with a gesture. "I'm good," I said. "Tell me what you know about Rita."

"Never met the bitch," Troll said. "But I did a fair amount of business with Riverside Dave, five or six years back. High Times ran a piece about Tujunga being speed capitol of the U.S. Brought unreal heat on all the cooks up here and back in the canyon. Things dried up fast.

"Looking for a new source, I found Angel Dave, fronting for some Challengers, a splinter group of the Slaves. He was bringing me five pound packages, every couple of weeks. He'd make a delivery, hang around for a couple hours to avoid the appearance of traffic. Dave's not much of a talker, he'd play pinball or video until it was time to go. Good dude, though. Count was always right, never whacked the dope.

"One day he showed up with an attitude, nothing too obvious, but I could tell something was eating him. I had to make sure it wasn't something was gonna affect my business, so I put in some time, played a little GTA, got him high on some shit that hadn't been around since the seventies. It got him talking.

"About a month earlier, his sister in law showed up from Alabama, kid in tow. Parked her ass in front of the boob tube and didn't move for a week. Meanwhile, Dave's old lady takes the ankle biter in hand, gets her started in school.

"Week two begins, Rita's still parked in front of the tube. Dave's at work when the Challenger's cook, cat named Pig, comes over for a tank of anhydrous ammonia."

"Another fat biker?" I said.

"Roly poly motherfucker," said Troll, "until he started cooking zip. He dropped about two hundred pounds in six months. Turned out he was a good looking guy under all the fat, and still in his early twenties, didn't end up with a bunch of saggy skin after he dropped the weight.

"He had a clicker for Dave's garage door. Pulled his car in, loaded the tank, then goes to the kitchen door to let Dave's old lady know he'd made the pick-up. She's fixing lunch, they shoot the shit for a couple minutes, Pig splits. A few minutes later, Dave's old lady hollers out to the living room, does Rita want some lunch? No answer. She goes to the living room, No Rita. Couple days later they find out Rita's in Apple Valley, living with Pig. Nobody knows how she went from vegetating in front of the tube to hooking up with a guy who was there may be a total of ten minutes, five of them with Dave's old lady. But when they got to Pig's place in Apple Valley, she walked in, took one look at the three bag whores who were always hanging around the place, spins around and shoves Pig right back up against the door, drops to her knees and gives him the best blow job he's had in his short sexual life. Then she gets up, wipes off her chin and tells the bag whores to get out and don't come back til she calls them. They split, Pig's whipped, Rita's the new speed queen of Apple Valley, and she don't do laundry.

"To give Rita her due, she took care of business, dope stayed good, Pig stayed happy. But Dave's old lady put her foot down concerning Rita's daughter. No way she'd let him send the kid out there to live in a cooking situation, not that Rita asked. Now, Dave's got his fourteen year old niece, and all her new girlfriends hanging at his house. His old lady's in hog heaven, Dave's another story. He can't hold any dope at his place, with all these underage girls hanging out, plus he's got half the driving age boys from the local high school cruising his street every night, hoping to hook up with his niece. Tells me he's gonna call in a few of his chapter's prospects to bang heads on the cruisers. I told him that sounded like a swell idea, if he wanted to end up in Folsom, or maybe one of the new ex-SAVAK designed corn hole resorts, loaded down with all kinds of anti-gang legislation beefs."

"Anybody ever tell you," I said, "you've got a real subtle way of pointing out people's errors to them, almost making it seem to them it was their idea? Anybody ever tell you that?"

"Fuck no."

"That's good," I said, "because you don't."

"Heh heh," said Troll. "Too chilly."

"You tell Dave he could get rid of the teenage cruisers by transferring his niece to a private school?"

"I told him there would be a lot less of them," Troll said, "and they'd be driving better cars. The girl tell you about that?"

"She was blown away," I said. "Dave paid for the school, bought her clothes, books, all that, and never tried to get into her pants."

"Dave's that kind of guy," said Troll. "But a story like that getting around could hurt a motherfucker's reputation."

"You still see him?" I asked.

"Talked to him, about a month ago. His money's tight since Pig went down.

"Couple months after she moved to Apple Valley, Rita had a birthday. She made Pig give the Challenger's prez a big issue of dope and cash, to party on, and she and Pig took off for a couple weeks in Rosarita Beach. That was her birthday present. Six months later, she started thinking about her next birthday, different story. She tells Pig she wants a new Vette. Well, business is good, Pig's raking in money with both hands, plus, he's whipped. No problem, he tells her, takes her to the local Chevy dealer to order it, lays out a big cash deposit.

"When the birthday gets close, business has slowed down. Anhydrous ammonia has gotten real controlled, Pig's using the iodine and red phosphorus method, dope's not as good, he's only raking with one hand, sees he's gonna come up short on the Vette. He goes to the Chevy dealer, since the Vette hadn't been delivered yet the dealer was willing to let him cut a new deal on a tricked out Camaro he had in stock. Pig cashes out the deal. Rita's birthday rolls around. Nobody at the party figured Rita was pissed about the Camaro, but she wasn't real thrilled, either. She was like, a new car, how nice.

"Couple weeks later, Pig's cooking up a twenty pound batch, and the drug task force comes calling, every brand of narc, federal, state and county, hazmat team, a real hootenanny. Pig's caught dead to rights, along with a handful of Challengers who were waiting to pick up.

"They all get piled into the sheriff's van, and it's like, where's Rita. Somebody says she took off to get groceries, about an hour ago. They figure, great, somebody on the outside to set up bail. Only Rita's never heard from again. After about a week, Pig tells the Challenger prez where his money stashes are. They turn up empty. Long and short, Rita took off with about forty grand of Pig's money, plus a couple grand she got from the DEA for ratting him off. Pig can't make his half a mil bond, cops a plea for fifteen years.

"The Challengers would love to get a hold of Rita, and spend about three days turning her out. Now, let's hear your tale of woe."

"I didn't think twice about it when she said she got my beeper number from Dave. I had that number for about five years, it was my money machine.

"When I returned her call, she said she'd just moved back from the West coast, and was shopping for a quarter pound. We set up a meet at a motel in Lagrange. We met, cash was right, we did the deal. She snorted up a couple rails right away, and asked me to stick around until she came onto it. Once the dope started to take hold, she tried to lay some leg on me. I told her I didn't mix business and pleasure, and got out of there."

"Lying sack of shit," said Troll.

"Rita was a good looking broad," I said, "but she was crowding forty, and I had a couple of superfine Emory grad students draining my precious bodily fluids on a daily basis.

"Week or so later, she beepers me again, ready for another QP. We meet again, same town, different motel. This time she's got her daughter with her. Unbelievably fine, and from the looks of Rita, going to be fine for a long, long time.

"After we do the deal, Rita says she has to make a couple local deliveries, and is it okay if her kid kicks it at the motel while she's taking care of business. I say no problem, give her the room key, and take off."

Troll said, "What lame excuse you come up with for going back?" I stared at him. He shrugged, "What I would have done."

"Told her I thought I forgot my beeper. And took out my dick."

Troll laughed. "That the only trick you know?"

"Only one I need," I said. "Anyway, I'm no good at small talk."

"Ever wonder why that might be?" Troll inquired.

"No."

"Mmmm," said Troll, "reckon not. I imagine Rita was thrilled to death."

"Didn't seem to bother her much, neither her nor Sweet Thing ever mentioned the age thing. I pegged her for eighteen, nineteen."

"Girl didn't talk much," Troll said.

"How you figure?."

Troll gave me a look that skirted contempt. "Sixteen-year-old girl wants to pass for nineteen, she keeps her mouth shut. How long before Rita started asking for fronts?"

"Didn't exactly ask," I said, "just started coming up short on the cash. I was delivering to her place. I'd putt down there on a scooter, drop off an issue, pick up Sweet Thing and run down to Gulfport for a couple days of serious gorilla-sizing. Rita got a new sound system, young boyfriend, big plasma TV, fat new Michelins on her Camaro."

"Fucking rat mobile," Troll grunted.

"But she's steady short on cash. After six months, she's into me for over a pound, so I cut off her credit, just let her have what she had cash to cover. She pissed and moaned, but kept buying. It didn't take long to realize she had no plans on paying up her fronts. I talked it over with Sweet Thing. She'd heard there was a police/ military joint drug task force working the area, and was worried about her mom getting popped, thought it would be a good idea to shut off supply for a while.

"I got Sweet Thing her own cell phone, and gave her a 4Runner I'd gotten from some Tekki for a couple ounces. I stopped answering Rita's pages, and Sweet Thing started meeting me a couple times a week in La Grange."

"Oh, Double D," Troll said in a high falsetto voice, "it would be so romantic to meet in the town where you first showed me your thing."

"You want to hear the story , or not?" I said.

"Oops," said Troll, "sorry. Go ahead."

A month or so later, Sweet Thing tells me the word around her little bum fuck town is the drug task force has moved on down near Pensacola."

"Good old Bum fuck, Alabama," said Troll, "remember it, well."

"Which one?"

"About four or five of them, around Benning, before I shipped out. Some fine-ass women, not too swift, though, not the ones fucking G.I.s, at least."

"Had Sweet Thing tell Rita I got a new connect, and was putting money together for a buy, would let her know when I was back in pocket. She sends a note with Sweet Thing a couple days later, saying she'll have some of the cash she owes me in a day or two, and will call my pager when she's got it in hand.

"Couple days later I call back at her page, she tells me she's got half what she owes me, and she's holding somebody's money for a quarter pound, if I can bring one.

"I was holding about six pounds in a Winnebago at the time, told her I'd see what I could do and be there around lunchtime the next day.

"Next morning I decided not to bring her an issue until Sweet Thing green lighted it, but went down to pick up my ducats. When I get there, Sweet Thing's 4Runner's not around, boyfriend's Mustang's gone, just Rita's Camaro in the yard."

"Fucking Rat mobile," said Troll."

"Rita takes me into the living room, says she'll be right down with the cash. Soon as she's out of the room I've got rednecks coming out of the woodwork, one skinny one and five fat "ones, throwing down on me with twelve gauge pumps. A couple of these assholes were shaking so bad I thought I'd end up dead by accident. I put my hands on my head, and said, 'I'm unarmed, fellows, so let's get some cuffs on me, and you can put those cannons away.' I wasn't holding anything, figured if I got out of the room alive I was home free."

Troll said, "What did they charge you with, statch? What's that carry in Alabama?"

"First they tore my Fat Boy apart, looking for the QP Rita told them I was bringing, fucked that bike up.

"Then things started to get hinkey. Instead of taking me to the Bum fuck jail, they carried me across the state line to Fuck Ewe, Georgia. They run me right into the sheriff's office, uncuff me, and back out.

"The sheriff's about our age," I continued, "about six five, in good shape, looked a lot like the dude that played The Rifleman."

"Chuck Conners," said Troll.

"Yeah. He starts in with, even though he's sworn to uphold the law, it pains him to perform his duty against a highly decorated Marine like little old me, and he's hoping we can reach some sort of accommodation."

"That's unusual," Troll said.

"How so?"

"Cops don't try to turn people into rats. They just load motherfuckers up with as many beefs as they can think of, and wait for the cheese eaters to approach them."

"Is that so?" I said. "I've never had much experience with cops."

"That's because every time you started catching heat, you beat feet," said Troll.

"Well, excuse the fuck out of me."

Troll shrugged. "Nothing wrong with it. When I'm catching heat I close up shop until they get bored and leave. This fucking neighborhood ought to give me a medal. Every street around here except mine got resurfaced while they had my house under surveillance. What did you tell The Rifleman?"

"I asked him when he was gonna Mirandize me. He has me sign the paper, then sits back, looking all expectant. I don't say shit. After a while, he starts to say something, but I rub my chin, and he shuts up. Awhile more, I can see he wants to talk again, I clear my throat. He sits back. Then, about the time he snaps to the fact I'm fucking with him, I hold up a finger, and say: Ten thousand gobs lay down their swabs, to lick one sick Marine. Ten thousand more watched from the shore, and swore it was the bloodiest battle they'd ever seen."

Troll wheezed out a laugh. "Fucking Double-D. How you scope him out as Navy?"

"What he wanted to know. I told him he had that look, the one that comes from sitting around off shore, playing cards and shooting craps, while other guys fight the war."

"That's choice," said Troll, still chuckling. "I don't think you want your Diablo brother, Hank, to hear you talk like that, though. Nice guy, but I never really wanted to see him pissed off."

"Wouldn't bother Hank," I said. "He didn't sit around off shore. He was on a river boat, having the time of his life. I'd like to see him."

"You'll have to drive up to Lompoc. He's two years into a seven year sentence, behind some Army C-4 he got caught holding."

"Hank and his goddamn explosives," I said.

"What's his trip with that?"

"Fuck if I know. He's never blown up anything, stateside, just likes having the stuff around, doesn't even keep detonators for the shit."

"How Sheriff Chuck react to all your shameless flattery?" Troll said.

"Called in a deputy and told him to book me for everything he could come up with, that would make it past the prelim," I said.

Next morning, at arraignment, the public defender waives reading of charges, has me plead not guilty to all counts, asks for a bail reduction hearing.

"Back in the holding cell, he tells me I'm looking at thirty to life. Couple days later, he tells me the prosecutor says if I decide to be a prick, and take it to trial, and lose, he'll ask for the death penalty."

"For statch?" Troll said. "Do I look extra stupid, this week?"

"Ever hear of aggravated sodomy?" I said.

"Like some fag aggravates you, so you corn hole him without the KY, and tell yourself you're not queer?"

"Or, "I said, "you hold a gun to a woman's head and make her suck you off."

"Never had to hold a gun to their head for that," said Troll.

"Easy to say, when you're holding the bag."

"I didn't invent bag chasers, but it's my patriotic duty to make them suck long wee wee."

"In Georgia," I said, "if they're under eighteen and you're over twenty-five, you let them have that meat whistle, no matter how bad they want it, it's aggravated sodomy, you might have to ride the lightning."

"What kind of freaks would pass a law like that?" Troll said with a look of wonder.

"How about a bunch of limp dick crackers, worried about their old ladies guzzling big, black loggerheads."

"Right," said Troll. "Like they'd really need a gun to their head."

"No," I said. "They just had to claim they did, and what else they going to say, if they got caught. No gun? He used his finger, and they thought it was a gun. Same thing."

"Bye bye, Rastus," said Troll. "So how'd your white ass end up riding that kind of beef."

"I fucked up. First, I never got around to calling Angel Dave, to check out Rita."

"That might have saved you some grief," Troll said, with the exaggerated gentleness one might use when addressing a dangerous psychotic.

"Rub it in," I said. "Here, let me hand you the salt."

"You take it to trial?"

"Wanted to," I said. "Got a hotshot criminal lawyer from Atlanta, speed customer, a couple connects downstream from me. Paid him in uncut dope. That probably wasn't the swiftest thing I ever did, either. It was like I'd gone so long without catching a beef, I started thinking I was immune or something." I shook my head. "My dumb ass.."

"Troll said, "You end up copping a plea?"

"Not much choice. My lawyer said they had tapes of me and Sweet Thing, in a La Grange motel, doing it every which way. Said, if a jury got a look at them, they'd give me life, just out of jealousy."

"Jesus," said Troll, "they went to that kind of trouble to set you up?"

"No trouble at all," I said. "La Grange is on the North/South coke route. Apparently, half the motel rooms around there have lipstick pickups in the ceiling lamps, so the cops can see who they might like to pull over for weaving.

"They offered ten years suspended, when I walk out I've got seventy-two hours to marry Sweet Thing.

"We get into court. The judge, who, by the way, I found out later was Rita's second cousin, says do I understand the charges, enter the plea of my own free will, no promises made, all that bullshit. I say yes, your honor. He says ten years in state prison.

"I'm standing there, waiting for him to say suspended, and the courtroom starts emptying.

I say what the fuck, to my lawyer. He says he'll be in touch, last I ever hear from him.

"Sweet Thing never came to court, didn't want to see me in handcuffs and leg irons. She was home, planning the wedding. Rita and Cousin Judge went to the Burger King across from the courthouse. I'm eating baloney sandwiches in the holding cell.

"One of Sweet Thing's girlfriends calls her up, and tells her Cousin Judge reneged on the suspended sentence, so she's going to have to push the wedding date up ten years.

"Sweet Thing freaks, takes her 4Runner into town, drives it right into the Burger King, parks it on top of Rita, Cousin Judge, and their Double Whoppers. Rita's dead at the scene. Cousin Judge gets off with a broken pelvis and some cracked ribs. Sweet Thing ends up in the happy hotel at Milledgeville, doing the Thorazine shuffle. I'm down the road with ten years. Just another Tale From the South."

Troll brooded into his beard. "I know some Challengers who'll be happy to know they can forget about Rita. I've just got one question," he turned a piercing gaze on me, "you catch a real early parole, or am I liable to have my door kicked any minute?"

I took The Document out of my wallet and handed it to him. He read it, and said, "I will be go to hell, a pardon. You always were a lucky bastard. I like lucky people."

"And you don't trust unlucky ones," I said.

"Fucking A!" he said.

CHAPTER FIVE

"So," said Troll, "you going to try to get Sweet Stuff out?"

"Sweet Thing," I said.

"What's the dif?"

"That was the name on her birth certificate," I said. "Her girlfriends just called her Thing."

"Fucking Rita," Troll said, shaking his head."

"Rita was dog shit, as far as I'm concerned," I said. "But she was Sweet Thing's mother. I can't be messing with anybody kills their mother."

He chewed on that for a while, then said, "Never really thought about it before, but I'd have to say you're right. Goddamn shame, though, sounds like she was a hell of a woman."

"She was," I said. "I don't want to think about what she might be, now."

Troll reached into one of the shelves built into the waterbed's headboard, and pulled out a black velvet jeweler's case, about the same dimensions as an eighteen count carton of eggs, but half the thickness. He flipped the top up, inside were ten disposable syringes, cradled in silk lined depressions likely designed for sickeningly expensive writing implements. The syringes contained varying amounts of amber fluid.

"Care for a jolt," Troll said, holding the case out.

A hundred pros and cons tumbled through my mind, as I said, "Thought you'd never ask," and picked up a medium size load. Troll took a full one, slid the case back into its shelf, secured a tan medical tie above his bicep (blindfolding the grim reaper), and pumped with his hand a few times.

I looked at a vein, pulsing lazily on my forearm, removed the orange point cover, and squirted the amber fluid into my mouth, then made a quick grab for my beer, and chug-a-lugged it dry.

"Gaaa! Shit tastes that bad, must be way good."

Troll looked up from the point resting against his skin. "Jesus, you ate it? Drink my beer, too."

While I did, he tapped in the point, drew a register, and emptied the amber fluid into a vein, flipped the used syringe at a dartboard mounted next to the bathroom door, where it stuck close to the bulls eye for a couple seconds, then dropped into the trash can below..

Troll did some heavy breathing as his metabolism went to overdrive in the space of a few seconds. It would require a half hour or so for my orally ingested dose to bring me to the same state.

After Troll's respiration caught up with his pulse, he said, "If you told me you were going to eat it, I'd have given you a couple loaded gel caps. Thinking about that shit, raw, hitting the back of your tongue, gives me some serious willies."

"Didn't know it, myself, until the last second."

"Why didn't you slam it?" asked Troll.

"I was looking at my freeway vein, feeling smug, that I wouldn't need to tie off. Somehow," I said, "that got me thinking about all the guys I've seen come out of lockup, and the first thing they wanted to do, before pussy, even, was slam a hit of speed. I couldn't think of a single one managed to stay on the streets longer than three months, and only a couple made it that long. So, I figured, fuck it. I'll wait six months, a year, if it seems necessary. I like being "an outlaw, and an outlaw in jail..."

Troll filled in my pause, saying, "Is no outlaw at all."

"You fucker," I said. "That should have been my line."

"It will be," said Troll, "when you visit Hank. If it makes you feel any better, I didn't just come up with it."

"Who did?"

"The best cocksucker who ever walked through my front door."

"Anybody I know?."

"Don't even think about it," said Troll.

"Yeah, yeah. Find my own trim," I said. "I can live with that."

"Easy to say," Troll said, "when all you have to do is take out your dick."

"God had to give me something to offset my bow legs and shitty personality."

"So," said Troll, "what's the plan? You need a place to stay?"

"Got one," I said. "Just haven't seen it, yet. You feel like running me up there in that hot little Cadillac you're waving in the pigs' faces? What happened to Mister Discipline, Mister Low Profile?"

"I won that little monster in a raffle, all legal and above board, complete with pictures of me, grinning like an idiot, in the Glendale and Tujunga newspapers. It cost me ten grand, over and above the price of the car, but it was worth it. Friendly Frank set it up. Remember him?"

"The guy could sell used rubbers. He's in no danger of slipping off into my unconscious memory."

"Where's this new crib, you haven't seen?" Troll inquired.

"Way out beyond that old graveyard on Parson's Trail," I said.

Troll stared at me, lips slightly parted. Within seconds, all the multitude in his range of expressions evaporated, along with the ever present tensions reflected in his face, even in repose, due to a lifetime lived so far beyond the lines of behavior most of the herd exist within. He'd been a source of wet dreams for ambitious law enforcement bureaucrats for thirty years, without one of them yet realizing those dreams.

He was facing me, but I doubt he was taking in any outside data, and he barely looked like himself, but I could fairly hear the synapses firing in his brain.

Was about to say, you okay? when his eyes refocused, and he said, "I will be go to hell, you're connected to that dude, Albert Brown."

"I think I told you once, I had a rich uncle," I said.

"When the place was under construction," said Troll, "security was like a secret government project, no local people worked on it, no stories in the press, or pictures in Architectural Digest. There's something like thirty acres, surrounded by wrought iron spears, mounted in white concrete, front gate looks like it could stop a tank."

"How about that ride?" I said.

"I'm motivated," he said, sliding off the bed and stepping into a pair of light weight hiking boots.

We went through the bathroom to the kitchen and out the back door onto the fenced off section of the driveway. Troll held the gate for me, and unlocked his car electronically, then secured the gate and joined me in the car.

"You know," he said, starting the car, "I hear your uncle sank about thirty mil into that place, and there's not a spot you can drive on this mountain where you can see any buildings on the property. You'll see fence up the ass, but no buildings, except, if you're on Foothill Boulevard or the 210 freeway, where they cross Big Tujunga Wash, down in Sunland, you can look up there and see a black triangle, floating in the air."

"You ready for a close up look?" I said.

"You know I am," Troll answered. "There's just one thing." I looked at him and raised my eyebrows. "Since your uncle died, the whole perimeter of that place has been crawling with rent-a-pigs, that's in addition to all the built in security the place already had. Nobody's allowed onto the property, deliveries, service people, even the rent-a-pigs. You still want to go up there?"

I was not surprised by the extent of Troll's information. Over the years he'd developed an intelligence network, based in Tujunga, but with lines all over SoCal, that would have made the OSS drool.

"As a matter of fact," I said, "my uncle didn't just die. He died and left me in charge. As my first official act, I believe we should go up there and send those chumps back down to The Valley, where they belong. How about it?"

"How about this?" Troll said, slapping the shifter into low, punching us out of the driveway and up the street with just enough fishtailing to kick the speed I was starting to feel into high gear.

I hyper-ventilated, pumping oxygen to the butterflies in my stomach, while Troll demonstrated his world class driving skills, flogging the turbo-charged little monster along Tujunga's narrow, twisting, poorly lit streets, at speeds that rendered lines of shoulder parked vehicles as a single amorphous blur.

After spending thirty seconds with my whole body clenched against the inevitable loss of control, I began to relax a little, as certain destruction passed harmlessly behind us, again. Glancing at Troll, his hooded gaze and erect posture suggested he was driving two or three crises ahead of me. I felt more at ease, and began to enjoy the ride, the likes of which you'll never find in an amusement park.

Troll brodied us through a right turn onto a one lane paved track that appeared to dead end at the base of a cliff, but I knew from previous experience it continued up the cliff in a series of cutbacks, each with its own hairpin turn. Troll took us up the cliff face, driving as if failure to negotiate even one of the hairpin curves in a four wheel drift to within inches of the sheer escarpment would leave him open to accusations of slip-shod motoring.

We topped out, and I caught a glimpse of the old cemetery's sagging chain link gates as we shot past. The road made a three-way fork, and Troll took the center one, marked with a reflective sign: Private Road. It was two lanes, with a rock retaining wall on the off-hill side, and took us up the mountain far beyond any signs of human habitation. Troll maintained a breakneck pace, slowing only when we passed a warning sign: Road Ends ¼ mile.

It ended not at a painted wood barricade, but in a giant paved cul-de-sac, a hundred yards in diameter and perfectly flat. Troll slipped the transmission into neutral, and we coasted to a stop, about thirty yards in.

Behind us, a quarter million dollar motor home was backed up to the low rock wall enclosing the off hill side of the cul de sac. It showed no lights or other signs of life.

Troll killed the headlights, leaving the parking lights on, and we sat in silence, looking across seventy yards of featureless black asphalt at a V shaped opening in the landscape formed by a canyon running into the mountainside. Entry to the canyon was restricted by giant steel columns rising from both the flattened canyon mouth and it's sloping sides, curving at the top to form one large arch, flanked by a pair of smaller arches. The six major columns supported a number of smaller risers between them. On each side of the massive gate the land had been shaved to create cliffs about twenty feet high. Narrow ranked wrought iron spears, set in white concrete, marched away from the gate's outermost columns atop the cliffs. About ten yards before the gate a curving piece of steel conduit stuck out of the asphalt, emitting a muted green light from its end. A pair of white wannabe police cars were parked nose to nose, twenty yards to the left of the gate.

"Well," said Troll, "What's it gonna be, rent-a-pigs or gate control?"

"I strike you as the kind of guy who asks permission? I said.

"Sure don't," said Troll, "but it was your call, and it looks

42

like," he held his right hand a foot above the shifter and wiggled his fingers, "gate control it is!" His hand dropped to the shifter, slapping it into low as he floored the accelerator. The late evening silence was shattered by the screech of tires on asphalt, the crisp mountain air became rank with the odor of burnt rubber.

I regarded the fast approaching sides of the two Crown Vics with some trepidation. Troll hit his high beams, wheezing, "Run, you sucker faces," at the four khaki clad men scrambling out of the vehicles. Then he cut the wheel, tromped the brake, goosed the gas, and yelled, "Just passing through, boys," as we spun away in a large smoking donut, coming to rest about five feet away from the curving section of conduit that housed the gate control. We were facing away from the gate, toward the still dark and silent motor home.

Troll glanced my way. "Want to catch the gate, while I turn this hog around?"

"Can I change my pants first?"

Troll said, "Heh, heh, heh," as I stepped out of the car, then, "Double-D, look here." I leaned down to look through the open window, and he held up a CD between two fingers. "George Thorogood," he grinned. "Get on!" He flipped the disc like a frisbee into a slot in the dash, and rolled away at a stately pace. I approached the green glow of the keypad, accompanied, like a second rate actor, by the high velocity strains of Bad to the Bone, belted out at a volume that was probably waking up people in Glendale. I inserted my color coded, key shaped microchip into the color coded key way below the green keypad. The pad turned red, and words streamed across the top: Enter new six digit command line and press #. I entered the short form of my mother's date of birth, The pad streamed: The six digits you have entered now control all coded entries on this property. Assign access codes to other individuals by following command line with asterisk, then entering five digits for main entry, four digits for exterior passages and three digits for interior passages. To disable a code, enter the code plus 9.

A Mag-light beam splashed the side of my face, I responded with a warning look.

"Lower the light, Junior."

He was a tow-headed beanpole with a serious case of jug ears.

He dropped the beam to a five by seven color portrait in his other hand, saying, "Sorry, I had to make sure it was you."

"How can you be sure?" I said. "That picture's over thirty years old."

"You can tell it's you, though," Ears replied..

It was a photo taken in my dress blues, just after basic training, firm, unsmiling chin, green as goose shit look in my eye. It had been commandeered by some dumb ass recruiting colonel for use as a poster, displayed in recruiting offices all over the U.S. for a year, after which I suppose, they found somebody even greener and dumber looking. Luckily, I was in the Far East that year, and spared the humiliation of seeing myself as poster boy.

Troll turned the car around and was creeping back in our direction, the volume of his sound system lowered. I told Ears, "Put that away, I don't want this guy to see it."

Ears stuck the photo in his pocket, and scowled in Troll's direction. "What's that guy's problem?"

I shrugged. "Limo company said he was the best."

"They were blowing smoke up your ass!,"

"You have to admit," I said, "you don't see driving like that every day."

"I hope I don't ever see it again," Ears replied with feeling. "Sonofabitch ought to be fired."

"There's an idea," I said. "I'll mention it to his boss. You have anything I need to sign?"

He pulled a leather clad invoice book off his belt, pointed out the relevant data he'd filled, and put a small check mark next to the space requiring my signature. "Just note the date and time along with your autograph."

"Hold on," I protested. "It says here twelve men. I only saw four bailing out of the Crown Vics."

His ears got red. "The rest of the team's spread out around the perimeter, keep anybody from activating the approach system."

"Well," I said, "okay." I printed the date and time, and scribbled my signature. "You seem like a pretty all right guy," I said, handing it back, "so I'm not going to hang around and count heads. Go ahead and wrap things up. You're off the clock."

"That's right," agreed a deep mechanical sounding voice that seemed to come out of the darkness around us. "Get your asses back down to The Valley, where you belong."

Ears was looking around for the source of the voice, one hand on his holstered sidearm. I noticed his three back-ups, who'd positioned themselves about fifteen feet away, doing the same. I was the only one to even glance at Troll, parked so near. He sat, one hand hung over the top of the steering wheel, looking bored and sleepy. I knew he was neither.

Ears looked at me and shrugged. "Probably that bunch in the motor home. They've got the sound equipment you'd need."

So did the little Cadillac, I mused, but said, "I thought that was with you guys."

He barked a laugh. "Don't I wish! I'm commuting from Lancaster every day. Nah. It's some ditzy broad, claims to be daughter of the deceased, and a bunch of her friends. What a crew!"

"Maybe she is the daughter of the deceased," I suggested.

"Don't know, don't care," Ears said, "nothing to do with our contract."

"Which was?"

"Any day Mister Brown didn't contact our office by noon, we were to have a team of licensed armed guards here by three pm, and keep anyone from entering the property until you or Mister Brown showed up."

"That happen often?"

"Three times in the past year. I think the first two times he was testing us. Third time, they were taking Mr. Brown's body out when we got here."

"Okay," I said, "thanks. What's your name?"

"Stout," he said, and stuck out his hand. "Tim Stout, Stout Security Systems."

"You affiliated with any of the security companies Al owned?"

"Nope, sole proprietorship. No idea he was in the business."

"He was in many businesses."

"You think it's weird he hired an outside agency?"

"No. Kind of makes sense, Now beat it."

"Okay. Keep us in mind."

"I'll do that."

I blocked the keypad with my body, shielding it, not from the departing Tim Stout, but from anyone who might be hunkered behind the dark windshield of the motor home with a pair of binoculars, and keyed my mother's date of birth, then slipped back into Troll's passenger seat, and said, "Home, James."

"Check this out," grunted Troll, gesturing with his beard toward the gate. I looked, but it took me a few ticks to get what my eyes were telling me. Four of the six main columns composing the gate's superstructure (all but the two shortest and outermost), were rising up off their footings, as if withdrawing into themselves, and carrying all the secondary risers up with them. In half a minute, half the gate's mass was gone, the other (upper half) forming a graceful arc across the paved mouth of the canyon. "That's disturbing," I said.

"Guess it's not a heavy as it looks," said Troll.

"Nor as tough," I said.

Troll cut me a sideways glance. "Nor?"

"Fuck you," I said. "Let's go."

The Cadillac's five hundred cubic inch mill was so silent and vibration free at idle, you could forget it was running. Troll goosed the accelerator a couple times, making it roar, and making the security men walking back to their vehicles jump as if he'd goosed them. They looked over with surly expressions. Troll gave them a friendly grin, said, "You girls drive safe, now," and burned rubber through the gate. He stopped at the first curve, and we both looked back, but the gate was already in its closed position.

"Quick," Troll said, and we continued up the drive, marked on both sides with reflectors. It curved in a wide arc to the ridge top that defined the canyon, then flattened for about twenty yards traversing the ridge.

Troll stopped the car before starting down the other side, and we stared at the lights of Los Angeles from a higher ground elevation than we'd ever seen before. Big Tujunga Canyon and the Angeles National Forest were behind us, dark and brooding, the land spread out before us was carpeted with light as far as the eye could see, some of it flowing like rivers.

Troll eased the car forward, lights began coming on around us, we'd activated a motion sensor. The double wide drive, sloping before us became illuminated by tiny white lights, spaced every foot or so in the middle of two retaining walls. It dropped down the mountainside atop concrete columns a yard in diameter, rising out of the chaparral every ten yards. The drive rejoined the Earth at the base of a large (ten acres, I guessed), flat shelf, a couple hundred feet below our once again stationary vehicle.

We sat in silence while outside lights on the shelf below activated, a few at a time. Al's new house became visible when low mounted flood lights came on, bathing it from below.

The house sat like a monolith, fifty yards from the outside edge of the shelf. It was a pyramid, about sixty feet high, set on a footing the height of a man, extending out around the pyramid on all sides.

Top third of the pyramid was featureless black glass, the triangle Troll said could be seen from down in The Valley when crossing Big Tujunga wash. Middle third was faced with limestone (joints between slabs invisible from our distance), and festooned with railed balconies, two to a side.

Only the four corner columns continued in an unbroken line to the footing. First floor walls were vertical, recessed beneath overhanging limestone faces.

A light blinking on drew my eyes left, to a large oval shaped swimming pool, thirty yards from the pyramid. While I stared at the turquoise oval, the Sphinx took shape out of the shadows, until half the pool was nestled between his paws. This Sphinx could be better described as a computer enhanced, pre-Napoleonic Sphinx (it had a nose).

Its non-committal face seemed to be staring past the pyramid at something in the vastness beyond the edge of the shelf. I imagined the lion body springing from its prone position, clearing the edge of the shelf in a couple bounds to confront an approaching enemy, then my disrespectful inner voice said, get a clue, dip shit, it's the guest house. And so it was. Hollow, and filled with every modern convenience, the impressive looking Sphinx could no more clear that shelf's outer edge in two bounds than I could.

After sitting awhile in silence, Troll said, "Looks like your uncle knew how to get the most out of his money."

"One of his talents," I said, "what would cost you or me a grand, he could usually nail down for two or three hundred."

"How long you going to be living here?" he asked.

"Until I get his daughter tightened up enough to deal."

"What's her story?"

I told him what I knew, including a couple tidbits from the video file I'd watched privately in Levy's office.

Went to work for her father fifteen years ago, after the breakup of her first marriage, to a professional baseball bonus baby with an incurable weakness for baseball groupies. She earned an MBA from USC in her off hours, and in five years worked her way from a data entry clerical position to executive vice-president of Brown Holdings, Ltd.

"Of course nepotism was involved," Al admitted on the video, "but she did that goddamn, boring data entry job for six months without a word of complaint, and became the fastest one in the department. Hell, if not for nepotism she'd still be there. She got so good at it, I kind of hated to move her."

During my last sojourn in Los Angeles, a week before my business at the cemetery, I attended her second wedding, a civil service in Palm Desert, to a hot shot commercial real estate broker, ten years her junior.

I liked the guy, a very polished soft sell type, who didn't come on, and was good company, could tell a joke. Figured they'd last three to five years, before he fell victim to Leni's measure of a man, drawn from Al whose money was the least interesting thing about him.

Leni sought an annulment after six months. She told the judge marriage had sapped her husband's will to work. He'd turned into a party boy, and his career went in the crapper. The judge granted the annulment, and Leni set up a modest annuity for ex number two, to keep him out of her hair. When he kept pestering her for more money, she moved up here with her mom and dad, where nobody could pester her.

About that time Aunt Ruth began feeling a little punk, a little worn out. She put it down to the stresses of packing and moving, and took a leave of absence from her teaching position at UCLA to relax and recharge.

When, after three months, she felt, if anything, worse, she went to UCLA medical center for a check-up. They found three types of cancer, running rampant through her thorax, none of them operable, all potentially fatal.

There were treatments available, Ruth declined, there wasn't one that did not include poison, baldness and nausea. She decided to enjoy her long awaited new house to the best of her ability for whatever time she had left, and mollified her doctors by bequeathing them her body upon her passing, trading her notarized signature on the necessary paperwork for a virgin pad of quadruplicate prescription forms from the chief of pathology, then retreating with husband and daughter behind the invisible, post state of the art walls of security encircling her new home.

Al and Leni attended her with no outside help for most of six months. In the final month, when the constant stream of pain killing chemicals had reduced her to an unconscious, shaking, sweating mass of protoplasm, Leni broke, and fled to the Venice Beach house.

Al waited another week before sending the nurse out of the room and increasing the morphine drip to end it.

When Leni showed at the memorial service, it was obvious she'd been hitting the bottle. But when she appeared at her father's Century City offices a few weeks later she was clear eyed and composed, applied belatedly for a leave of absence, explaining she'd joined a church that was helping her deal with the loss of her mother, without alcohol or drugs.

A relieved Al authorized paid leave of absence, for as long as she needed. His relief was short lived.

Over the next six months Leni ran through two hundred thousand dollars she'd received from Ruth's life insurance, fifty thousand she had in T-bills, and most of her salary, all spent (as opposed to donated) on church services, church publications, church lodging, etc.

She also donated the Venice beach house she'd just inherited to the church, to be utilized as an alcohol and drug treatment facility, operated by the church.

That one really stuck in Al's craw. "She got her name on the door, plus zilch," he said on the video I watched in Levy's office, "and those drug treatment scams are the hottest thing in medical services, these days."

Al was heavily invested in various medical enterprises as far back as I can remember, and referred to any and all business conducted in the medical community as scams. A cardiac clinic was a chest cutting scam; orthopedics, a broken leg scam; plastic surgery, a new you scam, and so on.

It was the fall of the Venice Beach house, Al admitted, along with his feeling he was running out of time, that got him thinking about who he might, without remorse of conscience, dump the Leni problem on. And, as he pondered, my image kept appearing in his mind's eye, accompanied by three words: I've got time.

When I finished filling him in, Troll said, "I knew that church was all about sucking bucks, but damn! The beach house, worth what, couple mil?"

"Assessed at two point five," I said.

"So, in six months they soaked your cousin for almost three million. That tells me something."

"What?"

"They've got no shame."

I shrugged. "Never heard of a church that did."

"And, with the amount of scratch your cousin's laid out, she either tows the true believer line or admits she's the chump of the century."

"If I sell her on chump hood," I said, "I collect long ducats."

"How long?"

"Private jet and helicopter owning long."

"Good luck," said Troll, and eased us down the elevated drive.

CHAPTER SIX

The elevated roadway widened to a parking area when it re-joined terra firma, and sent extensions to the guest Sphinx, into the canyon and straight to the pyramid, where it pitched down a wide gap under the footing. On one side of the garage entry, steps carved into the massive foundation curved up to first floor level.

Troll parked next to the steps, and we went up, activating more sensors, lighting the main entry. Smooth edged holes here and there in the surface we crossed sprouted a variety of indigenous desert flora and imported tropical trees and shrubs, softening the hard geometry of the building. The material underfoot appeared to be highly polished red granite, but the absence of any joints and the merest suggestion of give under my feet, made its geological pedigree suspect.

A pair of bronze griffins the size of sports cars crouched fifteen feet apart, guarding the main entry. Couldn't make out a front door in the featureless black surface of the first floor verticals, but noticed a familiar green glow on the back side of the right hand griffin and walked to the keypad;

Troll stood in front of the left hand griffin, examining its face. "Your uncle a tad enamored of ancient Egypt?" he said.

"Aunt Ruth," I said, "taught Egyptian History at UCLA for thirty years. Al was high tech, believed technology was the real magic. Seems they packed plenty of both into this place."

I entered my mother's DOB on the keypad and glanced over at Troll. He wasn't eyeballing the griffin anymore, but looking past it at the building with an expression I hadn't seen before. He looked dumbfounded. I glanced over my shoulder, into the building's interior. A hole, about ten foot in diameter, perfectly round except for a three foot flat spot at the floor, had appeared in the black wall.

"Jesus," I said, "where did that come from?"

"I think it opened from the center," said Troll. "But it happened too quick. Do it again, I gotta check this out."

"From the center?"

"Come on,," Troll said, moving toward the building, "quit fucking around."

I cleared the keypad with the pound key, and looked back at a restored solid wall. "Did you see it?" I said.

"Yeah, and it's a fast motherfucker. Hang on." He walked up and felt the wall. "Feels a little warm." He stepped back. "Okay, let her rip."

I re-entered the six digits, swinging my head around as I hit the last one, catching the barest flicker of movement at the edge of the hole. "You see it?" I asked Troll.

"Yeah. Good thing I didn't blink. It opened from the middle, but not like a camera shutter, like an eyeball." He walked over and felt the foot thick curving side. "Feels a little warmer." He grinned. "Double-D, this place is a trip."

I followed him into an egg shaped entry hall, where three passage ways and a curving staircase offered egress. The swooping walls were eggshell white, and the flooring looked like quarter-sawn oak, bleached white and coated with some shiny no-slip polymer, but still had that suggestion of give underfoot.

I had the feeling the surfaces we trod atop the massive footing had started life as a self-leveling gluey fluid, a new blend of polymers and esters, strong and light, hard but not brittle. If not for the total absence of joints between slabs of stone, and that hint of yielding underfoot, I'd have believed I was walking on red granite and quarter-sawn oak. You have to love those space-age polymers.

Troll stared down at a black and white rendition of the age old yin/yang symbol, a two-foot circle embedded in the egg's floor not far inside. He looked back and tapped the black side with his foot. Gaping hole returned to solid wall, tapped the white and the opening reappeared. He looked over at me.

"How's your computer literacy?"

"I was getting along on line pretty well when I got popped," I said. "But, after a year and a half," I shrugged, "whatever I haven't forgotten is probably obsolete. Why?"

Troll said, "I can think of two or three ways that door could work, in theory. But they'd all require the participation of a very large, very powerful computer. I've got a strong hunch we'll be running into something like that, here, before we get much older. I expect it will be pretty user friendly. Anyway, you've got some foundation, shouldn't have a problem."

"Nice to know I've got someone to call if I do," I said. "I take it you moved on from video games."

Troll said, "I still hit Game Dude once a month, but this guy I know, works at JPL, helped me set up a computer room in the little guest house out back, showed me how to take a bunch of laptops and turn them into one smoking monster, got me going in Linux. When we get back to my place, give me two hours in the computer room, I'll give you a binary tune up, have you running like a Ferrari."

"Bitchen." I said.

CHAPTER SEVEN

Three weeks later, awoke from a long bout of sleep in pitch darkness, felt a surge of relief, wasn't in prison. There are no pitch dark places in prison, I'd come awake out of another prison dream, nothing dramatic, an empty chow hall, me and some other white jump-suited prisoners playing poker for cigarettes at one of the octagonal, stainless steel chow hall tables. The guy across from me was on a winning streak, cartons of cigarettes stacked around him higher than his head. He glanced at his cards and looked at me, my shit bird cousin, Glen. No! not all those cigarettes and the West Hills Mall, too, I awoke thinking

I stretched and moved my arms and legs, like you do when you're making a snow angel, closeted in the top third of the pyramid, somewhere near the middle of Al's acre of bed, positioned at the center of the top level. It wasn't really an acre, but you could throw half a dozen tossers and turners on it, and they'd make it through the night without crowding each other.

I brooded, feeling around my perimeter for the clicker, free a month and still having dreams set in lock-up.

Prisons are depressing places, where time crawls. Half the people in them have no business being there, victims of stupid laws, vindictive bureaucrats and their own wrong-headed attitudes, but posing no threat or even burden to the community. The twenty percent of the prison population who really need to be there, make me glad we've got prisons.

I'd recently played cards and swapped jokes with men I would not like to see running around loose with access to weapons. Life's hard enough without assholes like them underfoot. Found the clicker under one of the pillows scattered around, and ran a thumb down the far right column, counting to seven, hit the seventh button once, moved down one button and held it in. The big triangular slab making up the sloping East wall atop the pyramid began to let in light. I released the button when the wall reached the density of welding goggles, passing enough half-light to navigate. The Sun looked like a badly smudged volley ball, near the top of the triangle.

Made my way to the edge of the bed on hands and knees, gathering up and pushing ahead plates, cups, bowls and flatware collected during a three day sleep-a-thon. Dropped the load in the dish hole when I got to the master suite's small kitchen, and was back in bed inside a minute, with a big, no spill cup of black tea, laced with sugar and heavy cream, and a jar of Wheat Nuts.

I left them on the bedside table, and crawled back out for the clicker. It had a hundred buttons, and capabilities I'd barely explored, the TV clicker from hell, but in a good way.

Propped myself up with some pillows and called down the giant flat screen to the foot of the bed. As a television it owned satellite access to a gross overabundance of channels. It could access digitally stored movies, hundreds of them. I could also view, after answering several questions Al figured only I could answer correctly, several hours of home video, starring Al, in which he explained many things, described in detail the cash engine whose care and feeding I must supervise, gave thumbnail sketches and detailed biographies of people I would be dealing with, described the structure and workings of the house he and Ruth designed (it was really two pyramids, set base to base).

The clicker also allowed me to view data collected and stored, or data being presently collected, by twenty eight digital video sensors scattered around the property. These micro-mini-cams were a product of nano technology, molecular world devices, grown rather than built, sensitive to double the light spectrum visible to humans, as well as sound frequencies. They were stupid but very durable sensors, expected to operate trouble free for two to three hundred years. The data they generated was useless without the participation of a powerful computer, like the one in the third level office next to the small kitchen, a featureless black slab (like that in 2001 A Space Odyssey), size of a tall filing cabinet, twenty years earlier it would have filled the Empire State Building. The multitude of complex duties it performs as the house computer (everything from security systems to pool maintenance, house-cleaning, internal and external communications, energy production and distribution) require less than one percent of its capacity.

I chewed some Wheat Nuts and keyed the nano-cam system, calling up a view from the leading edge of the pool's three-meter diving board. The big screen filled with a real time picture of the space between the Sphinx's fore-legs, most of the pool and its concrete apron, all the way to the open-air dining tables back in the shaded area beneath the Sphinx's big human face.

Near the body of the Sphinx, the pool's shallows let onto a concrete deck scattered with molded plastic chaise lounges, low, round glass-topped tables, and tall, broad-leafed shrubs in big, wheeled pots. One man and three women lay supine on lounges, slathered with sun block. I recognized one of the four, Lisa, a statuesque blond, who had been one of the group in the land yacht with Leni when I arrived. She was dressed in a modest, black one piece bathing suit. The two newcomer girls wore thong bikinis, designed not so much to cover as to draw attention to their female attributes. They were good looking girls, but in proximity to Lisa came off looking scrawny and a little desperate. They couldn't hold their space beside all that blond feminine pulchritude.

The new guy, positioned between Lisa and the thong girls, was slender but well-muscled and, except for head and armpits, appeared hairless. His Speedo was cut to display what he seemed to consider his best feature, if he'd been packing anything to be proud off he wouldn't have been able to get into it. The head of hair, though, was to die for.

The morning after my arrival, I returned from Troll's on the C90, and welcomed Leni back to her home, assigning her codes that gave her full access to the property, except for the top third of the pyramid, which was my domain, and some of the lower levels of the underground pyramid.

During the ensuing weeks a slew of church members availed themselves of Leni's open door policy. I kept my distance, cordial but reserved, and gave Leni free rein with the food service company and guest Sphinx, while exercising some free rein of my own with the nano-cam system to study the guests in their unguarded moments. Hey, I didn't ask for the job.

The church members were all good looking people. Based on the ones I saw, I'd have said that, notwithstanding the founding prophet, who was ugly as a carload of assholes, the church did not encourage the aesthetically challenged. Leni and Lisa aside, church members of both genders put in plenty of face time with the mirror, primping, making faces, trying out phrases and inflections. Leni would stare at herself ten or fifteen seconds, looking sad, then straighten her back, give her reflection half a smile, and turn away. Lisa always came in close, to examine her teeth, backed away for a critical once over, and grinned, "Pretty bitchen'."

Given a miasma of sexual tension, you could cut with a knife, and the unrestrained bandying of sexual double entendre, church members engaged in very little actual sex. Not unlike their secular sisters, it seems these ladies of the church do not believe half an hour of begging constitutes foreplay.

I chewed some more Wheat Nuts and pushed the zoom in and pan down buttons on the clicker until the big screen was filled with a close full shot of The Bod. I fantasized slipping the black straps off those tanned shoulders, pulling them down to expose the big white breasts. Lisa stirred uneasily, crossing an arm over them. A moment later she moved out of frame. I hit the zoom out button and got her luscious backside onscreen as she hit the water in a low, flat, shallow dive, then zoomed and panned my way into the outdoor dining area under the Sphinx's disinterested face. A quintet of round, glass-topped wicker tables could accommodate twenty-five in comfort, and offer an uncluttered view down the corridor between the fore legs of the lion body and the pool extending well beyond its paws..

A fair crowd was gathered around Leni, at the middle table, extra chairs brought over from adjoining tables and squeezed in. All present were drinking coffee and smoking like old diesels.

Sound quality was fuzzy from across the pool, switched to a nano-cam in the frame of an electric Hamms Beer sign, on the wall beside the table and felt like one of the gang.

Seated to Leni's right and left, Frieda and Edward had arrived with Leni in the motor home, and since shown no inclination to leave. Frieda's boyfriend, Jerry, behind the coffee bar, busied himself, serving up cappuccinos to the rest of the crowd. He is a perpetual smiler, and not without good reason. He's the only over nighter getting laid. He and Frieda have a stable-like sex life, and seem oblivious to how well sound travels at this elevation.

Jerry and Edward sport clerical collars. I suppose their positions in the church permit them this standard clergyman's accessory, but they wear them only on occasion, and I never did determine what prompted their appearance.

Edward seemed to be the senior member of the church hierarchy present. During my shameless peeping and eavesdropping, I gleaned the information Edward was the first to hear from Leni, her idea of turning the Venice beach house into a drug treatment clinic.

I didn't doubt it. He looks like he's straight out of the American Heartland, fresh off the farm, or ranch. He's not imposing, but has the kind of rawboned good looks enjoyed by actor, Viggo Mortensen, with maybe a taste of John Boy Walton rolled in.

Take away his fortunate physical appearance, though, and he's just another bureaucrat with delusions of a future in politics. He exhibited a proprietary attitude toward Lisa, but stopped well short of taking liberties that would be natural if there was any intimacy between them.

I doubted he facilitated the rapid transformation of the Venice Beach house, but he seemed a perfect choice to continue milking the cash cow.

I watched from the Hamms Beer sign, he said to Leni, "You know, Lenore, going back to your job might be the best way to get control of your inheritance."

Leni seemed to be thinking it over while she got out a cigarette, accepted a light from Edward, and blew a trio of smoke rings.

"I don't know, Edward," she said, at last, "I've scheduled and paid for the advance courses, and everybody else in my group is taking off work for them. That's supposed to be the best way to get the material, isn't it?"

"Sure. No distractions."

"And after completing them, I'll be more effective at work, right?'

"Of course," Edward said. "I just hope you're not being robbed blind while your attention is elsewhere."

"That's not going to happen. At least, not while Mark's head of the trust."

Edward said, "Can you spell unsupported premise?"

"Very funny. But answer me this.....You've had some

conversation with Mark, right?"

"Social intercourse," Edward replied, "nothing heavier than the weather."

"What do you think he'd do if he caught you stealing something from here, like, oh…that Picasso in the entry hall?"

"I don't steal," said Edward. "Anyway, that's just a print, isn't it?"

"I guess. But pretending it's real and you're a big art lover. In a moment of weakness, you decide you gotta have it. You've got it under your arm, heading for the door, then Mark comes in from the kitchen hallway and busts you red-handed. What would he do?"

"I don't know, smash my face in?"

"Come on, Edward. Use your head."

"You think you know him so well, you tell me what he'd do."

"Beats me," Leni said, and laughed. "But, I know what he wouldn't do."

"Call the police," said Edward.

"That's right," Leni said, "and make you wish he had."

"He's got you psyched out, Lenore. He doesn't scare me."

"Then, you're either stupid or crazy."

I saw a black expression flit across his face, as he looked down. He took a couple seconds to compose himself, then gave Leni a self-deprecating smile, and said, "Probably equal measures of both."

One of the women at the table said, "I wonder what he's doing, locked in the top of that pyramid."

"Probably sleeping," said Frieda.

"Or performing an unnatural act," Edward said.

"For three days?" Frieda sneered.

"Three days is nothing, to an unnatural act," said Edward.

"Sleeping is an unnatural act, around here," Frieda said.

Lisa came over, dripping from the pool, and oh so fine, she pushed in between Leni and Frieda, and reached across the table for a cigarette, holding her position waiting for a light.

Gazing at her prominently displayed backside, I dreamed of peace and plenty forever. Be still my heart (I'm not your heart, dick weed).

"Actually," said Lisa, expelling a cloud of cigarette smoke across the table, "our elusive host and guardian of Lenore's pocketbook may be watching our every move, hearing every word we speak."

A chorus of protest: "No way, Lisa"... "That would be so illegal"..."Not to mention creepy"... "In the shower, last night, I felt like I was being watched, I'm serious!"... "It's called wishful thinking, Brenda"........."Screw you, you little queer, It's called sniffing little boys' bicycle seats"... "I call that aroma-therapy!"... "You are nasty!" "You guys are out too deep!"

Lisa looked back over her shoulder. "Lenore, how say you?"

Leni said, "He could be, but he's got a low threshold of boredom, though he might be working up a pretty good stiffie, staring at your ass."

Lisa straightened up and adjusted the bottom of her suit. "You may not have been paying attention, Lenore, but he hasn't given me a second glance."

"I've noticed," said Leni. "It means he's hot for you."

"Come off it," said Lisa.

"I'm serious," Leni said. "He's had women figured out since high school. He flirts with all of them, except the ones he wants, he ignores them, totally. But whenever they're in his sight, though he won't look in their direction, he'll start imagining himself with them in all these really nasty sexual positions. Then, the first time he sees them alone, he walks right up and puts a lip lock on them. Says it works every time And, after he fucks them, if he decides he wants to fuck them again, he rolls on top of them, looks deep into their eyes, and says, 'What did you say your name was?'"

"He told you this?" Lisa said.

"Well," Leni said, "I was a nothing freshman, and he was a senior screwing the three finest girls in school. He was my cousin, so I asked him. He told me because he didn't want me falling for the same kind of bullshit."

Was wishing I'd been a little less forthcoming with Leni in high school when a flag on the upper left of the flat screen announced: Troll entering property. I switched to a nano-cam in one of the balcony railings on the pyramid's second level, opened to a wide angle shot of most of the Sphinx, driveways and parking areas, and the lower half of the elevated drive descending from the ridge top just as Troll came into frame, guiding his restored Apache pick-up down the slope.

He parked in the narrow shade of the pyramid's footing, and came up the steps, dressed in knee length cutoffs, flip-flops and dark Wayfarers, carrying a beach size black towel slung over one shoulder, he started across the slightly drooping wood and rope bridge, from the footing to the pool apron.

Reaching the pool, he kicked off his flops, dropped the towel on them, and the sunglasses on the towel, then climbed the diving platform up to the three meter board and stood there a moment, arms at his sides, shoulders back, stepping out smartly, coming down on the balls of his feet at the end of the board, causing it to dip so far I winced, expecting a loud crack, but it rebounded and he pushed off, launching himself high above the platform as the board chattered back to motionlessness. He got in a little hang time, toes pointed, head tipped back, a bearded, pot-bellied Buddha, surrendering to the Sun God. Then, started to drop, grabbed his knees, somersaulted backwards one and a half times, and kicked out to enter the water so arrow straight the resulting ten-foot column didn't vary a degree off the vertical.

He stayed under so long I got worried and keyed over to the nano-cam set in the metal ring around the pool light. Troll was swooping along, fifteen feet down at the bottom of the deep end, near the square drain grille. He reversed direction in a rising loop, and sped to the shallow end, finally coming up for air in four feet of water.

I keyed back to the view from the high dive, and the sounds issuing from the flat-screen lost their hollow underwater quality.

Troll sloshed up the curving steps at the shallow end of the pool, and stood on the edge, squeezing water out of his beard with one fist. "Afternoon, ladies."

"Mister, that was some dive," one of the thong girls said.

"Very impressive," Speedo threw in.

Troll ignored him and smiled at the thong girls. "Thank you kindly," he said, then, "I could teach you."

"Really?"

"Nah."

"That's mean."

"Well," said Troll, "you have to go through a lot of pain to dive like that."

"Pain?"

"Belly-flops, back-flops, face-flops."

"Ouch," the girl said, touching her face with her fingertips.

"Then again, I know other things I could teach you, wouldn't hurt a bit."

"I'll bet! Sorry, I have a boyfriend."

"I'm sure you do," Troll said, turning away, "but if you ever get to hankering for a man, give me a whistle."

Troll had gone three steps when a sharp wolf whistle cut the air. He stopped short and, after a moment, turned around. Lisa was returning to her chaise lounge, freshly lit cigarette in one hand. "Is that the kind of whistle you mean?"

He stood there, head lowered, watching as she settled back into the lounge and arched her back provocatively. "It sure is," said Troll.

"Just checking," she smiled. "Thanks."

Troll retrieved his towel, put his sunglasses on, stepped into his flops and proceeded to the men's shower room, in the Sphinx's right foreleg.

I was in the pyramid's huge main kitchen when he strolled in, flops slapping against the slate floor. "Smells good," he said.

I finished flipping a row of bacon slices on the central griddle of the commercial eight burner stove, and set the tongs aside. "Hungry?"

"Hungry and Horny," Troll said. "Not necessarily in that order."

"I can help you out with the first part," I said.

"Man, that blond in the black one piece is begging to get drilled."

"I'll see what I can do about it," I said.

"Better hurry," he said.

"Don't rush me," I said. "Take it out on Lori."

"You know I will," he said. "But if things don't work out with the girl.."

"You'll be the first to know," I promised.

Awhile later, we sat at a round table on the enclosed patio, just outside the kitchen, shoveling bacon, eggs fried in bacon grease, slices of beefsteak tomato, Haas avocado, red onion and fork-split sourdough muffins into our faces with an intensity that precluded conversation.

Troll ran a piece of muffin around his plate, wiping up egg yolk, popped it in his mouth and got up, taking his twenty ounce tumbler to the refrigerated milk dispenser. He lifted the ball-ended metal handle, filling the glass, poured it down his throat and refilled.

"Damn," he said, wiping his mouth with the back of his hand as he returned to the table. "What's a motherfucker got to do to get milk that good?"

"I think a motherfucker's got to own the dairy," I said.

"That figures," he said. "Guess you'll be seeing plenty of me."

"Always welcome," I said.

"By the way," he said, "I bumped into Sue, last night, down at Sunland Produce, told her you were back in the picture. She wanted your number, I gave her your e-mail address. You'll probably be hearing from her."

"Sue who?" I asked.

"Yeah."

"Oh. How's she doing?"

Sue Hu was a Vietnamese war orphan who'd set up house (or hooch) with a Marine Lieutenant attached to my company during the last year of the war. Jackson was a white boy from some wide spot in the road with a name, in South Mississippi. Having grown up on the edge of a swamp the size of Rhode Island, he was well suited for war in the tropics. Average height, whipcord thin, those stringy muscles like steel cable, and tireless. He'd gone native in the best sense of the word, fallen in love with the country and, by extension, one of its women. He didn't want to go home, and the more it became clear the brass wasn't going to allow us to kick ass, the more reckless he became.

He got caught in a crossfire, trying to cover the back of our forward observer, and I had to hump him back a couple klicks to the medevac perimeter, all the while he's telling me I've got to get Sue out if Saigon falls, and I'm huffing, "Shut the fuck up, you ain't dying." By the time we hit the LZ he had shut up, and made a liar out of me.

A sergeant major I was friendly with got Sue Hu and her tow headed infant on a cargo jet to Bangkok a week later, along with her dead husband's back pay.

I'd done my duty, and never gave her another thought, until I walked into a takeout place called China Sea, five years later, in a Sunland strip mall, and found her working the cash register, tiny, beautiful, and tough as a fifty cent steak.

Troll twisted a tuft of his beard, and said, "She's still one hot little package, especially when she goes: Me so hawney."

"She does that when she wants some dip shit to double his order, says it works every time."

"Naw," said Troll.

"You didn't when she said it to you?"

"I'd have to say I did," He shook his head, "even thought it was my idea."

"At least you've got the nuts to admit it," I said. "I admire that."

"I admire the breakfast you just put up," Troll said. "Didn't know you could cook."

"Didn't know you could dive," I said.

"Pennsylvania state champion, 1967," said Troll. "Qualified for the '68 Olympics."

"Didn't go?"

"No, too afraid."

"Of Olympic competition?"

"Nope, afraid the war was gonna end before I had a chance to get over there and get some slant-eyed pussy."

"You and half a million other swinging dicks," I said.

CHAPTER EIGHT

Troll left to make a speed delivery. I dumped our breakfast detritus in the patio dish-hole. What happens to it from there I haven't had time to look into, nor the inclination, no shortage of dishware or utensils being evident.

Putting away food items I'd left around the stove when Leni came in. She's a wiry little thing, takes big steps, has aristocratic features, framed by a half-tame black natural. Used to have a ready smile, and she seemed a lot less mopey now than when I first got here.

She made a beeline for the walk-in freezer. "Hey, Mark, were you spying on us earlier?"

"Who, me?"

Standing inside the freezer compartment, holding the door open with one foot, she grabbed a ten-pack of t-bones and a box of Australian lobster tails. Tendrils of ice-fog swirled around her and disappeared. She looked over.

"If you weren't, don't run and check now, but I think Lisa's getting a wide-on for you."

"A what?"

"Come on," she said, releasing the door to suck shut behind her, "guys get hard-ons, girls.. Jesus, where have you been living, Georgia? Oops!"

"Boy, is your face red," I said, "or should be."

Leni laughed. "You are too mean," she said. "Anyway, you've got your heads up on Lisa, she's unattached, but there are three church biggies in line, pitching hard.

"Edward thought he'd grab the inside track, bringing her up here, but she's playing him like a fish. She's the third generation of her family in the church, folks way up in the church hierarchy. So, she's a good catch."

"Not to mention having a bod that won't quit," I said.

"So, you did notice," Leni said, tucking the groceries under an arm. "Food will be ready in about an hour. You want to pop over for a bite, see if Lisa breathes hard, you know the way."

"I've got to go deal with my e-mails," I said, "then shit, shower and shave. Maybe I'll stop by before I go out, see if she wants to lay some old time religion on me."

"That's new-fangled religion, mister," Leni said, then grinned. "Only kind we're offering."

"Well, then," I said, "I might have to lay some old time religion on her."

"Yeah, right," Leni said. "Like the Church of your Dead Buddy?"

"Cult of the Dead Homey," I said.

"Whatever," Leni said. "I don't know how you came up with what you told them.."

"Pulled it out my ass."

"You made Jerry very nervous. And Jonathan was freaking so bad they had to send him home."

"I don't usually proselytize," I said, "but they seemed to be sincerely searching for answers."

"You gave them some. They think you're dangerous and unstable."

"They're half right," I said, "like their church."

"Oh, Mark, please don't break my balls."

"Sorry, Len." I tried to look contrite. "You know I love you."

"Always known that," she smiled, "at least since the day you saved me from the Mexican kid."

I searched my memory. "You mean the pencil-necked little prick, poking you with his finger?"

"Yeah, my first year at Reseda. The kid and his little band of no habla English commandos were ghosting me all week. I think he had some weird crush on me, he was creepy.

"When they caught up to me in the parking lot that day, I was terrified. He's poking me in the chest, telling me my new name's gonna be Puta Blanca. I saw you go by on the parking lot, but I was too scared to yell. Then, you did a double take, and stopped. You started toward us with a kind of skip, not running, but you were covering ground faster than I've seen it covered, and the look on your face would have scared the Devil in hell. The kid's little gang ran like maniacs, you snatched him out of my face by his neck, and slammed him into the side of that van, with his Converse kicking around two feet off the ground and whispered some stuff to him I couldn't hear, then tossed him away, like a flick of the wrist, but I'd swear he flew twenty feet."

"Have to give the little bastard credit, though," I said, "he hit the ground running."

"That's right, he did," Leni said. "And, you turned to me, with a big smile, like you hadn't even really been mad, and said, 'Rough day at school, kiddo? Well, that limp dick won't be giving you any more trouble. Come on, I'll give you a ride home.'"

"I remember giving you a ride home," I said. "Did he ever bother you again?"

"Are you kidding? Whenever that kid saw me coming, he booked, took off running and did not look back. People started being real friendly to me, the whole school was talking about it the next day."

The whole freshman class, maybe. None of my classmates found the incident worthy of comment, beyond a couple passing mumbles sounding suspiciously like big bully. I didn't voice these thoughts for Leni, I'll take any low-rent version of hero worship I can get. Most of the really heroic acts I've performed, I came away from the experience only grateful I was alive with all my appendages and wasn't up on charges.

Leni said, "The boy transferred, end of year, but for the rest of that year the only parts of him I ever saw were his skinny ass and the bottoms of his feet. What did you whisper to him?"

"Beats me, something scary, I guess. Seeing him poke you like that pissed me off ten times as bad as if he'd been poking me. I mainly remember telling myself, don't kill him, don't kill him, then tossing him away, so I wouldn't."

Didn't make Leni's barbecue, took me three hours just to deal with the e-mail that had stacked up while I slept. Most of them got something along the lines of, use your best judgment, and keep me posted. One got, You're fired. Return all company property in your possession, per attached list. Report to Personnel, to cash out your contract, and if you want a good reference, be civil.

The only e-mail I got a kick out of read: Double-D, Please come to see me at Sunland store. Me so hawnee. Sue Hu.

Reply: Sue, please put together three, no, make that six large seafood platters, pick up nine-thirty to ten. Thanks, DD.

The Albert Brown Family Trust (until recently Brown Holdings Ltd.) was domiciled in the top two floors of a Century City high rise. I had yet to visit the offices, but familiarized myself with their layout and activities by reviewing data gathered by thirty six nano-cams connected to their mainframe. I had looked over some of the data, mostly for the days following Al's death, and been bored to tears. The sheer mass of data was mind-boggling. Troll told me keywords of conversation and even body positions could be used to edit. My lack of interest had so far kept him from showing me how.

It was time to visit the offices in person, but not during business hours. I was doing well, establishing my authority by e-mail, had yet to accept any phone calls. Al suggested this as means of building a mystique and limiting demands on my time. He'd yet to make a suggestion I saw fit to disregard.

After showering and trimming my hair, beard and nails, I went into the walk-in closet that had been Al's, and browsed through the clothing he'd stocked it with, all new, my sizes. Aunt Ruth's closets and bathroom, on the other side of the big bed were completely empty. I later found all their clothing and personal effects neatly stored in the subterranean pyramid.

I put on some khaki pants, a purple wife-beater and an olive green sport jacket with no inner lining. I wavered between a pair of brown loafers and some tan leather flops. Laziness carried the day, flops.

Given all the high-tech goodies built into the pyramid, its elevator is surprisingly mundane, a big, oblong box, with doors on two sides and protective pads covering the walls. I took it to the parking garage, comprising the first level of the subterranean pyramid and mostly vacant, my motorcycle next to the elevator, Leni's Jag near the exit ramp, Al's and Ruth's cars side by side, his and her Lexus in matching eggshell white, Al's a big four door sedan, Ruth's a turbo-charged two door coupe. Leni had commandeered Al's car, leaving her Jaguar as a community vehicle for her friends. I was content to settle for exclusive use of Ruth's car, which could have given my C90 a run for its money, maybe caught it on a long enough stretch.

Al built and raced funny cars during the nineteen-sixties, and racing successes fueled his way into promotional and partnership agreements with several Southland auto dealerships. But off-track he drove like an old lady. Aunt Ruth, though, was fun to ride with.

It was dark when I pulled off Pico onto Century Park West. The building address was prominent, well marked, as was the parking entrance.

The uniformed attendant said, "Evening, Mr. Brown. If you'd like to hop out at the elevators, I'll be happy to park it for you and have it ready when you get back."

"Okay, thanks," I said. "How did you know my name?"

"Security briefing, sir," he said.

"Very reassuring."

A few minutes later I was sitting behind Al's desk, inside the top Northeast corner of the building. I had his chair turned around , and was gazing at L. A.'s downtown skyline, ten or twelve miles distant, from an elevation which, while nowhere near as commanding as that on which the pyramid was placed, nonetheless fostered a certain arrogance in me, due, I was certain, to the thrashing my self-esteem absorbed during the prison experience. Take a ride on the Ego Trip, asshole, I told myself.

Having my fill of the cityscape, I turned the chair back to the desk, switched on some light, and activated the desktop. While it booted, I dug a slip of paper out of my wallet, five passwords from Al's video.

There wasn't anything I could access on the office mainframe I couldn't have accessed through the computer at the pyramid. In layman's terms, the operating system in the pyramid's computer could kick the office operating system's ass, and make it give up everything it had. But Al, on the video he made, stressed putting in time at the office, after hours at first.

"You have a heavy presence," he remarked. "Might as well make it work for you."

During the course of his lengthy monologue Al alluded to perceptions from senses I do not possess. I was tempted to take those comments as allegorical, despite knowing from childhood he was the most matter of fact person in the family, least likely to ruminate or openly philosophize.

Yet, here I was, letting the office soak up my vibes.

I went into the personnel records, saw a check had been issued to the guy I fired earlier in the day, and shot an e-mail to his secretary: In five hundred words or less, convince me to promote you to Chester's job instead of searching outside organization.

I printed and signed three bonus checks, for people I'd found working whenever I keyed into the office nano-cam system, as opposed to working crossword puzzles, cruising internet porn sites or texting on cell phones held below the edge of their desks. I sealed the checks in white, business size security envelopes, each with a few words jotted on the back of a low-key business card. On the first I printed: When you'd finally convinced yourself that your good work and attention to detail were not even noticed, much less appreciated, and scrawled a barely legible MLB. The printed side of the card had The Albert Brown Family Trust across its face, on an invisible line between the upper third and bottom two thirds. In the lower left corner was M. L. Brown – Administrator, in the lower right my e-mail address.

Finished, I still had an hour to kill before heading to Sue Hu's. E-mailed Troll I'd be coming by between ten and eleven with long seafood, chose yes when his e-mail server asked if it should notify his cell as to the waiting message.

Drumming a four-finger composition on the desk, considering whether I wanted to call the garage and leave early, I realized I was not alone on the floor. I was surprised, but not concerned. Most of the security apparatus for the building's top two floors was either invisible (as the nano-cams), or disguised as something else (as the olfactory intakes). Everyone with access to the floors had a profile made up of sight, sound and smell data in system memory, and high speed processors silently, invisibly began constructing a profile on anyone coming within the building's foundation. Only authorized profiles had after-hours access to these floors, and, if through fluke or subterfuge, a profile-less individual did gain access to either floor, they would encounter one frustration after another in trying to leave The faint ding of the arriving elevator hadn't caught my attention, while I was talking with Troll's mailbox, but some other subtle input that followed left me no question I had company.

I could have scanned the nano-cams, and had an identity and location in seconds, but I preferred to sneak around and locate them myself. I stuck a flip-flop in each of my jacket side pockets, told the desktop to go to bed, locked the office's double doors, and went out a door behind the wet bar, into an executive bathroom larger and more lavish than a Wilshire high rise single.

I passed a wall-mounted toilet next to a wall-mounted bidet. A pair of recessed shelves in the pale blue ceramic wall they shared offered a selection of reading material. I looked through a tiled arch, into a semi-circular shower with multiple heads. The curving tiled wall clung at each end to a ten-by-ten foot slab of tinted window, looking across the Beverly flats and Sunset Strip at the Hollywood Hills. Beyond the shower was a lounge and dressing area, with a six-foot high pier glass in one corner and a couple four-foot high upholstered tables sticking out from one wall, prompting an urge in me for a massage, and a short nap.

Similarly woolgathering, I stepped through to an industrial carpeted rear passage and collided with a woman walking up the hallway. She stumbled back, the Styrofoam cup of coffee in her left hand tilted at me. I lifted the coffee cup with my right hand, holding it at arm's length while I caught her shoulder with my left. "Oops," I said.

"Jesus," she said, "where did you learn to move like that?"

"Acme School of Buffoonery," I said. "Sorry, I was daydreaming like an old hound dog." I handed the coffee back.

"You made a good recovery," she said. "Doesn't look like prison did you much harm."

"Only my pride," I said. "But you have me at a disadvantage."

"Of course, you don't remember me. Julia Hoffman, I grew up next door to Ruth and Albert. You saved my life when I was a baby."

"You're not the little crumb cruncher I found crawling around back in the alley."

"The very one," she smiled, "with the trash truck bearing down on me."

"The trash truck was still two blocks up the alley," I said. "But, your mom kind of over-reacted when I brought you in and told her she should try to keep you out of the alley on trash days."

"The way Mom always told it, you snatched me from the jaws of death."

"I was twelve, and self-righteous," I said, "probably over stated the danger."

"I suppose," she said with some reluctance.

She ushered me into her office, a ten by ten foot space, with unfinished sheet rock walls, it was the copying and fax room before desktop printing made it redundant. The space was bisected by a big clear Lucite desk, with enough space on one side to squeeze past. A couple long cork boards were mounted behind and down one side of the desk. Many letter size sheets of computer paper were pinned to the boards, all printed with large, round, multi-colored patterns, like mandalas.

The chair behind the desk and the two facing it from the other side, were three different versions of what I call back chairs, where you sit on one pad and rest your knees on a smaller pad a foot before and a few inches lower than the one you're sitting on, supposed to be good for your back. Julia Hoffman had good posture, I noted.

"How are you finding your new duties?" she inquired.

"Tolerable," I said. "Beats swinging a bush ax."

"What about that church? I've heard they can get mighty rude."

"That's difficult to believe," I said, "they're unfailingly polite, to me."

"I wouldn't get too comfortable,"

"Comfort's for sissies," I said. "I spit on comfort. What kind of job rates an office like this?"

"Astrologer."

"I didn't know astrologers got offices?"

"Well, I got this one, in perpetuity, with free phone and broadband."

"The place is starting to look a little more upscale," I said. "How did you go from being an escape artist in a diaper to an astrologer?"

"It started when I was a freshman at UCLA. Albert had been experimenting with moon and tide tables, trying to find correlations between them and the stock and commodities markets. He knew I'd won a couple math prizes in high school, and one day he brought my father a stack of basic astrology texts, and told him he'd buy me a new car, if I'd study them and report to him whether I found some validity to them, or just a bunch of hooey. I jumped on it.

"A few weeks later, I told him I needed more books. He set up an account for me at the Bodhi Tree Bookstore, and gave me money, to pay for classes at the Carroll Richter Institute.

"Six months later, I wrote him a fairly long report, telling him that I'd found astrology to be a vast field, with applications to every aspect of human existence. A certain amount of bullshit got into print under its banner, but the large majority reflected reality in ways I found downright eerie.

"He asked my what kind of car I wanted, I said, how about a used car, and keep my account at the Bodhi Tree open. He kept it open, and got me a Celica demonstrator, with five hundred miles on it, then asked me how I'd feel about doing astrology on a professional basis. I assumed he wanted to market astrology like those psychic hot lines that were big business at the time. I told him I didn't know if I'd ever feel comfortable doing it for money. He said fine, but should I ever changed my mind, please let him be the first to know.

"Seven years later, recently divorced, with a two year old daughter, and burnt out on insurance actuarial work, I called and told him I was ready to give professional astrology a shot. He set me up here, and told me I could have all the clients I wanted, as long as I put him first. I've been his in-house astrologer ever since."

"So, what do you do?" I asked.

"When I first started, it was a lot of comparing natal charts of prospective employees or business partners to his and the company chart."

"Companies have horoscopes?"

"Sure, usually the date of incorporation. Albert had so many businesses coming and going, I took the date and time of his first incorporation to compare with all his subsequent acquisitions. It worked real well."

"Did he always go with your recommendations?"

"No. But when he didn't he ended up wishing he had. After the first year, I had final say on hiring, and I never even met the candidates. By then I could take from a five second glance at a pair of charts what in the beginning took an hour of making notes and looking up stuff. Since I was eager to learn, I kind of became pro-active. I'd come up with things to try, and Albert was always willing. It was so much fun."

"What kind of things?"

"Oh, you know, not making big purchases or closing deals when the Moon's void of course, not signing legal documents or initiating legal action when Mercury's retrograde. Stuff like that."

"I can speak any language but Greek," I said

"And I started talking Greek. I'm sorry."

"Don't be. I didn't want to mislead you I was getting it."

"The function of the astrologer is translating the language of astrology into language the client understands, you were right to stop me."

"You're not in the payroll or personnel folders," I said.

"I'm a tenant, with my rent paid way in advance. Albert settled my consulting fees in cash. He also gave me small percentages on profitable business I recommended and for losses not incurred on situations I warned him off, not in cash. He made me a little cash engine with the money, so I don't have to sweat the basics, not until the collapse of Western civilization, at any rate."

"What info do you need to do my horoscope?" I said

"None. I've had your chart almost two years."

"What?"

"Well, I had to help Albert pick between you and your cousin, Glen, for the trusteeship. Boy, that was a tight one."

"What?"

"I'm kidding," she said, and laughed, "he was never in the running."

CHAPTER NINE

I drove like a maniac and got to Sue Hu's restaurant at ten after ten. It was in the same Foothill Blvd. strip mall it had occupied for twenty years, but now, instead of fifteen feet of curving storefront, it monopolized the entire C shaped structure.

The parking area, around the C's outer curve, was packed, but as I turned off Foothill, some back-up lights came on in the row nearest the building, and by the time I got there the space was vacant. Must be living right, I told myself, easing the Lexus in.

A pair of giant banana trees flanked the new front entrance. I walked between them into the building, stopping just inside to check out the re-modeling. The interior walls separating the various storefront units were gone, leaving a cavernous space that curved away in both directions, Dropped ceilings had been eliminated, and four-inch round steel columns installed where bearing walls had been removed. The steel joists supporting the roof were covered with vari-colored netting, and the under-roof between them painted as a continuous undersea mural, cleverly illuminated by little, hooded floodlights, mounted on the joists and pointing up at a wide variety of aquatic flora and fauna.

The food preparation area was to my right, separated from the lobby by an L shaped, clear sided tank, containing several thousand gallons of water, and a lot more seafood than you'd find on the ceiling, lobsters for days, climbing all over each other and waving their claws (held shut by paper rings), crabs, a baby shark or two, giant clams (letting it all hang out), cruising fish of wide variety.

On the far side of the tank six men prepared orders, with many stylized moves, their assistants decorated the finished product and slid loaded trays across the top of the tank, into a tube that conveyed them out of sight to the service area across the lobby.

The dining room curved away to my left, dotted with tables for four and six. Booths for larger parties were ranked below the windows on the curving outer wall. A blond hostess in a black silk sheath came out of the dining area, one arm cradling a short stack of leatherette menus beneath some mighty impressive cleavage.

"Reservation?" she said.

I gestured with my chin at Sue Hu, who was running the cash register from a tall stool behind a tall counter, the only thing about the place that hadn't changed. When I looked back at the hostess she was staring at me. "You're staring," I said.

"Oh," she put her hand to her mouth, the way young girls do. "I'm sorry. Can I get you something to drink? On the house."

"You old enough to serve liquor?" I said. She nodded. "A double Wild Turkey, on ice, please."

Sue Hu handed credit card and receipt to a young Latino wearing a crew cut, white wife beater, big denim shorts and black Converse sneakers. She looked from him to the woman, standing behind him with one kid riding hip shot, another distending her belly, and asked the only question she ever asked customers. "Food okay?"

"Great, like always," the guy said.

"Delicious," said the woman.

"Thank you, so much," said Sue.

I walked over as they passed, Sue scrutinized me with oriental inscrutability. "I thought you were dead."

"Only the good die young," I said.

"You're no spring chicken," she said. "Your phone got disconnected, your pager got me some guy who never heard of you, you don't answer email. Were you hiding?"

"Just keeping a low profile," I said.

"When the troll told me you were back.."

"It's just Troll," I said.

"Oh, sorry. Anyway, it was an answer to my prayers."

"Oh to be loved," I said.

"Needed," she said. "But I like you okay, too."

The blond hostess returned, bearing a small round tray with an eight ounce cut glass tumbler centered on it. The tumbler had been packed with ice and topped off with whiskey. I took a sip, to make sure it was real Turkey and not the eighty six proof crap, and said, "Thank you, very much."

"You're most welcome," she said without looking up.

Sue said, "Rebecca, please take over for me, we won't be

long. Oh, and please ask Vincent to put up six large platters."

"Yes, ma'am," the hostess said, and moved to the stool as Sue got down. I followed through a beaded opening behind the cash register, then out a door to the area enclosed by the C's interior curve. Half the space was now an Oriental garden, with winding pathways of polished pea gravel, small bridges over a sequence of connected koi ponds, riotous vegetation and a handful of tables, secluded and intimate. The outer half was paved and sported a loading dock. We crossed to the end of the building, Sue opened a steel security door, and I followed her into an office, with a big roll top desk and a computer module dominating half the room. A pair of papa-san chairs, set in the corners, lorded it over the other half, rattan footstools before them. I sat in one, put my feet up and sipped some cold, cold Bourbon.

Sue poured herself a glass of white wine, put the bottle back in a mini-fridge, then came and sat on the footstool, bumping my legs over to make room.

"Good looking hostess, out front," I said.

"My niece," said Sue, "good worker."

"Niece through Jackson?" I said, naming her long dead G.I.

She nodded, "His sister's oldest."

"It's great you're still close to the family."

"They're wonderful people. When I first came from Thailand, they sold their sugar plantation in Mississippi and moved to California, because they didn't want to expose me to Southern racism."

"Mighty white of them," I said. "Big plantation?"

"Pretty big. They bought a huge house in Benedict Canyon, and Andy's dad never worked again, plus he gave me the money to start my first store."

"What you've done with this place," I said, "I'm impressed."

"When the old owner decided to sell, I was able to move on it. But I got in trouble on the remodeling. I had to take on a couple partners, one to get the city and county bureaucrats off my back, the other bought a franchise from me for a hundred K, when I needed cash, now owns China Sea – Channel Islands and holds some non-voting stock in this place."

"How much?"

"Five percent, same with other guy."

"The one that got you out of inspection hell."

Sue nodded. He owns a piece of Neptune's Net, at County Line, belongs to the Marauders motorcycle club, but he's got relatives all through the local bureaucracies. His father's a big mucky-muck at DWP, brother's one of the top guys at building and safety, uncle at transportation, his mother and an aunt on the Coastal Commission."

"Is he the one got you pining for me?" I said.

"Both of them," said Sue. "They get together and do the seafood purchasing for all three stores, and they're good at it, but they became big buddies, and now they're ripping me off."

"Fuckers."

Sue Hu smiled. "I'm glad you see my side of things."

"Fuck them," I grunted. "They're dead men."

"No, goddamnit. I don't want them dead." Catching my sideways glance, she added. "They're good seafood buyers."

I nodded slowly, and prefaced my next question with a long, drawn out well. "How about wheelchairs and colostomy bags, for the rest of their miserable lives?"

"No! Jesus, Double-D."

"You don't want them killed or maimed, means you have wiggle room. If you have wiggle room, why you calling me?" We locked gazes. After five seconds, I moved my eyes from hers, like a lawyer leaving the courtroom to await a verdict. I took another sip of my ice cold Turkey, and felt thankful liquor wasn't one of the drugs I'd ruined for myself before developing a modicum of restraint.

"You're right," said Sue. "This situation has been eating me for a week. Then, when I saw the tr- excuse me, when I saw Troll at the produce store, and he told me you were living back in LA, I knew what I had to do, and knowing you were around gave me the nerve to do it. After what you did for me and little Andy, I've got no business asking you to help, but I could make it worth your while, financially."

"I've got a full time job," I said, "crappy salary but great benefits. Call me receptive. Let's start with what your partners did, what you did back, then move along to how I can help and what's in it for me."

"They bought a 747 full of sea urchins, real cheap, from a

coked out wholesaler who was in too deep to the air freight contractor, and was informed his urchins were grounded until he brought his account up to date. If they went bad in the plane, he was totally screwed, so he sold them Mutt and Jeff for three cents on the dollar, they told the carrier China Sea would cover the freight, China Sea has kick ass credit, the urchins go to Tokyo. Mutt and Jeff make a piss pot full of money, cash out the carrier, and no bill goes to China Sea."

"How did you get wind of it?" I said.

"The carrier placed a pending transaction on my bank account, took it off when Jeff paid cash, but I saw it next time I went on line. I called the carrier. Their office manager didn't know anything underhanded was going on, she told me the whole story, and I acted like I knew all along. I waited a week, to see if Mutt and Jeff would come clean, called them a few times on other matters, to see if they'd bring it up. Nothing."

"Mutt and Jeff?" I said.

"When I see them together, they remind me of those old cartoon characters. The biker's name is Michael Grover, he's short and stocky, very muscular. The guy that has my Channel Islands franchise is a tall and skinny Vietnamese, looks just like Mutt."

"How much they make off the urchins?" I said.

"If they got them as cheap as I heard, between two and three hundred thousand."

"Pretty healthy hunk of change," I said.

Sue Hu said, "Man is not satisfied by presence of wealth but by absence of avarice."

"These guys sound about run of the mill greedy, so far." I suggested.

"Greedy enough to steal from me, " said Sue, "from my good name."

"Low motherfuckers," I said.

Sue said. "I couldn't think what to do. If I sue them, lawyers just end up with both our money. When I saw the tr-woops-When I saw Troll at the produce store, and he told me you were living here again, it gave me back my nerve. I went to Oxnard Shores late last night.

"When I set up the store for the franchise, I had new locks and an alarm system installed. I had copies of the keys and a clicker to arm and disarm the alarm."

"Mutt know you have them?"

"I doubt it," she said, "they all still work. I went in about midnight, and started looking in all the spots I'd consider if I wanted to stash something in the place. Having set up the store, I know the place pretty well. Found it third place I looked, on top walk-in freezer, a locking aluminum case, like they use for camera equipment. Not locked."

"Probably figured nobody would be trying to open it," I said. "Full of cash?"

"Gold," she said, "little bricks, but there's a lot off buffer material, packed around the gold to keep it from shifting in the case."

"And you want me to hold it for you, until it cools some." I said.

She smiled. "You are so smart!"

"Don't kiss my ass," I said. "How long?"

"Two weeks to a month, I think. When I can take it, I'll turn it into some rare stamps those boys wouldn't know had value if they were looking at them. I was thinking ten percent for your trouble."

"Sounds good, at this point," I said. "And zilch to the wily partners."

She turned the inscrutable Oriental toward me, once again. "I can't very well reward people for stealing. It would set a bad precedent, don't you think?"

"No question," I said. "Just agitate their greed."

She told me my platters would be ready, and to tell Rebecca they were on the house. She'd meet me in the parking lot.

I picked her up out front, she directed me down to a side street, a few blocks off Foothill, and had me park behind a new Solara. She popped the trunk electronically, as we approached, and pointed at the round cornered case.

I picked it up. "Heavy little booger."

"You have a cell?" she asked.

"Let's communicate by email, for the first few weeks," I said. "But…"

"Hubba hubba hubba," I said, "who do you trust?"

"You're right," she said, "stupid of me. Thank you so much."

CHAPTER TEN

Troll's side of the street was lined with cars half way up the block. I drove to the end, u-turned through the T intersection, and came back down, parking directly across from his house.

Troll's redhead opened the door as I was reaching for a knocker, and said, "That's what I like, a man who delivers."

"Something besides empty promises," I said, and handed her three plastic handle bags, each holding a pair of big white thermal boxes. The white plastic bags were imprinted on both sides with a black, ten line sketch that somehow managed to convey the full impression of a Chinese sailing junk, running before the wind, China was above the line drawing in big block letters, Sea likewise, equidistant below.

Lori looked at the bags and said, "China Sea! I love China Sea.!" Then hefted the bags as I released them, and added, "Brother, this must have cost a mint." She moved off in the direction of the kitchen, working her way through a crowd of people.

I secured the door's barrel bolt. It appeared that all the cars lining the street were represented here. Six or seven people were crowded around the two pinball machines directly ahead. A five handed game was in progress at an eight sided poker table beside the empty stone fireplace. Beyond the pinball machines, near the kitchen entry, a high stakes dart game was in progress, everyone clutching greenbacks in their non-throwing hands.

"Time out," Lori snapped, pushing through the dart game, shoulders hunched. "Time out, you assholes!"

I leaned forward to peer through the door-less double door entry to the bedroom. Troll was holding court, his throne a folding kitchen step-up positioned before the airway of a large, through the wall swamp cooler. The current of cold air against his bare back as he leaned forward, palms resting on slightly bent knees, ran up the slope into his hair, which was blowing around his head in a sort of corona reminiscent of how Einstein's hair looked without any wind. It was not a warm night, had to assume he was wired to the tits. He gave me a fleeting look of greeting, and returned his attention to a stocky skinhead dressed in plaid Bermuda shorts, black, knee-length jackboots, and a red tank top emblazoned with: Give Me Head til I'm Dead.

Troll said something I couldn't hear, and the skinhead reached into a Trader Joe's paper grocery bag next to his chair, pulled out a nickel finished Colt .45 automatic, extending its grip first to Troll. Troll dropped the clip, ejected the chambered cartridge into his hand, and worked the slide to dry fire it a couple times. He looked closely at the firing pin, re-chambered the ejected round and slapped the clip back, thumbing the safety as he set it aside.

A couple hundred pairs of women's panties, seemingly no two alike, dangled from the ceiling above Troll's waterbed. He stood and reached into the crotch of one pair, extracting a small zip lock bag containing, to my experienced eye, three and a half grams of a substance that, taken internally, caused many people to talk real fast and answer questions nobody asked. He lobbed the eight ball to the skinhead, who snatched it out of the air as Troll returned to his half sitting position.

Skin was in motion the instant the bag hit his hand, thanking Troll rapidly but sincerely, letting one polite form of farewell cover the other three people in the room. He was heading for the door, gathering momentum. I slid the barrel bolt and held the door open.

"Thank you, sir," he blurted as he passed.

Walking to the vacated chair, I said, "Baldy's got to be heading toward some hot mama to move that fast."

"Right," said Troll, "the lovely and oh so slender Miss Plastipak Disposable."

Pete Black, 6' 7", 230 pounds of well-defined muscle, disgustingly good looking, but so unassuming nobody hates him for it, said, "How come I have to slam half a gram to get off like Baldy did just holding the bag?"

"It's good dope," said Troll. "Mexican Mafia finally got their shit together. When I was picking up this issue, soon as I touched the three pound package, I had to run to the bathroom and take a projectile crap. Kick up some green stamps and I'll let you put your hand on an ozee. It'll get you so wired, you'll have to slam half a gram to calm down."

Pete Black smiled and said, "You wouldn't bullshit me now, would you, boss?"

"B-bullshit," Troll sputtered. "I will be go to hell! Double D, tell him, you ever known me to bullshit?"

"Pete, old buddy," I said, "it's like this, every time Troll told me something I just knew was total bullshit, I found out later he was telling the god's truth. And every time I believed he was telling me the stone truth, he'd let something slip five minutes later that told me he'd been bullshitting like a water buffalo."

"Makes me feel better," Pete said. "I thought he only did me that way."

"I only do it to those I can," Troll said, "and that includes you and you," pointing a finger, then stroking his beard a couple times. "Damn! Now that I think about it, I guess it includes everybody. Heh heh."

I looked at Pete. "Is this goombah kissing my ass because he thinks I'm rich?"

"Hell no!" said Troll in a loud voice. "Get a grip. I know you're not rich. I mean, I understand that you're not rich." Looking at me with a serious expression, for about five seconds, then his lips started to twitch and his body seemed to shake with suppressed laughter, "BUT YOU MIGHT AS WELL BE, MOTHERFUCKER," he barked, raising an arm as if to explode in laughter, then stopping everything, dropping the hand back to his knee, assuming a deadpan expression, while Henchman Hank and Jimmy Stingray rolled on the floor laughing helplessly. Pete Black chuckled in a deep bass tone, I damn near smiled. Troll gave the two rolling on the floor a look of pity.

"How can you be so fucking funny?" I said.

"I've got funny bones," Troll answered, "but the rest of me is dead serious."

"That's what I like about you," I said.

"The funny bones?"

"Fucking-A," Pete Black and I said together.

"Well," said Troll, "I'd like to stay here and keep cracking you boys up, but I've got five wishers and hopers sitting in there at the poker table, and they won't go home until they're out of money. So, I'm gonna have to get to it." He stood up. "As a wise man once said, it's a sin to let a sucker keep his money."

"What's the game?" I said..

"Dealer's choice," Troll said, "but just poker, none of that acey-deucy or Mexican sweat bullshit. But I thought you didn't play cards."

"Didn't," I said. "Didn't read much, either. All that changed in the past couple years."

"I can dig it," Troll said. "There's a seat, if you want it. Dealer sets the ante, and it's table stakes, can't go into your pocket in the middle of a hand, you can go all in."

"They're your pigeons. You don't mind me horning in?"

"No sweat," Troll replied, rubbing his hands. "We'll skin them, real quick, and send them home. Then we can bump heads."

"I take it you don't believe in beginner's luck," I said.

"Course I do," said Troll, "and I'm real scared. But, I think," he sniffed the air like a bear. "I'm sure of it. I smell some of that uncle money."

"I'll have to show you the difference between smelling and winning," I said.

"Let's do it, Teach," said Troll. Lori met us halfway to the poker table, bearing a pair of oval platters, piled with seafood ranging from raw to deep fried.

"Why, thank you, lady," Troll said, taking one.

I took the other. "Thanks a lot."

She said, "You're welcome. And you're welcome." And more quietly, to Troll, "I left the rest out on the table, with some plastic plates and stuff. I'll fix Pete a platter, the rest of these Bozos can fend for themselves."

"Good girl." Troll smiled, patted her ass and turned to the poker table, hooking a chair with his foot and seating himself. I took one of the remaining chairs, put the platter on my lap and dropped a wad of greenbacks on the table.

I'd been introduced to everyone at the table over the years, though I couldn't put a name to every face. The man shuffling cards across from me, wearing a lime green Lacoste shirt, had the un-aggressive good looks and grooming of an insurance executive or TV pitchman. He glanced up.

"Double D. How you been?"

"Friendly Frank," I said. "Not bad, yourself?"

"Hanging in, hanging in. Never used to be able to get you near a card table."

"That was then," I said. "Now I fancy myself a poker player."

"Is that right?" Friendly Frank smiled, and placed the deck in front of the player to his right, for the cut. "Let's find out." He dropped a bill onto the center of the table. "Five dollar ante," he said, "best five out of ten, black deuces wild." He dealt five cards all around, then the five community cards face down, out near the pot. The rest of us tossed pictures of Honest Abe onto the table.

By 2:00 am it was just me and Troll, bumping heads. His stack of cash dwarfed mine.

While the others were in the game he'd controlled it by force of personality, punctuated with outbursts of temper, producing strange reactions in the other players. It seemed to me they wanted him to win, so he'd be his happy, funny self, if you can believe that. I couldn't beat him when the others were there, and only started to accumulate some winnings after folding every hand he stayed in past the second betting round, and betting like hell when he folded early. I was doing better with just the two of us playing.

I dropped tens full on his three queens, he rubbed his chin, "Good hand."

"Damn," I said, dragging the pot, "aren't you going to fling the cards, or tear up some bills?"

Troll chuckled. "Would if I thought it would work on you, Mister beginner's luck!"

"I never said I didn't play a lot, when I was a kid."

"Never said you did, either," said Troll.

"Family games, every Friday night. They wouldn't let me sit in until I was twelve," I said, putting down the deck for him to cut.

Troll cut the deck, and said, "Why twelve?"

"Because that's when I got a paper route and started having my own money."

"How did you do?"

"First year I never lasted past the first hour, they'd take my money and send me to bed. I'd lay in bed, trying to figure out why everybody always folded when I had a good hand. Second year I did better, got to stay up late. Third year I started reading them, and I began kicking ass. Trouble was, the stakes never changed, nickel dime poker, big money when I was twelve and losing, chump change when I was fifteen and winning. I drifted away when I was sixteen, found better ways to spend Friday night. Never played poker again until I got to the chain gang."

"Run into any poker players in there?" Troll asked.

"Nah, like taking candy away from babies, boring as everything else in there." I dealt us each five cards, and said, "Five card double draw low ball. On you."

Troll tossed in a bill. "Ten bucks, Buckaroo."

I tossed in a ten. "If you looked at your cards first, I'd be folding."

"I know," Troll said and discarded. "Gimme two."

CHAPTER ELEVEN

At 7:30 the same morning I woke up on Al's acre of bed, rousted out of sleep by a serious chill in the room, cold air was pouring in through a pair of six foot diameter holes, one in the East facing wall, the other in the Southern exposure.

The material forming the top third of the pyramid so impressively, as well as most of the vertical exterior walls of the first floor, was not glass as I'd supposed, but a type of smart plastic cooked up in a privately owned R&D lab in Glendale, ninety percent of its stock held by The Albert Brown Family Trust. The remaining ten percent was distributed among several young brainiacs employed at the lab, and would propel them into the ranks of the filthy rich before their thirtieth birthdays.

I'd mentally tagged it onyx at first sight, but when I discovered it had one tenth the weight of glass, could go from solid black to perfectly clear at the clicker's command, and grow holes at the click of a mouse, flubber seemed a better fit.

When I rolled in from Troll's, a little after 3:30, some mild Santa Anas were blowing warm, dry air down the mountain, so I went into the flubber control program and grew the holes before turning in, thinking to air the place out while I slept.

When I woke, chilled to the bone a few short hours later, tendrils of fog drifting past the holes told the story, while I slept a layer of cool air moved in off the ocean, across The Valley, and chased my warm winds back toward Palmdale.

I made haste to the bathroom, for a hot shower, making it gradually hotter over the twenty minutes I huddled in its downpour. When it began calling forth a dull itch from my skin, I shut it down and crouched there in the vapor for another minute.

The chill in the room faded, sunlight streamed through the hole in the East slab, and a faint odor of drying sage hinted the day would be a hot one.

In the office, I maximized flubber control and clicked the holes away, then opened the security directory and made a quick sweep of the nano-cams. Everything appeared normal, and none of the feeds displayed the blinking flag that would prompt me to scan back down the time line for unusual activity.

A cruise through the Sphinx revealed that Speedo and the thong girls had not spent the night. Munchable Lisa still slept alone, one breast peeping fetchingly out of the covers. Jerry and his girlfriend, Frieda, slept spooned, snoring in unison. Edward, in polo pajamas, tossed, turned, battled the bedding and moaned in his sleep.

Leni was not in her Sphinx room, the bedding undisturbed. I located her, sleeping in the pyramid's emerald suite, place she called hers when both parents were alive.

The home team jumps out to a commanding lead, I thought.

My dumb ass.

CHAPTER TWELVE

Since it was early and I was up, I decided to address a task I'd been putting off, down in the pyramid's second subterranean level.

Half the space on that level was given over to Al's conception of high performance heaven, and brothers and sisters it was good, programmable welders, lathes and other metal working machinery, hand held diagnostic computers, laser guided wheel alignment platforms and balancers. The equipment down there sported more lasers than a death star. I could go on.

Astride one of the two hydraulic lifts, her sixteen inch Michelin X's pigeon-toed two feet off the floor, a full size replica of the 1963 Lincoln Continental gleamed when light hit its clear coated aluminum body.

The sixty-three Continental had been my dream car as I approached driving age. With its suicide doors and low-slung elegance, it seemed to my fifteen and a half year old eyes the epitome of cool. If you couldn't get laid in that car, I remember telling myself, you couldn't get laid. My reality didn't quite attain that level of cool.

My father made it very clear, during the two years I approached driving age, in order to exercise my driving privilege I would have to buy, register and insure my own vehicle. He also declined to loan me money toward that end, saying, "The first rule of financial independence is don't go into debt over something that doesn't increase in value. You might as well learn it now." Then, in a burst of generosity, he said if I wanted to give the Beechcraft Bonanza he parked at Van Nuys airport a thorough cleaning, inside and out, say every Wednesday after school, he'd pay me twenty dollars a week. Twenty dollars in those days was nothing to sneeze at. I swallowed my pride and accepted.

My mother agreed to take me to the DMV on my birthday, and let me use her car to take the driving test, but warned, "After that, you're on your own. Don't even think of borrowing my car. I love my car, and if anything bad happened to it, and it was anybody but me driving, well, I would not want to be in that person's shoes. Do you know what I mean, darling?"

I knew what she meant.

At age fourteen, I'd begun spending frequent Saturdays at Al's, hanging out in the big detached garage that opened onto a paved alley behind his house. Al could be found there on any Saturday morning, working on his funny car, modifying, repairing, replacing, shaving weight, often preparing for a race the following day.

The first thing he taught me was the names of all the various automotive wrenches: box end, open end, combination, then the sockets and ratchets, drive sizes (1/4" 3/8" ½"), torque wrenches, feeler gauges. I was a quick study, soon manning a station beside the giant roll away toolbox, able to bring whatever tool he called for with quick accuracy. Within a few weeks, I could, by paying attention, anticipate which tool he'd need before he called for it, ready to slap it into his hand. From that point forward, he began describing the procedures he was about to perform, pointing out critical points as he went, even having me do some of the work, under his eye. A few weeks later, I was doing simple procedures myself, such as changing spark plugs and plug wires, while Al worked on the more demanding, installing new brakes or aligning the front end.

He'd listen to my gripes about my father with a tolerant smile, occasionally giving out a laugh, and saying, "You hot shit."

One Saturday, when birthday sixteen was bearing down hard on me, he said, "You saving any of the dough your old man pays you for cleaning the Beech?"

"About half."

"How much you figure to spend on a car?"

"Couple hundred." (In those days a running car could be had for a hundred)."But I hoped I could use the two for a down payment and get something slightly reliable."

"Don't fall for that happy horse shit," Al snapped. "Financing's for peasants, and that's how they stay peasants. It's throwing good money down the crapper, plus you'd have to insure the car, instead of just carrying liability coverage, more money down the crapper."

Financing's out, anyway," I said. "The old man won't cosign."

"That's good," Al approved, "good for him, good for you, though you probably don't see it that way, yet."

"I sure don't"

"You're one of the brighter members of your generation," he said. "You will."

"Really," I said. "When?"

Al stopped what he was doing, and gave me his full attention. "When you've got your two hundred together," he said, "bring it to me. Winning races has brought many acquaintances in the automotive industry, a number of whom will jump on any chance to make me happy. When it comes to car buying, a dollar in my hands is worth four or five dollars in yours, you follow?"

"You can get for two what would cost me eight hundred or a thousand?"

"Give or take," Al nodded. "Course, you'd have to trust me to buy for you. I'll be pretending I want a second car for myself, so you won't be able to check them out, and unless there's something seriously wrong with the car, I couldn't ask them to take it back, if I pick something you don't like."

"If I can drive it without working on it first," I said, "I'm a happy camper."

Three weeks later found me the proud owner of a three year old Dodge Van, 150 series. It had a three quarter ton under carriage, with a slant six engine mounted between the driver and shotgun seats, so it wouldn't be winning any races, and it wasn't my dream Continental, but I was not blind to its potential. By the start of the new school year, in September, I had it tricked out with chrome reverse rims and a wrinkle free white paint job. The large windowless space behind the engine housing and seats, I transformed, with massive application of web-reinforced industrial foam and a variety of heavy fabrics, into something resembling a corrupt pasha's tent.

Though it never attained the level of glamor attached to my dream Continental, in most respects it was better suited to my main reason for wanting a vehicle, to get laid. I don't think words can properly convey the intensity of my surprised delight as I discovered the large percentage of Reseda High School girls who wanted exactly the same thing. My well-thumbed collection of

Playboy, Penthouse and Gent lay forgotten in a corner of my closet. The more notorious the white van became, the faster my opportunities arose.

It all came to a screeching halt a few months before my eighteenth birthday, when my father found it expedient to settle an undisclosed sum on the parents of one of my harem, who, happily, weren't quite as Catholic as they let on.

After that was taken care of, he took me aside and said, "The only kind of discipline that's worth a good goddamn in this world is self-discipline. Since you don't have any of that, you'll have to make due with the other kind. Pick your branch of the service."

"What about high school?"

"You'll get a GED."

More to spite his Naval Aviator ass than any other reason , I said, "Marines."

It's an indicator of how pissed he was he didn't turn a hair. "Fine," he said, and drove me down to the Marine Corps recruiter.

When the recruiting sergeant said, "He's only six months from graduation, don't you think..?"

My father broke in, "He's got too much testosterone to be trusted in high school."

"Ah," said the recruiting sergeant, "ladies' man, eh? Well, sir, " he said, sliding a paper clip over forms we'd filled out, "I'm certain The Corps will be able to accommodate your son very nicely." and shot me a mean grin.

I thought about the overweight desk jockey from time to time, a year or so later, while I was sneaking around the jungle, murdering people and tigers and water buffalo at a rate that would cause the most prolific of serial killers to hang their heads in shame. (I never could bring myself to kill an elephant, and still feel pretty bad about the water buffalo.) I thought about him, and the walls of his crappy office, plastered with posters of me, but only fleetingly and not that often. I had to keep focused on what I was about, or wind up dead myself.

The replica Continental on the lift puzzled me. I found no mention of it in the video instruction Al prepared.

On the other hand, it had been my dream car only during the three year period he and I spent time together. Not long after I could have bought one had I wished, but by then was more interested in big fast motorcycles. I mothballed the '63 Lincoln along with other adolescent fantasies, professional baseball and undersea treasure hunting. They paled to insignificance when I discovered my highly developed talent for waging war.

Physical appearance aside, the car on the lift bore as much relation to the '63 Continental as the Continental did to the Model T, and the more I thought about it the more I came to suspect it was there as a repository of information Al either couldn't or did not wish to transmit through written or spoken language. When first the idea crossed my mind I dismissed it as ridiculous, but it kept coming around, like a pesky ex-girlfriend, and I finally had to admit to myself I could not conjure a better reason for the vehicle's unlikely and very pricey existence.

It seemed to me the first step in unraveling the riddle of the car was to drive it, well, the second step. Unlike the other vehicle Al got me, I couldn't drive this one without working on it. The transmission was cradled on a transmission jack next to the lift, the drive shaft in an open wooden box on one of the work benches, nestled in a bed of curly paper.

I developed into a competent mechanic in my teens, under Al's guidance, but he'd been unable to instill in me the relaxed enjoyment he derived from doing the work. I'll do anything short of letting somebody else work on my vehicles to avoid getting my hands greasy. Thus, I had no problem finding things other than the transmission and drive shaft to occupy my time and mind for over a month, though they intruded into my thoughts at many odd moments, distracting me from matters at hand.

Stepping out of my long hot shower that morning, I considered, I'd already spent twice as much energy not doing the job as it would have taken to do it.

I followed a light breakfast of toast, bacon and coffee with a gelatin capsule full of Doctor Troll's Verdugo Hills Diet, within half an hour was motivated to do auto mechanics.

Every popular drug from heroin to methedrine has a game it plays on the mind. Knowing the game and being able to compensate for it is referred to as maintaining.

Part of the game speed in its various forms plays on the mind, is increasing one's motivation while decreasing one's ability to do things well. It's not uncommon for people under its influence to hurry through a task in such slap dash fashion they'd have been better off doing nothing, or to get so progressively sidetracked into smaller details of the job they've undertaken that, two hours after they set out to clean up their back yard, they find themselves on their knees at the edge of the patio, hammering two by fours together to make a concrete form, so they can re-pour the corner that broke off two years ago. Meanwhile, the rest of the yard still looks like an un-reclaimed section of the Bronx.

I realize many people have these experiences without taking drugs, but I refuse to dwell on it.

The elevator's dual doors slid open at the pyramid's second in-ground level, I stepped out one side, into high performance heaven. The other side led to a couple smaller workshops, devoted to technical disciplines mostly beyond my ken, and to a small shooting range with a weapons collection G. Gordon Liddy would have creamed his jeans over. I'm not one to get excited over implements of destruction more than any other type tool, but even I got a case of the warm fuzzies, strolling around the walk-in the gun safe.

With the heel of my hand on the lift control lever, bringing the Lincoln to an elevation I could walk under without bumping my head, I regarded the transmission jack and its cargo. The jack rested on three steel ball casters at the ends of a wide beamed T. An inch or so from each caster, short, thick risers buttressed the heavy open framework of the cradle and its load, a five speed automatic. The jacking mechanism wasn't apparent, but I had no worries. Having grown complacent about Al's front gate and front door, I was ready for anything.

I checked the torque converter for fluid, then began pushing the jack under the car, it said, "Please position my wheels on three red dots to fore of lift." I did so without comment, and the jack said, "Thank you."

I didn't bother respond, but began pulling mounting bolts off the flywheel housing. A quiet series of hums sounded behind me. I pulled the last bolt and turned around, coming eyeball to pilot shaft with the transmission. The jack said, "Please remove obstruction from path of splines." I got my head out of the way, and the jack sent forth three tiny beams of laser light, triangulating them to the pilot bushing at the center of the flywheel, then rolled forward under its own power, bringing the splined shaft through the center of the torque converter, and the transmission to its installed position with such fluid ease, I stepped in to spin the top three mounting bolts in finger tight with an irrational resentment toward the jack growing in me. In under a minute, it had rendered my hard won skill at stabbing transmissions crude and obsolete. When I got the first bolt finger tight, I turned my eyes toward a low hum, and saw the jack, rolling from under the car, while lowering its cradle. I scowled.

The jack said, "What?"

Unresponsive, I started the rest of the mounting bolts, and torqued them down with an air powered ratchet, then secured the rear transmission mount the same way, popped the shift linkage into place, and plugged in a pair of electrical connectors.

I got the drive shaft out of its bed of curly paper, and slipped the female splines of the front piece over the male splines on the transmission's rear shaft, sliding it into the trans, walked back to the differential and rested the shaft on my shoulder while I pulled a couple u-bolts out of my pocket and stripped off their paper wrapping.

The transmission jack rolled back under the vehicle, and said, "I am programmed to support drive shaft while u-joint is assembled."

"Bully for you," I said. "Now, fuck off." I slid the u-joint into place on the differential yoke and started securing the u-bolts.

"That was uncalled for," said the transmission jack.

"I'll be the judge of that." I said. " And from now on don't speak to me unless I speak to you first". I knew I was talking to the black slab, by proxy, but what the hell.

"How will I know you are addressing me?" said the jack.

"I'll say, hey, jack off."

"Very well."

I won't abide mouthy machinery. Intolerance, you say? Bigotry? Call me un-evolved. Like it's not bad enough certain people can talk (and you all know who you are). How lonely does one need to be before conversation with a machine becomes appealing?

It was sweet to hear nothing but the hiss of escaping air when I lowered the lift, bringing the car back down.

The vehicle's two-inch thick shop manual lay open, face down on the bench, gold lettering on its front cover and spine: The Albert Brown Replica 1963 Lincoln Continental. It was comprehensive to a degree found only in manufacturer's shop manuals, covered every detail of the machine, except a sealed polymer cylinder (about the size of a three gallon water bottle), mounted in the V of the engine, where you'd expect the intake manifold. The shop manual displayed injectors, connecting to a generic oval within the V. Inside the oval, the notation: Refer to fuel type appendix appropriate for your vehicle. The 48 valve V-12 came with three fuel options: gasoline, diesel or hydrogen. The back pages of the manual had fuel injection schematics for the first two, bearing no resemblance to what I had. If you opted for hydrogen, and required information or technical support, the manual advised: Consult with fuel provider. Hand written in the margin: H suppt. Brian 8185556969.

I punched in the number on my wireless, to make sure it was a working number and connected to someone who could provide hydrogen, should the need arise. It was answered on the first ring.

"Brian McIntyre."

"Hello, Brian, my name's Mark Brown," I said.

"Don't give me that crap! Who is this?"

"Did I mumble?" I said. "Is it a bad connection?"

"I heard you fine, but you used the wrong name, slick," he said. "Mark Brown doesn't talk on the telephone. Better luck next time."

"I'd send you an email," I said, "but I only have this phone number."

"What's the call in reference to?"

"I called this number because it's written in the shop manual of a car I'm preparing to put on the road, the number for fuel support."

"What kind of fuel?" Brian said.

"Hydrogen."

"The Continental?"

"Yes."

"What's the problem?"

"Where do I gas up?"

"Is there a white plastic tank connected to the fuel injectors?"

said Brian.

"There is."

"Then, you're good to go. Fill it just like you would a real '63 Continental, except the tank only holds ten gallons, and you fill it with water instead of gasoline. Tap water will do, but distilled is better."

"You're shitting me," I said.

"I wouldn't shit you, you're my favorite. Oops, sorry, Mr. Brown, forgot I was talking to the boss."

"Forget it," I said. "Don't apologize, and never explain. What's up with the polymer tank?"

"Fast reaction chamber," said Brian, "detaches O molecules from the water, delivers hydrogen to the injectors, on demand. Much more elegant than driving around with a bunch of pressurized hydrogen gas, not to mention safer."

"Doesn't that make it the most valuable invention of all time?" I said.

"Next to the medieval catapult, yeah," Brian said. "Trouble is, it's so damn simple, almost anyone could figure it out, if they cut the tank open. So, we're not going to sell them, one year leases only, and we've designed it so if the skin is breached, the tank implodes to mush."

"Thanks for the info," I said. "My number's in your phone, don't give it to anyone, and don't call me. You wouldn't like me when I'm angry, understand?'

"You're the boss, Boss. Could you email me something, though, referring to this call? I could use a little more pull around here."

"Sure," I said, "you've been helpful."

"Great," said Brian. "I mean unless you plan to start talking to other employees."

"No," I said, "this was purely accidental, didn't know who I was calling. You could be the only one in the organization whoever gets a call from me."

"That would give me beaucoup leverage," Brian said. Pumping ten quarts of synthetic ATF into the transmission dipstick tube, from a pull down hose, I checked the other fluid levels as a matter of course, pulled the engine dipstick, and a thin yellow tab popped out at a right angles below the splash guard, warning in red letters: Do not remove this tab before replacing break-in oil with full synthetic at 500 to 600 miles.

It appeared I'd be driving like an old lady for a day or two.

I returned my unsoiled cover-all's to their hanger, and walked around the Lincoln, pushing the lift arms out of the way with a foot, appreciating how well the buffed aluminum finish suited the car's body, making it seem more contemporary.

The interior demolished all ties to 1963, designed to seat four, in maximum comfort. The dash and instrument panel would have looked right at home in a Learjet. The fuel gauge read full.

I adjusted the driver's seat, rested my right foot on the brake, and kicked the engine over.

The V-12 came to life without fanfare, and idled at 600 rpms, vibration more suggested by the tachometer than actually felt. I put it in gear and glided up the ramp to the parking garage, slotting it across from Aunt Ruth's Lexus...

I sat awhile, perusing the user's guide, familiarizing myself with the instrument cluster and other features. After fifteen minutes, I hadn't penetrated far into the GPS options, but could make the car do some catchy dance moves with the hydraulic enhanced suspension, had the entertainment accessories down cold.

Stepped out of the Lincoln, hot wind blowing down the entry ramp. Leni's Jag and Al's sedan absent, indicating I was home alone, might get in a swim without having to interact with any church members. I went back down to the second level and took a tunnel to the hallway between the gym and changing room in the Sphinx's right foreleg.

A pair of black baggys in the men's bin looked about right, so I tore out the net like inner lining and tried them on, they rode low on my hips without falling down, and came to mid knee, perfect fit. Cranked the timer switch for the sauna, and went out, head first into the pool, down to the layer of cold water in the deep end, luxuriating in its chill until my diaphragm started heaving, got out near the diving boards, climbed the three-meter platform and discovered I was not alone, after all.

CHAPTER THIRTEEN

The occupied chaise lounge, invisible from pool level behind a bushy potted plant, was fully exposed to the high dive's perspective. Did I believe in God at that moment? You know I did, and thanked him profusely.

The admirable issue of supposed semi-divine entities at the inner circle of Leni's church, lay motionless as a slab, her modest one-piece bathing suit draped modestly over the back of a nearby chair.

Lisa was sprawled immodestly, and seemed more naked than regular people ever do. I climbed back down, slipped into the pool without a sound, and floated to the shallow end, with languid movement of hands and feet.

Before stepping out of the pool I submerged for a moment, then walked over and dripped on Lisa's unveiled perfection. She squinted up at me, "Do I get a towel with the shower?"

"If you promise not to wrap up in it," I said.

She rolled her eyes. "I hoped you weren't one of those bozos who gets overwrought at the sight of a woman's body," she said with contempt.

"I'd like to deny it," I said, propping my right foot on the edge of the chaise, a couple inches from her elbow, "but you'd see right through my lame lies, to the hard truth."

She broke eye contact, and directed her gaze up the right leg of my trunks, where Mister Happy, swollen and twitching, lurked like a cyclopean moray eel at the mouth of its cave.

Lisa stared without moving for a long time, and Mister Happy, ever the attention hog (pardon my pun), preened. When she raised her eyes back to mine I couldn't determine if they held a question or just anguish.

"Go ahead," I said, "touch it, it doesn't bite."

She shifted her eyes again, seemed to be thinking it over. I kept silent. She reached out a tentative hand, then paused and looked up again. "Maybe we could continue this conversation indoors."

"I turned the sauna on," I said. "Race you to it."

"Care to bet on it?"

"Ten minutes of head, loser gives."

She smiled, "Done," then bounced off the open side of the chaise, cutting the water before I got turned around. I tried to catch-up, and just missed her ankle, as she surged out of the pool, found no reason to hurry beyond that point.

Rinsed the chlorine at the outside shower, entered the sauna carrying my trunks, and pulled the heavy door shut, throwing the dead bolt.

Lisa was standing hip shot, back to me, directing the spray from a hand held shower head at the ceramic baffles enclosing the heating coils, blasting the room with steam. She pushed back her hair with her free hand, looking at me over her shoulder.

"Not bad," she said, "for an old man."

"Young punks," I said, "always trying to make a reputation off me."

"I won fair and square, " she said, and twitched her perfect, dimpled behind."

"You won," I said. "Let's leave it at that."

"Sore loser, eh?" she said.

"I pay my gambling debts," I said, and wagged my tongue at her.

"A man of principle." she said, "how nice," then turned her face up, and let the shower spray run over her head and down her body. She squinted in my direction. "Come on over here, you big beautiful thing, and bring the guy with you, if you want."

"That's cold," I said.

"Do you have any idea how long I've waited for a guy I could say that to?"

I shook my head.

"Well," she said, "never mind. How about a little less chit-chat, a little more head?"

"Why do I get the feeling your idea of foreplay is snapping your fingers and pointing at your crotch?"

She replied with a slow-motion pantomime, snapping her fingers and pointing at her crotch.

The redwood benches on the long wall of the sauna look like a three step section of a giant's staircase, three foot risers to three foot deep steps, only enough clearance above the third to lay on its shelf.

I sat on the first step, and spun around on my back, resting my calves on the second step and hanging my head off the first. Lisa looked just as fine upside down.

"I like you," I told her. "As long as I've got a face, you've got a place to sit."

"But, if I sit on your face, next thing I know, you'll be wanting to hold hands."

"Only one way to find out," I said, and wagged my tongue again.

"I'd better cool you off first," she said, and turned the hand held shower on me, soaking my legs and midsection with the cold spray. "And, I don't know where that face has been," she said, moving the spray to my head.

I snorted and shook the water out of my eyes. Lisa replaced the shower head on its yoke, and stalked toward me through the steam, stopping when my head was bracketed between her thighs. "I'll let you know when ten minutes is up," she murmured.

The floor was where we sprawled at last in the slowly cooling sauna. I lay flat on my back. Lisa was positioned with her head propped on my thigh, gazing up at flabby Mister Happy like he was the cutest thing since Sponge Bob. Is it possible, I wondered once again, to be jealous of your own dick? Nah.

Lisa said, "It can only be Edward, nobody else would knock half as long."

This referenced a monotonous pounding on the sauna door, going on about twenty minutes. It was annoying, but easier to ignore than get worked up about. "Is it a problem for you?" I said.

"Go away!" she yelled, then, "Edward's a pretty skillful ass kisser, but his nuts are non-existent. I was fanning false hope in him, when I agreed to join his little expedition in support of Lenore. I was coming up here anyway, as Lenore's friend, but I did him a large favor. Having any third generation church member attached to your project gives a big leg up in dealing with the church bureaucracy, and I like to think I bring a little something extra to the table."

"You do," I glanced at the door, the knocking was decreasing in volume and number. "But no good deed goes unpunished," I said.

"That says it all," she looked rueful. "He knew I was doing him a favor, and he took it as a sign I was warm for his shrimpy form. Can you imagine?"

"No accounting for taste," I said.

"He's so far out of his league it beggars pathetic."

I looked at the door, now emitting a sound like the last feeble scratching of the buried alive. "He's no Energizer Bunny, either." I said.

A little later, Lisa said, "You know, tempting as it is to rub Edward's nose in us, I've never been one to pull the wings off flies, disgusting as they are."

"Keep talking," I said, "I'm impressed."

"I'm thinking, if you'd be willing to follow my lead, when I open the door, it wouldn't be difficult to make Edward believe nothing happened between us." She looked up at me and gave Mister Happy a little squeeze.

"Piece of cake," I said. "We've only been locked in here for about forty minutes, he knows of."

"He wants to believe nothing happened," she assured me. "If you don't mind acting a little wimpy in front of him, he'll believe. Can you handle that?"

"Sweetie," I said, "for you, I'd act wimpy in front of the Oakland Hells Angels."

"You must be tougher than I thought."

"I have to keep a .38 in the bathroom," I said, "in case I shit a wildcat."

She laughed and clapped her hands. "This will be great. You put your trunks on. Damn, my suit's outside, throw me that towel, will you? Oh, and make sure nothing is dripping down my leg."

"I'll have to look into that."

Lisa pulled open the sauna door, wrapped in an oversized white towel, a smaller one turbaned on her head. Edward stood there, fingering his clerical collar.

Lisa snarled, "What the fuck do you want, Edward!" then back at me, "Mister, the only way you're ever going to hook up with a girl like me, is in your dreams. So why don't you go take a nap?"

"But, you didn't even give me a chance," I said.

"A chance for what, to make my flesh crawl? You did that when you grabbed my breast!"

"Aw, come on, Honey," I pleaded.

"Don't you honey me, you creep! You... you suppressive old geezer!" she spat, and stormed off, elbowing Edward to one side and looking more edible than See's candy.

Edward stood there, holding the door half open with one foot, staring at me while I stared at the floor, shaking my head. When after ten seconds he hadn't moved, I raised my head and locked eyes with him. "You," I said, making my voice hoarse. "If you hadn't kept banging on the door like that, she.."

"What?" Edward smirked. "She'd have sucked your middle-age dick? Don't make me laugh.."

"Things were going good until you started that pounding," I said. "You ruined everything, damn you. I'll make you pay!" I leaped in his direction, my fingers curved like claws. And he was gone, disappeared so completely I never saw him again, though I did speak once to his secretary, on the phone, briefly.

CHAPTER FOURTEEN

Having backed Lisa's play with whines stolen from the great Woody Allen, I wasn't anxious to do any explaining to Leni, saw nothing to be gained by further terrorizing Edward.

Decided to remove my whiney presence from the equation, and let the stirred pot simmer. Mister Happy opposed the idea, anxious to do more spelunking in Lisa. Overruled his motion, promising not to beat him.

Back in the top third of the pyramid, dressed in gray denim, black penny loafers, tan sleeveless tee shirt with purple lettering: Why walk around half dead, when, in Tombstone, we can bury you for twenty-two dollars. Got an off white linen jacket out of the closet, to take along, should the need arise to appear respectable, then secured the top of the pyramid, pocketed my wallet and phone, and rolled out the Lincoln for its shakedown cruise.

Showing off the new wheels to Troll meant waiting until I'd posted the break-in miles and switched from thin break-in oil to full synthetic. Until then, I needed to baby the V-12 like the newborn it was, so moving parts needing to wear a little to their optimum condition would wear gently, evenly. Why not just run synthetic from the gate? Because then those parts wouldn't wear at all, no internal combustion engine creates sufficient pressure against its moving parts to break through the synthetic's high tensile strength and make metal to metal contact. Stopped at a wide spot on La Tuna Canyon Road, before the I-210 access, to consider whether to head East or West, and to program some sounds for the drive. The Lincoln's radio covered all bandwidths from AM/FM to Police and Fire and Citizens' Band. I could speak to truckers by thumbing a little button built into the steering wheel. Music selections were available from a five terabyte hard drive, three tenths of one percent of its disc space occupied, the range and number of musical selections was mind boggling. I finally settled on Love: Forever Changes, followed by Best of Chris Rea, followed by Bright Eyes-Live, and rolled onto the 210 West as the

Sun settled behind the Santa Monica Mountains.

Stayed to the extreme right lane, a leisurely fifty-five, other vehicles whipping past on my left at eighty-plus, annoying but expected. More aggravating were the dip shits who got behind me and started flashing their high beams. I quickly tired of giving them the finger out the window, and switched to holding my fist out and making the jacking off gesture, much better, really pissed them off. I don't get road rage, I give it.

The sound system was still on the first album when I hit 210's terminus at Interstate 5, the major West coast artery, reaching from the Mexican border to Canada. Went North, and ran into some rush hour gridlock, easing shortly as Palmdale/Lancaster commuters exited to the 14 freeway.

Passed Magic Mountain's grip of roller coasters, getting a little further North on this freeway than I cared to be, took the next exit, Route 126, headed for the coast.

North of where I exited, civilization thins abruptly, and there is only the multi-lane masterpiece of civil engineering, plowing through mountain ranges like cubes of butter, skirting the strange and desolate Pyramid Lake (another engineering wonder). Then comes a thirty mile downgrade, The Grapevine, at the bottom of which you are no longer in SoCal and you know it.

I first transited the section of Interstate at thirteen, on a family vacation, watching the countryside from the rear of a Travel-all my father piloted up the recently opened freeway. Slouched on a pillow against the rounded wheel well, eating sunflower seeds and watching our back trail, an unusual lassitude descended on me accompanied by a foreboding feeling these freshly scarred mountains did not like me or the engineering marvel I rode in on.

The few times I've taken that stretch of road on a motorcycle (especially the night rides), I had the impression winds were trying to blow me off the road, and being damned strategic about it.

Route 126 had been widened and upgraded almost to freeway status since I'd last seen its country ass, it brought me to coastal 101 North just as Chris Rea began crooning On the Beach. Aside from the one incredibly clear morning I saw Catalina from the pyramid, I had not seen the ocean since returning to L.A.

Got off 101 at the first exit, Seaward Ave., banged a left over the freeway and rolled down to a small traffic circle where the sand began. About to exit the car, On the Beach ended and Looking for the Summer (best of Chris Rea's best) began. Raised the car on its hydraulics and looked at the ocean over the low retaining wall while the song played out.

Walking down to the water, bare toes clenching against the sand, I stared at three offshore oil drilling platforms to the North, lit up like Christmas trees across the water, brighter than marine and aircraft safety would demand, and offensive to tree huggers traveling the Northbound 101 in their Navigators and Suburbans, in route to hug perhaps a redwood. This sickening (to the trees) hugging might be stopped in an instant, if only the hapless hugees could convey to said huggers the distress of trees being groped by things whose sole attractive feature lay in the scrumptious dining experience their decomposing bodies might one day provide. Sadly, their shudders of revulsion are too subtle to penetrate the huggers' trance states.

Dropped my clothes behind a clump of kelp at the high-tide line, and walked into the wash from waves cast in reflected shore light, fifty yards out. When water reached my hips, I was obliged to dive under an incoming wave, surfacing on its backside in time to catch the next one and ride it back to the beach.

Stood naked in the tangle of kelp, brushing my feet through it, to remove most of the sand, and stepped back into my jeans, then carried my shirt back to the car, where the scanner in the door handle read my thumbprint and let me in.

Sitting in the car's open doorway, checked the bottoms of my feet for tar, found none, brushed off the residual sand and slipped my shoes back on.

Trundled back to the Northbound 101, passed downtown Ventura, and exited to Highway 33, heading back inland, following it nearly to Ojai, a hotbed of shameless tree huggerey, turned left onto Route 150 before I got there.

Five minutes later, I drove through a grove of avocado trees my parents bought and moved to shortly after my father was informed he could no longer fly airliners, except as a passenger.

The house and its outbuildings sprawl near the top of a hill, center of the twenty acre grove, main residence a one story L shaped affair, tan stucco, red tile roofs, deep verandas along the outside of the L, and fifty feet of lawn between house and grove.

Half a dozen trees dot the lawns, two lemon, two orange and two grapefruit.

A building facing the house's Southern exposure has a three car garage below and one bedroom apartment above, reached by a wooden stairway on one side. The paved area between the two provides guest parking.

I pulled in there, activating some floodlights on the garage, and gave my horn a couple taps. When my father showed, at the veranda steps, I made the Lincoln do a little jig with the hydraulics, then shut it down and got out.

"Hey," Dad said, "Number one son. Nice wheels. Where did you find a beauty like that?"

"In your little brother's basement," I said. "Appeared to have my name on it."

My father threw an arm across my shoulders and knuckled me in the ribs. "I always figured you were the favorite nephew."

"The car's nice," I said, "but the get out of jail free card, Jesus. How did he conjure that?"

"Not a big deal," said Dad. "Had the legal department of a life insurance company he controlled down there look into your case. They reported back, between Alabama law enforcement delivering you to Georgia without extradition, and a judge who should have recused himself at the outset, you had so many grounds for appeal, they were shocked you were still in custody.

"The lawyers wanted to file immediately, but Albert nixed that, had them give the report to the company CEO, who plays golf with the governor every Tuesday. You got out that Friday, is how Sid Levy tells it."

"Al had to spend some currency more potent than cash," I said

"Better believe it," said Dad. "But having the facts and the law on your side got him a hefty discount."

I followed him to the informal dining area, an open space between the kitchen and living room, The formal dining room was through a set of bat wing doors on the other side of the kitchen. I sat in a swiveling barrel chair at a barrel table, next to a sliding glass door shielded by vertical blinds.

"Drink?" my father asked.

"One of your famous whiskey sours would hit the spot," I said.

While fixing the drinks, Dad said, "Atlanta's an oasis of civilization in a desert of Southern Gothic. What were you doing, hanging around those small towns?"

"As Popeye would express it," I said, "wimminks."

He gave me a look, and laughed. Albert was right, you're a hot shit. It's hard to see when it's your own kid."

What's different?" I inquired.

He shrugged. I guess I don't feel so guilty, anymore, about forcing you into the service."

"You should never have felt guilt. My life began with recon school, but I'd never have got there on my own volition. You played your part so well, I had to prevail or die."

He set a whiskey sour down in front of me, and said, "Maybe if it hadn't turned out to be such a stupid, unjust, unnecessary war."

"Don't look now, Dad," I said, "but they're all stupid, unjust and unnecessary. How do you make these things so good?"

"I suppose it's natural you'd think that way," said Dad. "I make my own sweet and sour mix, fresh squeezed lemons, right off the tree, and dark Karo."

"Nectar of the gods," I said, smacking my lips. "How many missions do you think you'd have flown if Roosevelt had had the balls to go put in a little face time with Hitler in 1936, maybe sent MacArthur to Tokyo for a tête-à-tête with Hirohito.?"

"I'm sure that didn't even occur to anyone, at the time," said Dad.

"Don't kid yourself," I said. "It's called a lack of nerve at a critical moment. When a soldier has one he dies. When a head of state has one lots of innocent and not so innocent people die."

"You stayed there to the bitter end," Dad said. "I never understood that."

"It's like they say," I told him, "fame is a drug."

"You wanted to be on another recruiting poster?"

I got my hand over my mouth in time to keep from spewing whiskey sour across the table, and ended up in a coughing spasm. "Jesus, Dad," I gasped, while he pounded me on the back.

"How could I know?" Dad protested. "You refused to even mention it in your letters."

"Because it was an embarrassment, but at least I was an

anonymous dufuss face. I'm talking about the enemy. I was famous on the other side. They had a bigger bounty on my head than Westmoreland's. It was like being Elvis. They wanted my ass so bad, whenever they got me in a tight spot, they got all excited and blew it. The guy who took me down would have been set for life.

"They regarded American soldiers the same way we'd have regarded them, if they came sloshing ashore at Malibu, heavily armed and sporting woodies. But I was Ghost Marine, the dream prize and the nightmare all rolled into one. And these guys were probably the best fighters the world had seen since Genghis Kahn rolled out of Mongolia. There's no way I could have left early. It wouldn't have been fair."

"I assumed it was a woman kept you there," Dad said.

"That's a good one, Dad. I went through serious sexual deprivation for The Corps. , talk about self-discipline."

Dad freshened my cocktail from the carafe he mixed the sours in, and said, "Sounds grim, cut yourself down to once or twice a day, did you?"

"Try once or twice a year."

"Come on, son. I was born in the morning, but not this morning."

"I'm serious, Dad. I couldn't get close to any locals without putting them and their families in deadly peril, not that the Cong didn't have female agents waving pussy at me on a regular basis, but Vietnamese women aren't that forward, and I wasn't quite that stupid.

"In five years I got laid by half a dozen military nurses, three of whom I wouldn't normally have thrown rocks at, and one Penthouse Pet the USO brought over."

"I owe you an apology, then," Dad said. "For a young man, that is pretty rough going, especially the Penthouse Pet."

"It was brutal," I said, "but there's nothing like severe lackanookie to get a fella in the mood to kill."

"Ain't that the truth," Dad grinned, and refilled my drink again.

My mother came in, flush with bingo winnings. She fixed big mugs of cocoa for the three of us, then dragged Dad off to bed. I was wide awake, still feeling the wire from the loaded gel cap I'd eaten at breakfast.

The guest bedroom's wall of built in shelves made the room a catch all for used reading material. I settled on an old paperback, Treasure, by Robert Daley, and lay in bed reading about a real life treasure hunter until nearly dawn.

Looking out the room's open French doors, I could see the glassy surface of Lake Casitas glinting, down and away in the distance. I dog-eared the book, pulled the top sheet over my head and managed to get a couple hours zone-time before my father came barreling in at seven, full of piss and vinegar, making fake bugle sounds through his curled thumb and index finger, and otherwise exhibiting the obnoxious early morning high spirits common to those who never learned to stay in bed until a civilized hour.

CHAPTER FIFTEEN

My mother is a gunslinger in the kitchen, so adept at her craft, she was able to milk me for information about Leni, her emotional condition, associates in the church, and other complicated issues, while serving up three platters of peerless huevos rancheros (corn tortillas steamed to the verge of disintegration, fine shredded lettuce nesting fried eggs under melted cheeses and ranchera sauce), without missing an intonation or messing the kitchen. The avocado slices topping the melted cheese were a grade you'd have to be friendly with a grower to appreciate.

By eleven o'clock we'd exhausted conversation, my folks having been somewhat circumspect with me since I returned from five years in Southeast Asia, uninjured and with no glaring psychological problems. We said goodbyes and Dad walked me out to the car, telling Mom he was going to hike into the grove and confer with Javier, the ranch foreman, who lived in the garage apartment.

He ruffled my hair. "Take care, son, and good luck with Leni."

"Thanks," I said, then, "Hey, Dad." He paused and looked back.

"Do you know Julia Hoffman?"

He thought a moment. "Tom and Midge Hoffman's little girl? Haven't thought about them in years."

"You didn't know she was Al's astrologer?"

"Didn't know he had one."

I retraced my steps, back to the 101, and headed South, torn between the urge to hurry home and do unspeakable things to Lisa and my desire to arrive with five hundred miles on the odometer. After serious struggle I reached a decision and exited the freeway at Las Posas Road, turning right off the ramp toward the coast..

Driving fifty-five on Las Posas didn't make me an object of ridicule, though everyone not driving a farm tractor still passed at the first opportunity.

Las Posas ran out of continent at coastal Route 1, terminating before one of the entrances to Point Mugu Naval Base, just beyond a pair of ramps providing access to U.S. 1. On a sudden urge, I took the Northbound ramp, and made my way around the base to Channel Islands Marina, found the local China Sea franchise in a shopping center across the boulevard from the commercial dock.

It was strictly take-out, with a few tables out front, and a lunchtime line out the door. The guy manning the register looked just like Mutt, of Mutt and Jeff. I parked a couple car lengths from the storefront, and studied him from behind the Lincoln's light sensitive windshield. He was very friendly to the customers, and kept the line moving at a good clip, bagging orders as they appeared through a wide opening from the kitchen. Nothing in his demeanor hinted he was missing a cool quarter mil.

By 1:30, I was down coast, at county line, parked on a shelf between the roadway and the sea, fifty feet or so above a narrow, rocky strip of sand. Out on the water, some local wavers were working medium surf with short boards.

I left the Lincoln there, and strolled across four lanes of temporarily empty highway to Neptune's Net, where I bought an order of deep fried fish, a bottle of Fosters, and took them to one of the small tables strung out along the front porch. I hadn't seen any potential Jeffs inside the building, and now had a seat were I could observe arrivals and departures without showing interest. I nursed the beer along after inhaling the fish, and was about to get up when a trio of guys flying Marauders' colors, parked their hogs next to the porch and shut them down.

The first two proceeded straight inside, but the third paused to hail a waitress re-setting the porch tables with cutlery and condiments. "Hey, Sissy."

The girl looked over her shoulder. "Hey, J.C., what up?"

"Mike around?"

"Called early, said he'd be out until lunch, tomorrow."

"Damn! He's killing me."

"I know, sweetie. It's hell paying for beer."

"It is if you're riding with Walt and Larry, broke fuckers."

"Don't worry, good-looking. I know Michael would want me to give you boys happy hour pitchers, 2 for 1.

"You're a doll, Sis. How come we've never done the nasty."

"Because you're afraid of my old man."

"Oh, yeah. I knew there was something. You'll let me know if you two split, right?"

"You'll be one of the first ten guys I call."

I came in sight of Santa Monica Pier's roller coaster at 3:00 P.M., decided not to get onto the Western end of Interstate10 and join the Eastbound crawl choking the artery every weekday afternoon. Caught Ocean Ave. exit, and made haste South, out of Santa Monica into Venice. There's something about Santa Monica, so squeaky clean and politically correct, it creeps me out.

I paid for parking in the big municipal lot at the end of Rose Ave., parked the Lincoln where it had no close neighbors, secured it and strolled onto the World Famous Venice Boardwalk, stopping briefly at the Fig Tree Cafe for a triple cappuccino to sip as I continued South.

The house Leni donated to her church, to be utilized as a substance abuse scam, had been one of the last single family dwellings with boardwalk frontage. The building appeared unchanged, but the white picket fence enclosing the lot had been replaced by six foot high screened hurricane fencing, topped with small coil of razor wire. The entrance, on the Southwest corner, was fashioned from a pair of electrically controlled gates, containing a six by four foot passage between them. The place must have been bristling with surveillance equipment, it wasn't showing any.

I cut over to Speedway, a patchwork paved alley running behind the boardwalk properties, reported to have been a real race track in the previous dispensation, and followed it back, cutting down to the boardwalk at Dudley Ave., between the Cadillac Hotel and Henry's Market.

When I opened the Lincoln my phone was making a racket on the passenger seat. "Hello."

"Hello, Mark. It's Julia Hoffman."

"My favorite astrologer," I said.

"Know quite a few, do you?"

"Just you."

"I'm on my Astrology laptop, and I just pulled up your birth chart. Sometimes I like to talk to clients off the top of my head while I'm looking at their chart. Albert said many of what he considered priceless tid-bits came out of my mouth, when I wasn't writing things down and editing myself. Do you have time to talk?"

"I do," I said. "Your timing is good."

"Are you at home?"

"I'm at Venice Beach."

"Looking at the house Leni donated?"

"You know about that?"

"I almost cried when I heard. Ruth used to let my folks rent it, one week every summer. It held great memories, for me."

"Don't feel like the Lone Ranger," I said.

"How's it look?"

"Fenced off like a minimum security facility."

"What a shame."

"I'm authorized to buy it back for the trust," I said. "It won't be quick, I don't want to get soaked. But, soon as I can finagle a bagel, I'll get rid of the chain link eyesore, make the place respectable again."

"That will be very cool."

"How is my horoscope looking?"

"You were born with Uranus in the fourth house, the fourth represents, among other things, your home. With Uranus posited there, I imagine you've had some unusual abodes."

"Do now," I said.

"That's right," she said, and laughed. "I wasn't thinking. Any others?"

"When I was living in Milwaukee, I bought an abandoned power switching station auctioned off by the city. It had been stripped out and deserted since the fifties, but the structure was solid as a bunker. I got it cleared out, core drilled where I needed to install plumbing. They left a stack of those big old ceramic insulators out back, I used to decorate the exterior. Put a couple heat pumps on the roof, turned it into a two bedroom, two bath house, big and comfortable."

"Sounds fairly Uranian," said Julia Hoffman. "Still own it?"

"Sold it, when I moved to Boston, to a couple nerds who wanted to turn it into a techno-club."

"Very Uranian, indeed," she murmured, then said, "This evening, a couple hours from now, the Moon, out in the sky, will cross the degree occupied by Uranus in your chart, as it does once a month. However, since last month, Uranus, out in the sky, has moved to a close aspect with your Moon."

"The Moon to my Uranus," I said, "and Uranus to my Moon?"

"Very good," she sounded pleased. "We call that a double whammy."

"A technical term."

"Exactamundo."

"What does it portend?"

"Unexpected incidents, involving women."

"Happened yesterday," I said.

"Yesterday," she said. "Venus transited that point. Hot monkey sex, delivered to your home. Hot, quick, and over."

"I'm sorry to hear that," I said, "the over part."

"I just call 'em like I see 'em, big boy."

"You sounded pretty positive about the sex," I said.

"Venus transiting that fourth house Uranus of yours set the stage," she said, "but some reinforcing transits to your Venus and Mars pretty much made it a done deal. Done and done."

"Remains to be seen."

"Only for you, baby cakes."

"Are all astrologers so arrogant?"

"No, just the ones who've gotten sick of saying I told you so."

"What should I expect?"

"Uranus generally manifests as, Surprise, Motherfucker! The houses involved , the fourth and eighth, your home, other people's money."

"Is there any other kind?"

"With your eighth house Moon, it probably doesn't seem like it. But then, that's also responsible for your fulfilling sex life."

"Jesus Christ."

She laughed. "Anyway, sweetie, tonight the Moon will be fat lady in your personal opera, she'll start singing, at your place, about two hours from now.

"Won't be there," I said.

"You don't want to hear the fat lady sing?"

"I hate opera."

CHAPTER SIXTEEN

Left the beach, tooling up Rose Ave. to Lincoln Blvd. (US1 to LAX), where rush hour was in full crawl. I parked on Rose, pocketed the Robert Daley paperback my parents let me take, and went into La Cabana, Venice's answer to El Coyote. Finished the book while tucking in spinach enchiladas. beans and margaritas.

When I came out, at 7:30, traffic was still heavy, but moving.

Rolled South out of Venice, down Lincoln, through Marina del Rey, past LAX, where Lincoln merged with Sepulveda Blvd. which became US Route 1, continued on through El Segundo, Manhattan Beach, Hermosa Beach, turning left at Artesia Blvd., inland, while Leonard Cohen played out on the sound system and Billy Idol took over.

After a while, Artesia expanded into Highway 91, I stayed with it until Highway 57 showed up, choosing the Northbound connector. 57 brought me past the community of Diamond Bar, named for a ranch to which its acreage once belonged.

Driving there prompted memories of an old lady who owned an apartment building near the Venice beach house, and of the curious story she told me about Diamond Bar Ranch.

I lived rent-free in the beach house that winter, a year or two before the resurgence of Venice's popularity sent property values and rents through the roof. Al and Ruth were grateful to have me there, unoccupied houses during the period frequently got squatted by transients who, once in, were difficult and expensive to evict.

Dealing quarter pounds of H.A. crank, at the time, I made deliveries to dealers in Venice, Santa Monica and much of the Westside.

One of my customers lived in the old lady's building, and I walked a QP over there once or twice a week. She'd no idea of the reason for my visits and, once accustomed to my comings and goings, seemed to take a shine to me.

Our relationship consisted of smiles and nods, an occasional wave and comments on the weather, until one gray December morning she came shuffling by my porch, on the way to her place from Henry's Market, barely able to support the small bag of groceries she carried, a shadow of the woman I'd seen a week earlier dressing down one of her tenants with attitude and energy a Marine Corps top kick would have envied.

I vaulted the porch rail, landing next to her. "You don't look so good," I said. "Let me take that bag for you."

She managed a weak smile as she released the bag. "Been in the hospital all week, guess it shows."

I put a hand on her shoulder, and guided her through the gate. "Come and sit on the porch for a few minutes," I said, "then we'll get you back to your place."

She sat on the porch glider, folded her hands and smiled at me. "Thank you, you're a lifesaver."

Seventy-nine years old, five feet tall, ninety pounds fully dressed and soaking wet, she still looked good enough to let you know she'd been a stone fox in her day.

"Sit tight," I said. "I've got some Russian black tea on the stove, stuff will raise the dead."

"Cream and sugar, please." she said.

After she downed half her tea, and was getting some color in her cheeks, I said, "Let me give you some friendly advice, stay out of hospitals, people die like flies in those places, half the time from something they didn't have when they got there."

"I know that," she said, "but I had no say. I was unconscious when they brought me in."

"What was the matter?"

"Poison."

"You ate poison?"

"Not on purpose!"

"By accident?"

"Not that, either," she said.

"You think somebody tried to poison you?"

"Tried, Hell! If one of my daughters hadn't been visiting when I keeled over, I'd be pushing up daisies, right now."

Somebody who'd do that is lower than whale shit."

"Apt description," she said.

"Any idea who it was?"

"Course I do. I'm not senile."

117

"Well?" I said.

"Well what?"

"Who was it?"

"If I tell, you can't repeat it."

"Who would I tell?"

"Promise me."

"I won't repeat it, while you're alive," I said. "If you turn up dead, I'm liable to shout it from the rooftops."

"That would be acceptable," she said then turned and looked out to sea, lips tight. "It was my twin."

"Your what?"

"My goddamn twin. My sister."

"You have a twin sister?" I said.

She and her boyfriend have been living in my building since they came back from the Yukon, almost a year. You've seen her, and him, too."

"When?"

"Lots of times," she said, looking impatient. "She was always having him push her up and down the boardwalk, in that wheel chair."

"Dark haired guy? Horn rimmed glasses? Always dressed in khaki?" This was a man I'd seen often, about half the time pushing a hospital issue wheel chair, bearing what looked to me like a scaled down version of Jabba the Hut, rolls and rolls of jiggly fat, assembled into vaguely human form, bevy of chins propping a chubby little head with reptilian eyes.

"That's him," she said, "the boyfriend."

"The one in the chair is your twin sister?"

She nodded with vigor.

"I don't see the family resemblance," I said. "She looks like Jabba the Hut's sister."

"I'm telling you, we are identical twins," she insisted. "In high school nobody could tell us apart. She used to have sex with my boyfriends, pretending to be me. It was terrible."

"How did she get so fat and ugly?"

She shrugged. "I suppose that's what happens, when you go around poisoning people."

"She's poisoned other people?"

"That's how I knew she did it to me. That and the fact she'd been cooking my meals for the two days before I collapsed."

"She cooks from a wheel chair?"

She waved her hand. "She can walk fine, just doesn't like to."

"Who else did she poison?"

"Her husband," she said. "He owned Diamond Bar Ranch, found out she was playing hide-the-salami with his ranch foreman, and was fixing to divorce her. She got wind of it, and she and her boyfriend slipped him a mickey, then injected him with amyl nitrate. Destroyed his heart and left no trace. Claimed he had a heart attack while she was blowing him."

"And got away with it?"

She gave another wave. "I think the local assistant D.A. was sweet on her. She made millions, selling off that ranch, her and the boyfriend."

"He was the ranch foreman?"

"For about a month," she said. "But that's another story. Anyway, they were living it up on the ranch money. But when the tax people came, looking for their share, she wrote them a check on a closed account, then took off to the Yukon, her and that boyfriend of hers."

"She in jail, now?" I asked.

She looked surprised. "Jail? Certainly not. I can't have that kind of scandal in my family. I own an apartment complex, in Riverside. Made them move down there."

"The boyfriend," I said. "I thought he was her son, or something."

"No," she shook her head. "We are all the same age. I met him first, at a USO dance in "Hollywood during the War. He wanted me, but I wouldn't cheat on my husband, not with him, anyway." She ducked her head, and looked embarrassed. "So he went after my sister. Hired on at the ranch to get close to her, made foreman in about a week. Seems he knows everything and can do everything, came out of The War a full Colonel. Only bad move he ever made was helping my sister kill her husband. Been stuck with her, ever since. She swore, if he ever left her, she'd confess to the murder and implicate him. I think he planned to get rid of her, up in the Yukon. But she wrote me a letter, all about the murder, and told me, if a month ever passed without a letter or a phone call from her, I was to send it to the District Attorney. I guess she showed him copies of the letters, so he was stuck, still is, no statute of limitations on murder."

"Did you ever consider giving the letter to the authorities, anyway?" I asked.

She mused, "No, not really. She was my sister, after all. Besides, her husband was a real asshole. I never liked him."

"How about the boyfriend?"

She propped her elbow on one hand, her chin on the other. "I never could figure that man, at all. Nothing ever seemed to bother him, still doesn't. You'd expect he must hate my sister's guts, but he treats her just fine, never so much as a dirty look in her direction. Never a complaint from her about him, though she damn sure complains about everything else under the Sun. No sir, I don't understand that man, at all."

I remembered the man very well. I'd seen him often, pushing Mrs. Hut (as I'd christened her) along the boardwalk, or drinking coffee with her at an outside table. He seemed to find the boardwalk foot traffic endlessly fascinating, and always seemed on the verge of smiling. His girlfriend seemed entirely self-absorbed and indifferent to her surroundings.

He was a rugged, good-looking man, I could imagine right at home in the Yukon. The black horn rim glasses he wore took nothing away from his aura of competent masculinity.

We'd never exchanged words. In passing, he generally favored me with an ironic half-smile and a one finger salute, to which I automatically returned the full military response. Once I knew his real age, I figured my instincts were good.

The ringing of my phone cut short my reverie as I approached the 210 at San Dimas. I picked it up, read Troll on the display, and slipped it into a receptacle on the center console, pulling down my sun visor. "What's happening, Troll?"

"Question," he said, through the sound system speakers. "Know any Marauders?"

"Can't say I do."

"One of them was down in Sunland, today," Troll said, "asking about you."

"Got a name?"

"Mike," said Troll. "Misdemeanor Mike, they call him."

"Never catches any felony beefs?"

"Reckon not," Troll said. "Ring any bells?"

"Not so far," I lied. "Any idea what he looks like?"

"Short guy," he answered, "but husky. Pumps iron for bulk, not definition. Word is he's a pretty bad little motherfucker, but doesn't walk around selling wolf tickets. Decent business rep, into some ducats, too. Never met him, though."

Jeff.

"Something's niggling at my brain," I said. "Let's talk in person."

"I'm good with that. Tomorrow?"

"How's three?"

"Good, for me. Oh, one other thing."

"Shoot."

"I told Lori about your digs, up there. She gassed on it, had to tell her friend, Tuesday, all about it. Word is, Misdemeanor Mike drops by to bone Tuesday, whenever he's in the neighborhood. Fair chance he knows where you live, sorry about that."

"Don't be, I'm not shy about meeting people, and he damn sure can't sneak up on me. I appreciate the heads up."

"All right," said Troll, "later."

Pushed my visor back up, ending the call, eased my speed down from 65 and rolled through the night toward San Bernadino, a destination I calculated would bring me home with the miles I needed.

After tonight this car would only see 55 on surface streets.

CHAPTER SEVENTEEN

At 10:30 pm, I exited the 210 via Lowell Ave. Twenty minutes later, I was rolling through the gate, watching it drop noiselessly behind me in the rear view mirror.

When I crossed the ridge, and lights began coming on all over the property, I realized I hadn't seen the place blacked out since the night of my arrival. Coming down the elevated drive, I noticed the motor home was gone from its hook-ups behind the Sphinx.

My motorcycle and Aunt Ruth's Lexus were the only vehicles in the subterranean parking. I eased the Lincoln down the ramp to high performance heaven, remembering Julia Hoffman's words, Uranus generally manifests as surprise, motherfucker. I was not amused. I put the Lincoln on the lift, and drained the break-in oil into a wheeled twenty gallon drum, with a catch basin on an extendable neck. If the thing tried to talk to me, I'd have kicked the crap out of it, and ended up with used oil all over the floor.

While oil drained, I used the local terminal to scan through the property, nobody else home, no surprise. I ran some time lines. Edward and Jerry (sans collars) rolled out in the land yacht, at 6:31 pm, Lisa and Frieda left in the Jag at 6:42, Leni was five minutes behind them, in Al's Lexus. So much for the home team jumping out to a commanding lead.

Julia Hoffman wasn't half bad looking (if you like willowy, small breasted blonds), At around 4:30, she told me the fat lady would sing in two hours. She knew something I didn't, and I hoped it was just astrology.

Went back to the Lincoln and spun in a fresh oil filter, replaced the drain plug and brought down the lift, pumped seven quarts of Amsoil into the engine, then broke off the yellow tab on the dipstick and drove back up to the garage.

After pushing the elevator call button, I remembered something and went back to Ruth's Lexus for the aluminum case, shifting it to the Lincoln's trunk. Somebody would need my left thumb or a high speed grinder to access it there.

The sour mood was lifting, first time I felt really alone in almost two years. I got a small tri tip out of the fresh meat compartment, sprayed it with soy sauce and placed it in the instant barbecue box, above the big stove's splash plate, set the selector on black & blue and closed the door.

When I returned from the walk in freezer a minute later, with a couple Australian lobster tails, the door sighed back open, releasing fragrance that nudged my memory to family Fourth of July picnics at Tapia Park, in Malibu Canyon, when my father and Uncle Bill were undamaged war heroes, Uncle Max was a budget accountant for Dave Selznick, Aunt May worked in wardrobe, and Al was just a hotshot pharmaceutical salesman, who bought cheap tracts of land in Thousand Oaks with his buddy, Eddie Janss, and dragged his girlfriend, Ruth to car races on weekends, while his newlywed sister, June, scornfully declined repeated offers of movie stardom from Hollywood big shots.

Time's a funny thing, and I don't mean funny ha ha.

Slid the blackened tri tip onto a fourteen inch platter and put the tails in the box, giving them each a squirt of soy, and turning the selector to Seafood. While I was taking melted butter from the microwave, the door eased back open to reveal the tails, plump and steaming, sporting slight tans. I put them on the platter with the blackened meat and melted butter, filled the rest of the platter with tomato wedges and hunks of cucumber marinated in Caesar, grabbed a cold liter of Coke, and took it all across to the pool, dining atop the platform of the three-meter board, a place now considered my lucky spot.

The Valley light show while I ate was impressive, but knowing there was not a human being within a mile made the food extra tasty.

Took the platter and butter bowl back to the pyramid, and dumped them in the kitchen dish hole, then went up to the mezzanine via an enclosed stairwell just off the kitchen.

The stairwell let onto an interior terrace overlooking much of the first floor's three thousand square foot living room, while serving as a common area for three full suites: Sapphire Suite, Ruby Suite and Emerald Suite, so named because their entry portals were colorized flubber, shaped like enormous cuts of the three gems. The Emerald Suite's giant fake stone was missing,

Leni hadn't closed the door when she left.

I walked through the open portal, crossing a short entry to the sitting room, where everything visible reflected the emerald motif in endless shadings and blendings of green.

Leni's choice spot in the room was at once obvious, a two-toned, seamlessly upholstered chaise cum love seat, with six legs of dark hardwood, each carved in the shape of a great bird's three-toed talon clutching a piece of translucent jade the size and shape of a baseball.

A large hardcover book lay open, pages down, on the center of the chaise, a bulky and weighty tome, penned by the prophet of Leni's church. I dog-eared the open page, and cruised the book for several minutes. The sheer volume of words made me dubious of their conveying any ideas of real significance. When the author had gone on for six pages without completing a round robin I set it aside, thinking, speed freak.

A house phone lay keypad up on a side table, whose three carved legs ended in green glass spheres the size of golf balls. The table also held a purple tulip shaped ashtray (half full), a quarter mug of black coffee and a black pack of American Spirit cigarettes, pink mini-Bic tucked inside the cellophane.

Shook out a cigarette and lit it, my first in nearly two years, a rush to remember.

Pulled up the last incoming call, and called it, puffing away.

An electronic Betty White voice answered. "Thank you for calling the blah blah offices of the blah Church blah blah. Our switchboard is closed, you may key ahead if you know your party's extension, or call back during business hours. Thank you."

I usually press 01 in these situations, and this was no exception.

"Pastor Nevins office." She sounded very young, her tone hushed.

I took a shot. "Edward there?"

"I'm sorry, Pastor Nevins has gone for the day."

"But he said I could reach him here."

"It's very late, sir."

"How about Lisa? She around?"

"She's hosting our celebrity coffee house, tonight."

"Oh crap," I said, "it already started?"

"An hour ago!"

"Oh, Jesus," I moaned, "she's going to rip my lungs out."

"Oh, man," she breathed. "I wouldn't want Lisa Leopold mad at me."

"But the directions she gave me flew out the window," I wailed, "now I'll never find the place."

"Lisa invited you to CCH?" she sounded wary. "How famous are you? I don't recognize your voice."

I raised my register an octave, "I have many voice, young rady."

"Ohmigod! Is this Jackie Chan?"

"Please, he's B-list."

"Give me a hint."

"Can't risk it, sweetie," I said. "If my agent catches me hanging with you people, he'll drop an intervention on me."

"Get off it," she said. "He can't do that."

"Can't he?" I said. "I don't suppose the letters CAA mean anything to you."

"Oh, shit."

"Maybe I should just forget this whole thing," I tried to sound scared.

"No!" It was almost a shout. "Don't let those suits bully you. Lisa can show you how to handle them. Are you coming by freeway?"

"I'm coming down the 101," I fibbed.

"Okay, you're gonna exit at Sunset."

"Do you know if Lisa's friend, Lenore, is there?" I asked.

"Lenore Brown? Probably, I always see them together."

"Here comes Sunset," I said.

"Turn right at the top of the ramp. You're not Josh Brolin, are you?"

"Come over, and see."

"Yeah, right," she said. "I'll just waltz right in."

"Why not?"

"You kidding?" she said, "the only way you're gonna see me at CCH is if they need another peon to serve coffee and kiss ass."

I broke the connection, and went upstairs, diving into what I found myself thinking of, more and more, as my acre of bed. I rolled around for a few minutes, enjoying the feeling of stretching

125

out all my long muscles, then fell asleep.

CHAPTER EIGHTEEN

Came awake, somewhere in the wee hours, from a dream crowded with Lisa, Edward, Jerry, Frieda, the thong girls and a couple dozen strangers (all church members), milling around all over the property, calling, "Lenore, Lenore."

I yelled at Lisa to get those people out of there. She yelled back they were just trying to help. This sparked such a rage in me I woke up, surprised to find I'd been dreaming, and relieved.

The dream was disturbing enough for me to consider getting up, until I realized there had been no prison people in it. I rolled back into sleep.

Got out of bed at 7:00, shuffled into the small kitchen and grabbed a bottle of Trader Joe's tangerine juice off the refrigerator door, shook it, swallowed half its contents, and took the rest with me to the office, where I removed the hundred button clicker from its charger, and used it to change the whole top of the pyramid from transparent black to clear.

While the walls became invisible much that was inside them did not, plumbing pipes, electric cable, fiber-optic bundles, a/c duct work, but none of it rose more than three feet above the floor, so the clearing of the flubber was pretty dramatic.

I walked around, finding the uphill panoramas as impressive as the downhill. The overall effect was like walking on a small mountaintop without leaving the comforts of home.

It was a clear morning, and I could see the rush hour traffic away down in the distance where Foothill Blvd. and the 210 freeway bridged Big Tujunga Wash, the long haul rigs on the 210 looked like matchbox versions of themselves. The Valley floor was smudged with haze, but the mountains on the far side stood out in sharp relief. The 405 freeway floated a river of cars up through Sepulveda Pass at the speed of lava. The far horizon blended sea and sky invisibly.

Finished the tangerine juice and clickered the flubber back to sunglass tint, then sat on the edge of the bed and keyed Leni's phone on mine. Voice mail.

"Call me, kiddo," I said, keeping it light. "Let me know you're okay."

A call came in as I broke the connection. I checked the display, not Leni. "Hello, Julia," I said into the phone.

"Good morning, Mark. Sorry to bother you, but it was either call or spend all day wondering what kind of surprise Moon/Uranus had for you last night. I hope it wasn't too aggravating."

"Would have been more annoying without your timely call," I said.

"Sometimes a little advance notice lightens the emotional charge," she said.

"I'd have sulked for hours instead of minutes," I said.

"Could never get those hours back."

"By the way, I fired Chet Bowles, yesterday."

"Ohmigod, I love you. I'm sorry, that was mean."

"Al said you'd picked yesterday as a good day to give him the boot."

"That's right," she said, "I did a few dump Chet elections a couple years ago, I 'd forgotten all about them."

"Al thought it would be a good way to snap the rest of the staff to attention, or he'd have fired him a year ago."

"You have a replacement?" asked Julia.

"Al suggested moving Linda Herrera into his spot, and moving Walker, the A/R guy over to be her assistant."

"Linda's great," she said. "Walker's got a pretty lucky birth chart, and he seems nice. What about his job?"

"Al suggested finding an MBA, who's a real asshole or a cast iron bitch, and let them think they've got a shot at the controller's job."

"Ah yes. The obligatory asshole."

"What's up with that?"

"It predates my history with him," she said. "Albert thought friction to be a vital ingredient for a business, and was always on the lookout for good trouble makers, so he wouldn't have to play the role."

"Is that what Bowles was?"

"No. He didn't become a problem until Albert gave me that

old copy room as an office, and made me his in house astrologer. It made Chet furious when Albert followed my suggestions over his, then crazy when it resulted in huge profits. Plus, the poor man and I were so incompatible, astrologically, we couldn't stand to be in the same room."

"He's gone, now," I said. "Think he'll be tough to replace, irritation-wise?"

"When you've got a hot prospect," she said, "give me their birth data. Month day and year should be sufficient, if you can get time and location so much the better. I've got charts on all the employees, I can throw your candidate's planetary pattern onto their charts, and let you know how disruptive they're likely to be."

"You'll be hearing from me on that," I said. "I take it you've got Leni's chart?"

"Of course."

"She and her church buddies were all gone when I got home last night. I haven't been able to get her to answer the phone."

"Did the two of you have a falling out?" Julia asked.

"Not that I could tell."

"I'll pull up her chart, call you back in a little while."

"Okay, thanks."

I was in the office, dealing with emails, when the house line rang, Troll. "Hello."

"Hey, now."

"Troll," I said, "I was just thinking about coming down and giving you a ride in my new car."

"The hot little Lexus?"

"Nah. This will whip that Lexus like a red-headed step-child."

"Sounds like a ride I'll have to accept," Troll said, "but maybe I can save you the trip down."

"What do you have in mind?"

"I've got a couple girls here, cleaning my house," he said. "You can probably hear the vacuum going in the living room. The other one's doing the kitchen and laundry."

"You want to get out of their way," I said. "Come on up."

"It's not quite like that," said Troll. "They showed up and started doing all this stuff, dressed in string bikinis."

"You must be living right," I said. "Fucker."

"Bikinis," Troll said, "and a lot of jewelry, armbands, layered necklaces, heavy eye make-up, too."

"Ah," I said.

"They haven't said a word since they got here, went right to work. I think I'm supposed to be Mr. Sensitive, and invite them to swim between the paws of The Sphinx, that is, if I'd like to enjoy this type of service again."

"They're very subtle," I said.

"Yeah," said Troll, "like a kick in the nuts."

"Have I met these girls?"

"Lori and her cousin."

"Annette?"

"That would be the one," Troll said.

"How's she looking?"

"Pretty bitchen."

"What time should I look for you?"

"One, one-thirty, said Troll.

"Don't eat lunch," I said. "I'm up to my ass in t-bones and lobster tails."

"Okay," said Troll. "Bring you anything? Beer, wine, speed, weed, ludes, acid?"

"Some herb might be the ticket," I said. "I haven't gotten stupid since the day I moved up here."

"Annette's holding some chronic," he said, "knock about twenty points off your IQ."

"You remember the gate code I assigned you?" I said.

"Sure do."

"People who have their own gate code don't need to call first."

"I appreciate that," Troll said, "but I didn't want to, you know, cramp your style."

"I got no style," I said. "It's lonely at the top."

"What happened to all those religious freaks?" said Troll, "and that one fine motherfucker?"

"Took off like a herd of turtles up a dry creek bed."

"Leni, too?"

"Yep."

"Fuck."

"See you after a while." I said.

CHAPTER NINETEEN

Linda Herrera's email was next up: "I won't make you read five hundred words. I've been doing eighty percent of Chet's job for the past eighteen months, while he played politics with Mr. Brown's money and reputation, and thought up new ways to make life miserable for Julia Hoffman. I kept my mouth shut and got the work done, because it needed to be done and I'm not a tattle-tale. But now that Chet's gone, God, it's good to tell somebody about it."

I typed: "Move into Bowles' office. Remodel as you feel necessary (anything over a grand comes out of your pocket) Instruct Walker to move to your present office, as your assistant. Your next paycheck will be commensurate with new title. Congratulations".

I copied the email to the controller, adding, Eighty percent of Bowles' salary, no change for Walker.

The next two received this reply: Don't waste my time with this crap. If you need advice call Julia Hoffman, that's what I do.

Next was a fairly long email from the Law Offices of Levy and Fleece, regarding blocks of voting stock held in a couple of the trusts, that weren't proxied out and had to be voted this month.

When Al and Sid Levy set up the trusts about three quarters of all voting stock were provided with proxies to take effect upon Al's death. The quarter remaining would be voted by the administrator of the trust where the stock reposed, but required co-signature of the administrator of The Brown Family Trust (expected to be Leni, at the time), to be binding.

During his last year, as Al despaired of leaving Leni in charge, he contracted Levy and Fleece to provide information services to whomever became principal of the trust, notifying them of voting situations as they developed with un-proxied holdings.

The two trust managers handling the blocks to be voted sent emails, with rudimentary descriptions of the issues. They seemed expectant I'd rubber stamp their decisions. The info paks Levy and

Fleece provided were sufficiently comprehensive to undermine those expectations.

They sketched the issues at conflict with no wasted words. One involved a stock swap acquisition, proposed by a medical equipment supplier who wanted to own their chief supplier of medical gases, possibly, suggested the analyst, so they could manipulate gas deliveries to competing equipment suppliers, with great caution, of course.

The other was a national chain of Mexican style cantinas, wanting to take on huge short-term debt, to go into China.

I emailed the respective managers, approving the first, nixing the second, then shot one to Levy and Fleece, thanking them for the in depth analysis, not expecting a reply, much less a quick one.

hv vtng stk bth cos. Bcm aqtd w/A bmpng in2 hm at stckhldr mtngs, bcm frnds. Sid.

Good to know, I typed back, thanks again.

Lk medgas?

Yeah.

Mex?

No.

Mt rcnsdr, cld b big.

Ok. Have finegirl send five years annual reports.

Wildo. How Leni?

Pissed at me, I think.

Y?

No clue, yet.

Wr frnds. Drpd me wn Rth die. Nt tlk snce.

Likely due to influence of her spiritual advisers, I typed.

Fucking assholes!! Mst go, T off 15 min.

Ok, later.

Went off-line, into the security system, I wanted to time line Leni's suite.

Nano-cams inside the pyramid were not spy friendly. Each mezzanine suite had one, positioned, it seemed, only to see whether the suite was occupied. Panning and zooming were disabled. Sound pick-up was also restricted.

The one in Leni's suite showed just the lower third of the green chaise, and I didn't note her presence until she got up and left. I ran it back from that point, and determined she'd been sitting there over two hours.

She'd received a call on her cell, around 5:00, I could make out an occasional word spoken by her, and zip from the caller, took a systematic tour of all the other nanos, at the time of the call, and found Lisa on the little roof deck behind the Sphinx's head, talking on her cell. Nothing disabled at that location, I was able to hear both sides of the conversation, while looking down the front of Lisa's v-neck.

LISA: Hey, girlfriend, what are you doing in that big old pyramid?

LENI: I'm finally getting through the reading assignments you gave me.

LISA: I thought maybe you were hiding.

LENI: The house is wide open, and so is my door. Won't Edward let you come over? It's not like Mark is lurking over here.

LISA: It's got nothing to do with your cousin, he didn't do anything wrong. But I was a little rough on Edward, so I'm feeling obliged to respect his position in the org, in spite of my personal reservations about him.

LENI: He sure turned into a petty dictator, in the twinkling of an eye.

LISA: He won't show it, but he's hurt you won't come with us.

LENI: He should have said please, instead of issuing orders. Anyway, don't worry, I'll be along directly. Just, don't tell Mr. Bossy.

LISA: I can keep a secret.

LENI: So can I, you don't even have to ask.

LISA: I would never ask.

LENI: I wish I had your nerve

LISA: Stick with me, I'll show you how. Frieda's coming, talk to you later.

I'd been lax resupplying the kitchenette in the top level, so I put on my camo shorts, put the clicker from hell in one of the big thigh pockets, phone in the other, stepped into my flops, then into a large round hole in the floor, at one corner of the office, landing light as a feather on the faux bleached oak floor of the egg shaped entry hall, twenty feet below.

Al said, on his video, he couldn't explain how it worked,

didn't fully understand it, himself, but it conformed to the known laws of physics, and used no power. One of the theoretical brainiacs at his R&D facility in Glendale had dreamed it up and built it, the effect, a fleeting soft spot in the unbending law of gravity, within ten seconds arc of the bottom of our gravity well. So far, it was fail proof.

Despite such assurances, I'd tested it by dropping several breakable, and increasingly heavy objects, through the hole, before taking the leap, myself. I refrained from using it when there was any possibility of being observed. The young scientist who dreamed it up and built it is loathe to release his drawings to the U.S. Patent Office. My generation had to learn not to trust the government, these youngsters coming out of our top schools seem to have been born that way.

In the big kitchen, I took a couple swigs from a quart bottle of vitamin/mineral elixir. The profusion of vitamins, minerals, amino acids and other goodies listed on the bottle, prompted the notion that chewing a piece of cardboard (for fiber) would make it a well-rounded meal. I did something similar: Toasted some frozen waffles, slathered them with butter, Log Cabin and sour cream, then made them disappear at a rate that was probably sickening to behold. I chased the gooey sweetness with a quart and a half of very cold milk, thus was well fortified when Julia Hoffman called back a few minutes later.

CHAPTER TWENTY

"How's it looking?"

"Pretty disturbing, I'm sorry to say."

"Swell. How much can you tell me?"

"You seemed to catch onto the transits I described to your chart, yesterday."

"Uranus to my Moon, in the house of sex and money," I said, "and Moon to my Uranus, in the house of home. They acquired meaning pretty quick, when I rolled in last night."

"Leni had a couple transits becoming exact during the same time period. Her Moon's in the fourth house, opposing her tenth house Pluto. Last night, Mars in the sky conjuncted her Moon, as it does once every couple years, opposing her Pluto. She had that same transit occurring when she left her second husband, though it was reinforced by Saturn making a bad aspect to her seventh house Venus. The seventh rules marriage and the spouse. Saturn afflicting put this attractive guy in a very unflattering light, Mars hitting the Moon/Pluto configuration on the same day provided the drive to tell him off and leave, which she did."

"You see it coming, or see it after it happened?" I asked.

"I called it ahead of time," she said. "I'd been looking at Leni's chart a lot, because she was just at the beginning of a brutal Neptune transit, that's been messing up her life, ever since."

"Care to elaborate on that?" I asked. "In English?"

"Sure, Leni was born with Moon, Mercury and Mars all within the last three degrees of "Scorpio. That makes her a very ballsy girl."

"She's always had a lot of nerve," I said, "but thinks of herself as chicken shit."

"When three planets are so close in somebody's chart, one gets transited they all get transited.

"I think I'm getting in over my head, here," I said. "What's a brutal Neptune transit."

"You might find it easier to grasp if I tell you first about a more or less benign transit of Neptune, one you've experienced."

"Okay," I said, "lay it on me."

"The outer planets have very long orbits, compared to ours, and spend long periods where, from our perspective, they appear to move backward instead of forward through the Zodiac. Neptune's orbit takes one hundred fifty five years. When he makes a transit to a planet in your chart, his influence can last, depending on where your planet falls in relation to his retrograde periods, from one to three years.

"Neptune transited your Venus, by trine, starting about two and a half years ago, a particularly pleasant transit, Neptune is considered the upper octave of Venus by most Astrologers. You may have met your ideal woman under this transit, or at least one who seemed to embody your ideal while the transit was in effect. On the downside, you may have had to contend with a certain amount of deception from females during the same period, especially if they felt you had unreasonably high expectations of them.

"As Neptune transits go, it was brief, a little over a year. Your legal troubles began as it was separating from your Venus, because at the same time Saturn moved into your ninth house, almost immediately forming a very stressful aspect, called a square, to your twelfth house Jupiter. You follow?"

"I think so," I lied. "Can we cut to the chase?"

"Okay, Saturn in the Ninth, where you find governing bodies, courts, the law, putting a bad juju on Jupiter in the Twelfth, where you find prisons, hospitals, asylums. Meanwhile, Mercury's retrograde in your seventh, opposing your Mars and Ascendant. You're lucky you weren't killed."

"Are you making this all up, as you go along?"

"Oh please!"

"It sounds mighty goddamn pat."

"Many people experience legal difficulties under Saturn square Jupiter. They may have to pay a fine, or do community service, or get nicked for back taxes, or lose a lawsuit. Most of them don't get ten years for corrupting the morals of a minor."

"Contributing to the delinquency," I said

"Whatever. Anyway, you were already in prison when Albert brought me your birth data, so, if it makes you feel any better, this was all hindsight on my part."

"Look," I said, "I apologize. I got pretty lazy, mentally, the past year or so, now I'm trying to get back up to speed. After meeting you, I did some fast forwarding through a kind of training video Al prepared for me, to see what he had to say about you, and when he'd get around to saying it. He doesn't mention you until the last five minutes."

"What did he say?"

"He said the thing he's proudest of, in his life, is being responsible for you becoming an Astrologer, you are what he believes all good Astrologers will be, two or three hundred years from now, cautious, precise, confidential, and scornful of self-promotion."

"You're making me cry," she sniffled.

"Sorry," I said. "He ended the training video with a promise."

"What did he promise, if it's not too personal?"

"He promised, if I could get you on my side, my job would become ten times easier."

"That sounds about right," she said primly, "if you don't keep thinking I'm bullshitting you all the time."

"Okay, okay. Jesus."

"Can I call you later? I'm too emotional, right now."

"Call me anytime."

CHAPTER TWENTY-ONE

Warming up a small section of the big pit barbecue, just outside the Sphinx's kitchen, I saw Troll and Lori stroll across the rope and redwood bridge and drop their towels on the back of the one-meter board. Lori smiled a greeting, took a couple running steps to the edge, and headed for the bottom. Troll walked out on the low board and gave a couple test bounces.

"Annette beg off?" I said as I approached.

"Checking the panorama," said Troll, pointing behind with a thumb, then bouncing off into a deep dive, clear of where Lori's head surfaced.

I stood at the edge of the pool, studying Troll's surprising speed and grace underwater. On land, he carried himself with an unhurried force and momentum that often put me in mind of a rhinoceros. In the water, he became a sea lion. Watching him now, rumors of his lone exploits on Vietnamese rivers, I'd regarded as heavily embroidered G.I. scuttlebutt, began to seem more plausible, though I wouldn't express it to him. He never showed inclination to rehash those days, and the idea he'd entertain opinions of his wartime conduct would not occur to anyone with more than a nodding acquaintance of the man.

I crossed the bridge, and walked around the Pyramid on its footing, winding my way past water heavy desert flora, and leafy tropicals sprouting out of round edged depressions in the, better than real, fake red granite.

There was a small population of horned-lizards on the footing (everyone referred to as horny toads). The surrounding mountainside supported chipmunks, coyotes, a skunk or three, some raccoons, migrant mule deer, rattlers and king snakes and, to harass and fuck with them all (the nearest police station being way down in The Valley), the energetic and ever present crow, unofficial bird of Los Angeles.

When I came around to the off-hill side of the building, Annette was visible, up slope, at the apogee of the hundred and twenty degree bulge of mountainside, its elevation extending the horizon's distance out to a line (when clear) where blue sky met blue Pacific, and thus all Los Angeles fell within the frame.

I went down from the footing and up the slope. She had her back to me, and didn't move as I approached, until I said. "It always amazes me how a beautiful woman can make a boring old landscape suddenly interesting."

She turned with a smile, "Keep talking, I know it's bullshit, but you do it so well."

"Play your cards right, little lady, this could all be yours, someday."

"Really, mister? What would I have to do?"

"Never mind about that, nothing difficult."

"But I was hoping for something hard."

"I could follow you to the pool, and see what pops up."

"I don't normally allow a fellow to stare at my behind for that long at a stretch," she said. "But, buddy, when you move into the neighborhood, you really move into the neighborhood. So, get an eyeful, but be careful." Annette started down slope , looked back as she tugged her bikini bottom down a hair. "If you feel yourself getting dizzy, look away."

"If I can."

"Want to cut through the house on the way to the pool?" I asked, as we neared the footing.

Annette paused. "Don't we have to walk around to get in? No doors on this side."

"I can fix that," I said, pulling the clicker out of my flapped pocket. I pointed it at the balcony recessed in the limestone face of the second level, and pushed a button. Nothing happened. "Shit." I studied the buttons.

"Will clicker man save the day?" asked Annette, in talking head cadence, "or will they have to walk around. The tension mounts."

I saw I'd neglected to reposition a rocker switch, by which the clicker's buttons all did double duty. I flicked it, said, "I believe you meant to say, Mister Clicker Man," and pushed the same button. The lower edge of the balcony spewed a long, narrow ribbon of chain mail, its stiff leading edge dragging a shifting mass, like flowing gold in the sunlight. When the unbending edge hit the footing, the flowing mass of metal behind stopped moving, in the shape of a curving stairway.

Annette turned a dazed expression at me. "Is it safe?"

"Solid as ice," I said. "Give it a try."

"I'm going to have to be from Missouri, on this one," she said. "You first."

"You just want to look at my butt," I said, starting up.

"Well, yes," she said, "but I'm nervous, too."

When I got to the balcony without incident, she came up. I pushed another clicker button, the shining stairs went limp and were sucked back into the floor beneath our feet.

Annette was examining the seamless transparent wall for a way inside.

"Say, open says me," I suggested.

"Open says me." Nothing happened. "Wise guy, eh?" said Annette, raising an eyebrow.

"Damn," I said, and rubbed my chin. " Try clapping twice."

She looked dubious, but clapped twice, and the wall dilated. "Jesus," she said, walking into the common area of the mezzanine, "I'm on Star Trek."

I showed her the ruby suite, then took her down, through the kitchen and across to the pool. I knew she had a million questions, but didn't ask. I like that in a woman.

Troll was fussing with the steaks and tails, while I smoked a joint and sipped margaritas with Lori and Annette. We were seated at the same glass-topped wicker table Leni and her pals congregated around, a few days before. Now, I had to restrain myself from shooting glances at the Hamms Beer sign, where something too small to see was processing light and sound values, effortlessly, endlessly, to the black slab's memory.

Troll hailed me, and I looked over. He held up my phone, I'd left near the grill.

Went over and got it, the display said: Text message Leni. "About time," I said, showing it to Troll, then keying to read: You have something belonging to me, you must return. Stand by.

"Check this," I said, and showed Troll.

"What do you have that belongs to her?" he asked.

"About everything except her car."

"Try calling," he suggested

I did, got voice mail. "Hey, what's up?" I said, and broke the connection..

"Might as well eat," said Troll, "while we stand by."

When we finished eating and the girls cleaned up the mess, Troll tossed his keys to Lori, and said, "Take the car down to my place. We'll see you there after a while."

The redhead caught the keys on the fly, and said, "Okay. Should we answer the door, if anybody comes by?"

"Nah," said Troll, "don't bother. We won't be long."

Walking them out to Troll's car, I opened the passenger door for Annette. She brushed my cheek with her lips and got in. "Thanks for a wonderful lunch," she said. "It was good seeing you again."

"Thank you for coming," I said.

CHAPTER TWENTY-TWO

Troll was still in the cutoffs and flops he'd arrived in, I in my black baggys. He hadn't brought anything to change into, but we'd both dried enough to sit in the car. I gave him one of my 'Don't Forget to Think About Your Dead Homey' v-necks, put on a gray tank top, and took him down in the elevator to the parking garage.

"Now look here," Troll said, and walked in a wide arc around the Lincoln, nodding his approval. He started to get in the front passenger seat, but changed his mind, and got in the back, fastened his seat belt and said, "Now, James, I know you think I'm sitting back here so I can profile. But the real reason is, every time I see a car with two guys sitting in the front, my first thought is they're either cops or queers, and I don't want to put you in a bad light."

"You don't want anybody getting the notion I'm a cop."

"There it is."

"Mighty considerate," I said.

"Drive, James," he said. "And don't spare the horses."

I took us off the property and down through Tujunga to Lowell Ave. at a sedate pace, while Troll peppered me with caustic comments: "Well. come on, let's see what this thing can do. I'm ready to be scared."

"All in good time, my man," I replied. "No sense terrorizing the locals."

"Creeping around like this won't even get them nervous."

"Keypad for the sound system's under that flap on your armrest," I said. "Find some tunes."

I turned left onto the 210 East at the bottom of Lowell and, finding the ramp clear, floored the accelerator. I was pushed back into my seat, and heard noise from behind me like Slim Pickens riding the bomb down in Dr. Strangelove. I couldn't steal a glance at the speedometer until we were in the diamond lane and I'd eased up with my right foot, 140 and falling. I let it drop to 110 as we approached the exit to the Glendale Freeway, and, once we were on the wide seven mile downgrade, put it back to 130. Except for the cars racing past us in reverse, it felt like 80. Troll had Radar Love pounding from the speakers. I noticed the driver of a CHP cruiser, on the other side of the freeway, doing a double take as we passed and flipping on his flashers. I'd have scanned the police bands to see what kind of description he was putting out, but didn't want to break the ambiance, so I kicked it up to 160. Now, that felt fast.

In less than a minute we were off the freeway, and doodling along San Fernando Road at a mellow 25. Troll found Steve Miller Band's Sailor album:

Frank James, Jesse James, Billy the Kid and all the rest
Yeah, some bad cats, way out in the West
Those cats would've dug me and my gangster ways
They'd have hung up their guns, dug me to the grave
Cause I'm a gangster, a gangster of love.

"So," I said over the seat back, "what do you think?"

"I think your uncle loved you," Troll said.

CHAPTER TWENTY-THREE

Saw the numbers I was looking for, up ahead on the left, and pulled to the right side of the road, stopping to check the paper I'd written the R&D lab's address on. Correct digits, but it was a couple acres of fenced asphalt, sandwiched between San Fernando Road and the North/South railroad, with a big World War Two vintage quonset hut near the back fence, a dozen or so cars parked willy nilly in its vicinity. It didn't look like a high tech research lab, more like an extra inventory lot for one of the big auto dealers.

I waited for a hole in the traffic and pulled across, into the open gated entry, stopping next to a flimsy guard shack. The fellow at the window dog-eared a Carlos Casteneda paperback and turned to me. "Good afternoon, sir."

He was in his mid-twenties, blond crew-cut, white tee shirt and air of easy confidence uncommon to private security personnel. I said, "Is this Brown Micro Labs?"

"Sure is." He gestured to the empty lot. "Park anywhere you like."

"Thanks," I said. "Go Rangers."

He gave me a tight little smile. "I know a puking buzzard when I see one."

He stood and saluted. "And I know a Navy Cross when I see one, sir. Have a nice visit."

I raised my window, eased onto the lot, rolling toward the Quonset hut. "Sonofabitch."

"What's up?" Troll asked from the rear.

"I thought I was making a surprise inspection."

"Hey now," said Troll, "this gets interesting."

"Wouldn't want you to get bored."

"And you know I appreciate that."

A steel door at one end of the Quonset hut clicked free of its latch as we came to a shaded entry bristling with pointy leafed desert trees. Troll, half a step ahead, pulled it open.

We entered a pleasant, air-conditioned waiting area, with

comfortable seating around a kidney shaped coffee table, its surface strewn with an eclectic selection of periodicals and newsletters.

A reception desk of blond wood, straight out of the fifties, bisected the hut across much of its center. A tall surfer type in jeans and a pullover had one hip propped on an edge of the desk, chatting with the receptionist, a severe looking woman in late middle age. She glanced as we entered, and he looked back over his shoulder, then came around the desk, greeting us with a smile that said we were making his day.

"Mister Brown, I'm Bob Mosher," he said and we shook hands. "Delighted you've found time to come see us."

"Please don't mention it to the people at Century City," I said.

"Well, okay. But I can't control the grapevine."

"I know. I just don't want them to hear it from the head honcho."

"My lips are sealed."

"Good man. This is my associate, Mr. Salvatore."

Mosher's eyes narrowed as he shook hands with Troll, and he said, "Mike Salvatore?"

Troll's grin didn't slip, but there was a bit of steel in his, "Nice guess."

Mosher laughed, a little nervously. "I'm no psychic. J.J. Kline was my PhD thesis adviser, and he's on payroll here as a consultant."

"My computer guy," Troll said to me. "How did J.J. happen to mention my name?" he said with a lack of concern I knew was manufactured.

"As I recall," Mosher said, "it was at a weekend seminar J.J. holds once a year, Artificial Intelligence. Only honor students are invited. You've got a bunch of youngsters with top heavy IQ s discussing the nature of intelligence, pissing contests are inevitable. Who was smarter, Einstein, Fermi, Feynman? At one point, everybody's looking at J.J. to settle a question, and he says something like: I deal with geniuses like you people year in and year out. Most of you are super talented in one or two areas, above average in a couple more, and clueless about the rest of the world. But for unshackled, hitting on all cylinders, pure smoking brain power? I'd have to say the smartest guy I ever met is a biker up in

Tujunga named Mike Salvatore."

Troll snorted, "J.J.'s got rocks in his head!"

Mosher looked at me askance.

"I brought him along so he can explain things to me, later," I said.

"You're a knuckle head, too," said Troll.

Mosher smiled. "Let's go downstairs, fellas, I'll show you some weird science."

"Now you're talking," said Troll, and started for the pair of giant escalators on the other side of the reception desk.

"Sir, sir!" the receptionist hailed Troll in a loud voice. He pulled up short and gave her a curious look. She held up a credit card sized piece of black plastic. "You'll want to put this in your pocket before you step onto the escalator."

Troll took the card and shoved it into a pocket of his cutoffs.

"Got one for me?" I asked.

"You don't need one, Mr. Brown. Your profile is in our system, that's why the door opened at your approach. You have full twenty-four hour access. However, we generally have several experiments ongoing, so we'd appreciate a little advance notice, if you intend to drop in between midnight and six am."

"I have no problem with that," I said. "You're Mary Kelly?"

"At your service."

"According to Al, my main duty in this operation is to keep you from retiring."

"Set your mind at ease," she said, smiling a bit, "I have no ambitions in that direction. I know it's inevitable, but I won't be shuffling off to some plastic senior condo. I prefer a nice snug pine box."

"I think I'm falling in love," I said.

She sniffed, and turned back to her work. "Don't even think about it, you're not getting near me with that thing."

"There really is no privacy in this world, anymore."

"There never was," she said without looking up. "I heard about you when you were a teenager."

I retreated toward the escalators. Mosher flipped his sun bleached hair out of his eyes with a couple fingers, and extended his arm toward the down escalator. "After you, Mr. Salvatore."

Troll stepped onto the stationary top plate, then paused, as my phone sounded. I dug it out of the pocket of my baggys.

"You guys go ahead," I said, "I'll catch up."

I headed back to the outside door, heard Troll ask Mosher, "What would have happened if I stepped on this thing without the card? All kinds of alarms go off?"

"You'd have done the funky chicken, for about three minutes," said Mosher. "That would have been pretty alarming."

"You got that right," Troll's voice faded as the escalator carried them down, "I'm a shitty dancer."

My phone's display showed the call was from Leni. I thumbed the answer icon as I stepped outside, stopping in the shaded entry. The display said: Live video feed. Linking. A blurry image cleared to a live talking head on CNN, then narrowed to the date and time flag in one corner of the screen. It blurred again, and when it cleared I was looking at Leni, in profile. She was sitting on the edge of a bed or cot, forearms resting on her thighs, staring at the floor.

"Okay, honey," a masculine off screen voice prompted, "your cousin's hooked in. Just read what's on the card to him, then we can get you back to your place."

Leni looked over at the camera, then down at a three by five card in her hand, then back to the camera. She sent the card spinning at the camera. "Fuck you, fat boy," she said. "When my cousin gets his hands on you, he's going to rip your ugly head off, and shove it up your ass."

"Goddamn it, Leni!" I heard, then the display read: Transmission ended. I saved the clip and went back inside.

"That was quick," Mary Kelly said.

"I hate talking on the phone," I said, trying to match her faint smile, all the smile I could muster at the moment."

"Yes, I've heard."

"I do answer emails promptly," I said

"That I hadn't heard. We'll do fine."

CHAPTER TWENTY-FOUR

I rode down the over-sized escalator, spotting Troll and Mosher near the middle of the cavernous underground space, half an acre, unobstructed but for an occasional thirty-foot column and two concrete sheer walls flanking the pair of rotating stairs.

Walking to where they waited, I passed a man and woman in lab coats, playing cat's cradle with a loop of optic fiber. Another woman, very well constructed and wearing a tank top with Dream On across the front, sat at a console, entering numbers the others uttered as the loop passed from one pair of hands to the other, changing color and assuming new geometric patterns, none of which I recalled seeing when playing the game as a child. They paused for half a beat to smile and nod as I went by. I winked at the woman in the lab coat.

Troll's back was to me, and he motionless, gazing down at a long glass case, such as might be found displaying precious trinkets at a retail jeweler.

Mosher, who was monitoring my progress, turned as I came up. "Great," he said, "short and sweet. I didn't want to move ahead without you. This is cutting edge."

He continued, "You're staying at Fort Tujunga, you've become familiar with the surveillance system? "

"Thanks to Mr. JJ's got rocks in his head, here," I said. "Creeped me out at first."

Mosher grinned. "They do refine the term hidden camera, eh?. We're going to keep them quiet awhile longer, getting ready to test a self-propelled version, able to navigate inside a living body. If it tests out, we'll go public, medical applications will be endless. We plan to seed the technology in countries with universal health care. But, since Mr. Brown died, well, we're all trying to lower our profile. We stopped applying for patents three years ago. We'll keep our own secrets, thanks."

"Fine with me." I said..

"We've got some of the most conceptually creative guys on

the planet here. Employment is by invitation only. Pay's great, benefits? Fuggedaboudit. But the clincher? No government contract work." Mosher said, "Most of the guys working here came to our attention when they were fourteen or fifteen."

"How do they come to your attention?" I said.

"Five of us are team leaders, at any given time, and are much sought after as guest speakers at high school science fairs, in this country and Canada. We each manage to attend seven or eight fairs a year. When we meet kids who interest us, we stay in touch, make friends with their folks, help grease the wheels of the educational system for them. The small fraction who end up working here are the real stars."

"Is Brian McIntyre a star?" I asked.

"J.J. Kline says he's the best practical physicist of his generation

"This place is privately owned, right?" Troll said without looking up."

"And closely held," I said.

"Then, what's up with a Ranger manning the velvet rope out front?" said Troll.

"Part of a Delta team," Mosher said, "protecting two miles of track, and some secret comm installations. They asked to use our guard shack, we weren't using it, so we said okay. They owe us one, and keep out solicitors and Jehovah Witnesses. Guys rotate back to training every three weeks, they think we're down here, pounding out code, day and night."

"Good, good," Troll looked up. "People hear the word, coding, they go into a fog that's never known curiosity. You guys aren't so dumb, for a bunch of geniuses."

"I don't know whether to say thanks or demand satisfaction," Mosher laughed.

"Don't bother with either."

"I've got a couple questions," I said.

"Fire away," Mosher smiled.

"What's he looking at in the empty case?"

"The future," said Mosher. "Look closer."

I sidled over next to Troll, and stared where he seemed to be looking. The focus of his attention was a small pile of dust. It was invisible from a few feet away, but was the only thing keeping the case from being empty, unless you counted a piece of paper or plastic stuck to the clear bottom surface, six inches from the dust pile. I took it to be a piece of manufacturer's label.

"The way you're staring," I said, "I know there are naked women in there, but I can't see them."

"See the thing looks like a piece of label?"

"Yeah."

"It's twice as big now as when I got here, and the dust pile is getting smaller.

"What do you make of it?"

"According to the Big Kahuna here," Troll said, jerking a thumb in Mosher's direction, "what we are really seeing is hundreds of real tiny machines, picking up raw material from the pile, transporting it six inches away, and assembling it as a two dimensional figure, in this case, a triangle."

"Boring to watch," I said.

"Worse than a Dodger game," Troll said, "but the implications are mind-bending."

"Tell me,"

Troll said, "If the little fuckers can make a good triangle, they could build skyscrapers."

I turned to Mosher. "How much magnification does it take to see these guys?

"About ten power," said Mosher, "to know they're there, not much detail."

"You have a ten-x glass handy?"

"I think we can accommodate you," he said, and bent over a keyboard attached to a small monitor next to the case. He did some insanely fast typing for about fifteen seconds, then straightened up. "There," he said, "just lean over so you can look straight down."

Troll and I glanced at each other and leaned as one over the bubble that appeared on the top surface of the case. The entire area between the pile and the developing triangle was crowded with shiny little dots, moving at incredible speeds in both directions. As we watched, a head on collision occurred, and the pair of dots lost their shiny quality and lay still.

"Whoa," said Troll, "fender bender."

The moving dots swung around the crash victims with no appreciable loss of speed, and I quickly noticed three other crash sites. "Reminds me of the one-ten at rush hour," I said. It also reminded me, somehow, of battle scenes in biblical epics.

"Programming is still rudimentary," Mosher said. "In a couple years, though, we'll have them doing some complex behaviors, serious shit."

"What's next?" asked Troll

"Want to see some anti-gravity experiments?"

"Sure," we both said.

"You said you had a couple questions," Mosher prompted me.

"I was wondering," I said, "are you a real surfer or a Sears surfer?"

He replied. "I live at Silver Strand, but have a little winter place at Rincon. Days we've got heavy storm swells pounding, I take vacation time."

"Very good," I said. "How did you know I was coming here today?"

Mosher grimaced. "Your phone gave us a heads up, when you got on the 2 freeway."

"GPS?"

"Right. Only we can access it.. Nobody can eavesdrop on your calls."

"Leni's phone is like mine."

"Yeah. She wanted to get some for her new associates, we had to tell her no."

"How about my associate, can you fix him up with one?"

"Sure, no problem."

"Can you tell me where Leni is, right now?"

"If she has her phone with her, I can. Let's go to my office."

Mosher's office was back behind the escalators, large and tastefully appointed, no clutter, and big, converging corner windows which, if I hadn't known better, I'd have testified looked out over Wiamea Bay, on a winter day. Troll and I watched jet skis, towing surf maniacs to take off points on monster, man killing waves, while Mosher contacted Leni's phone.

"At this moment," Mosher said, eyeing his monitor and manipulating a track ball, "She's traveling South on the 14 Freeway, just went by Sand Canyon Road."

Troll and I crowded one side of Mosher's desk to get a look at his flat screen, displaying a map much like a page out of the local

Thomas Guide.

"That's her," Mosher said, using a laser pointer to indicate a pale cursor mark, the only thing in motion on screen. "She's moving right along, doing about ninety," he shot me a look, "probably beat you home."

"You haven't seen what I'm driving," I said. "But if she doesn't go home, can we see where she goes. I mean, what kind of range have we got?"

"Plenty," said Mosher, "she could be in Australia and we'd be getting the same real time data, maybe a second later."

"Pretty impressive," Troll said.

Mosher said, "This place is Sat com City. Satellite communications was invented down here, a couple generations before me, I can't take credit."

"So basically," said Troll, "you guys own the sky."

"Hush," said Mosher, "we can't have any talk like that going around."

I asked Mosher, "Mind if I use your land line?" gesturing to the phone on the desk.

"Mi telefono es su telefono," he said, pushing it across, "and I mean that literally."

I punched in Leni's number. It rang in my ear five times and went to voice mail. The only difference between this and the other times I'd called was the five rings. I had no message to leave and hung up.

Troll said, "She stopped moving."

"Don't bet on it," said Mosher. Troll shot him a glance. "Stopped too quick," Mosher told him, "Can't go from ninety to nothing that fast, in a car."

"She tossed the phone." said Troll.

"Be my guess."

"Let's go get it," I said.

"Good idea," Mosher said. "I'll keep an eye on it here, call you if it moves."

"Thanks," I said. "We'll call when we get out there, and you can talk us to it."

Mosher opened a desk drawer, as we were turning away, and pulled out a cardboard box the size of a pound of butter. "Mr. Salvatore." Troll paused to pluck the box out of the air. "Your phone. I think you'll find it simple to use."

"Thank you, Bob," Troll said. "It's not really a cell phone, is it?"

"Course not," Mosher said. "Cell phones are for the peasantry."

CHAPTER TWENTY-FIVE

"Feel like driving?" I asked Troll, as we approached the Lincoln.

"You know I do, but, before the new is worn off?"

"I want to get there quick," I said, "and you know the territory better." I unlocked and started the car electronically, got in the shotgun seat. Troll adjusted the driver's seat and mirrors, and took us out of there, sparing the gatekeeper an abbreviated salute as we passed. We went back up the Glendale Freeway to the 210 West, Troll commenting the 5 was a parking lot this time of day. He exited the 210 near Sylmar, before it merged with the 5 and followed surface streets to Canyon Country, putting us onto the 14 South at Sand Canyon Road. Bob Mosher called, and told us where to pull over. Troll turned on the Lincoln's emergency flashers and moved us into the breakdown lane. I jumped out as we stopped, phone to one ear.

The you're getting warmers changed to you're on fire, and I was picking up Leni's discarded phone from the base of a small yucca.

Made my way back up to the roadway and stepped over the guardrail, showing the phone to Troll, positioned behind the rail, ten feet to the rear of the Lincoln, and waving on good Samaritans who slowed inquiringly as they passed.

We got back in the car, and Troll blasted us out of there. Mosher gave me some simple directions for uploading the call records from Leni's phone, and said, "Once you've got them in memory you can boogle them and find out more about their owners than you want to know."

"Boogle?" I said.

"Our private search engine. Better than Google. Way better."

"Cute," I said.

"Cute is what we strive for," said Mosher, "cute and harmless."

"Thanks for the help," I said, "and for being up front."

"Not at all. I'm counting on you to cover our asses."

"I'm on it."

Troll stopped the car in front of his driveway. "Coming in?"

I demurred. "Too much to do."

"Need anything?"

"Since you ask," I said, pulling my phone out, and calling up the saved video, "Take a look at .this, tell me what you think."

He watched twice and chuckled without humor. "Your cousin's got some brass ovaries," he said. "Guy's voice didn't sound to me like he'd take many insults. And who's driving her car?"

"Think it could be Misdemeanor Mike?"

"Never have heard his voice, Lori might have. Think he's graduated to felonies?"

"No reason to, except this looks, sounds like kidnapping, just after he showed up."

"I know a few Marauders," said Troll. "I'll check around."

"I'll copy this to you," I said, taking the phone back, "so Lori can get a listen."

CHAPTER TWENTY-SIX

Rolling onto the big asphalt circle fronting Al's property, I passed a dusty, brown Crown Vic, backed up to the off hill retaining wall. Curious, I pulled next to the gate control, instead of using the gate clicker clipped to my Sun-visor. The Vic flashed its headlights and pulled up on my right. I rolled my shotgun window down. The face framed in the Vic's driver's window had the looks and grooming of a mid-level enforcer from Gary.

The face said, "Your name Brown?"

"It is."

"Officer Sand, Foothill Division."

A name well known within Tujunga's drug sub-culture, it came up during the poker game at Troll's, a few nights before, prompting half the guys at the table to whip out their Officer Sand horror stories.

"What can I do for you, Officer?" I said.

"A Lexus registered to this address was abandoned on the lawn at Richie Valens Park, keys in it. Captain McNeil sent me to return the keys and offer transportation to the vehicle."

"This is unreal," I said. "Had no idea the LAPD was so accommodating."

Sand seemed to experience sudden gas pains. "Somebody at this address is a friend of the Division." No hint in his tone the friend might be me.

"Let me put the car inside the gate," I said, "and we can go."

I slid into the shotgun seat beside the infamous Officer Sand, and used my heels to shove a layer of fast food packaging under the seat. We drove down the mountain in silence, but I had the feeling Sand wanted to talk. My peripheral vision caught movements of glances he shot at me. What you looking at, sucker? Watch the road, I thought, but said nothing, appearing to enjoy the scenery. I could wait all day. The older I get the less I feel like talking, and I never liked it all that much in the first place.

Down off Mt. Lukens, we were on Foothill Boulevard over by

Hansen Dam when Sand broke the silence. "I came goddamn close to nailing you, what was it, twenty years ago?"

"Something like that," I said.

"We kicked your door at five in the morning," Sand said, "house was clean as a whistle. Dishes in the dishwasher were still warm. You couldn't have been gone more than a couple hours."

"I left at 2:30," I said.

"Who tipped you?"

"A bad feeling," I lied. "I'd gotten wind some Mongols I'd been selling to were talking about sticking me up."

"You ran from a pack of bikers?" said Sand with naked scorn.

"Like the wind," I said. "I was holding three barrels of mini-whites, (100,000 pills to a barrel), a couple jars of Abbot yellows, (1,000 pills to a jar) three M-16s, half a dozen live grenades, five thousand hits of windowpane and twenty grand cash. I couldn't have dealt with the kind of heat dead Mongols on my property would have generated. Plus, I'd made a rule for myself, just a few days before, not to kill people stateside. I'd have felt like a real asshole, breaking it so quick."

"Hmmph," replied Sand, a real conversation stopper for which I was covertly grateful.

When we got onto Laurel Canyon Blvd., half a mile from the park, it may have occurred to Officer Sand his opportunity to question me without advising me of my rights was slipping away.

"Word on the street," he said, "is a hefty package of golden triangle heroin has gone AWOL."

"I don't fuck with junk," I said, "or know any junkies."

"You know dealers, you can find things out."

"Not heroin dealers, are you shitting me?"

"Oh," said Sand, "so, they're down low because you are high up."

"I've never been desperate enough for money to deal to people who are likely to rat on me, their mother, granny and little sister, after twelve hours withdrawal in a cold cell.".

"If I got a lead on this parcel, I'd be willing to show my appreciation." Sand offered, pulling to the curb in front of Ritchie Valens Park and lobbing Leni's keys onto my lap.

"In what way?" I inquired.

"I could take some heat off your buddy, Salvatore."

"Interesting," I said, stepping out of the vehicle. I put one arm atop the open door, propped the other on the roof and ducked my head back inside. Sand jotted his cell number on the back of an LAPD card and slid it across the seat. I picked it up, "From what I hear, first time you raided him, you found half a gram of speed on a gem scope, he got drug diversion classes. Second time you raided him, didn't find shit. Miss again and it's harassment suit city. But thanks, thanks for the swell offer."

I put the Lexus in the garage, then hiked back over the ridge on the elevated drive for the Lincoln. I paused atop the ridge, put the car in Park and doused the lights. Afternoon Santa Ana winds had scrubbed The Valley's atmosphere, giving the night time light show a rare diamond like clarity. The ground lights around the pyramid complex had dimmed to ten percent, default night setting when nobody was in the common areas.

Looking across the brilliant megalopolis, I pondered the odds of finding Leni. Without further contact, minuscule. I needed to talk to Sue Hu, because if Misdemeanor Mike was involved, she had seriously fucked up. Debating whether to call or go down there was left unresolved, my phone intruded.

"Hello, Julia. Feeling better?"

"Yes, thanks. Any word from Leni?"

"Not encouraging. It looks like she's been kidnapped."

"Damn! If they get her on one of those ships.."

"What ships?"

"Their goddamn missionary ships. I read about a reporter that went on board one in Naples, nobody heard from him for six months. He finally escaped, in Hawaii."

"The church?'

"Duh! Who did you think?"

"Not them," I said. "They all left within the same half hour. But Leni left last, in Al's Lexus. She didn't want Edward to think she was just falling in line."

"Who is Edward?" asked Julia.

"Church biggie," I said. "Seems to be Leni's case manager, ordered the exodus. Leni never has been one for taking orders."

"But why did he decide to clear out? Oh shit, Mark, you did not have hot monkey sex with a church member."

"I did."

"Oh man," I sensed a certain glee in her tone, "I just don't see how you could do that."

"I couldn't discriminate against her because of religion," I said. "She's too fine."

"No, no, that's not what I meant, at all."

"Then what?"

"Let me tell you about the only other person I've known who got involved with that church."

"Go ahead."

"His name is Alan England. He was Senior Actuary in my department, when I began work in the insurance industry, right after college."

"Alan was brilliant, a math prodigy, and rich. He came from money, had a big trust fund, and got paid more than anyone in the company except the CEO and CFO. If you're picturing some nerdy guy with a big head and glasses, forget it. Alan England looks like a Greek god."

"I hate his guts, already," I said.

"The first time I laid eyes on him," Julia continued, "I assumed he was gay. I mean, the looks and perfect grooming, unreal taste in clothes, effortless good manners. Let's face it, most guys that fine are queer as a football bat."

"Thank God," I said.

"I was shocked to discover Alan didn't have a gay bone in his body. I was having a conversation with him in the copier room, one morning during my second week, and I felt something brush my hip, but his hands were right in front of me, holding a file. I glanced down, and there's this tent pole in his pants, touching me. I was going to knee him where it would hurt, but he started apologizing and blushing, saying he couldn't control it. He made it seem so damn flattering, if I hadn't just had my honeymoon before starting the job, I'd have blown him on the spot."

"Sure," I said, "then gone ballistic when you caught him tent poling some other girl, at the water cooler."

"Probably," she admitted. "I ended up being the only married woman in the office who didn't have a fling with him."

"Want a medal?" I said, "or a chest to pin it on?"

"How clever," she cooed. "I believe it's the first time I've heard that one. Today."

"Sorry," I said, "it just slipped out. I'm really not much of a tit man."

"It's obvious, you're an ass, man."

"Ouch. So, wonderful Alan got religion?"

"He heard about a church in Hollywood, rumored to be crawling with attractive young women. He took a look, liked what he saw, started attending, classes, seminars.

"Pretty soon, the office hotties, who were generally at each other's throats on an ongoing basis, buried the hatchet and put their heads together. You see, Alan was spending all his free time at the church, had no more time for any of them. This went on for a couple months, during which Alan showed up at work looking a little more haggard and shopworn, every day. The girls were furious, thinking those church bitches were sucking him dry."

"When he was really suffering from acute lackanookie," I said.

"How did you know?" said Julia.

"I'm a guy."

"He stopped going, but by then he was walking around shell shocked. He was good enough at his job to do it on auto pilot. To his female fan club, he was polite but distant. He confided in one account executive, an older man.

"The account exec told me Alan had been unable to get past first base with any women in the church. Never had he been so totally shut down, hadn't heard the word no from a woman since he was fifteen. It boggled his mind, as if the law of gravity had been rescinded."

"Mercy fuck him?' I asked, skeptical.

"No. By then, I'd gotten his birth data and compared our charts, no Venus/Mars compatibility."

"Which means?"

"Sex would have been unsatisfying, for both of us. We'd each have thought the other bad in bed, didn't smell right, too hot, too cold, made the wrong moves at the wrong time. My body knew, and was about to knee him in the cojones, that day in the copier room. I couldn't accept it until I saw his horoscope. Alan wasn't having any, anyway.

"He was struggling to figure it all out. He'd sit in his office for hours, not moving. You could almost see smoke coming off his head. Those church ladies had knocked his wee-wee in the dirt, and all his brilliant mind now fixated on them.

"He figured something out. Everybody noticed the surge in his energy level, he seemed to glow. Then he was gone. Gave the company notice, took vacation time in lieu of working his last two weeks, and headed balls-on back into the church.

"I guess he did well, last I heard he was running his own church franchise, in Portland."

"And all the sanctified pussy he can handle." I said.

"Sure," Julia said, "but what he had to go through to open those slippery portals. You understand now what I meant when I said I didn't see how you could do that?"

"Yeah, I get it. Show a little more faith in your astrology. You said, I could hardly avoid getting laid that day, and she was the only girl in my vicinity. Too bad astrology can't tell me where Leni is."

"Maybe it can, It's a good subject for a Horary chart."

"What's that?"

"One of the older branches of Astrology, perhaps the oldest. I've been studying it for about five years. You erect a chart for the time a question is asked, and apply the rules of Horary to it. What time have you got?"

"Twelve past ten."

"Same here. I'll set up the chart for eleven past, and get back to you."

"You're serious, you think this can tell where Leni is?"

"I've never tried to find a missing person, but I've helped find plenty of missing objects."

"Like what?"

"Lost keys, jewelry, a stolen mink coat, a missing will."

"They wouldn't have been found anyway?"

"Who knows? But it's a pretty big coinkydinky that they were all found by people looking where I told them, wouldn't you say?"

"It would seem, and I'm not exactly loaded with options at this point. Let me know."

Rolled down from the ridge, parked under the pyramid, across from the reunited his and her Lexi. I checked the time, 10:30. China Sea's hours were noon to midnight during the week, open until 3:00 am Friday and Saturday nights. Today was Tuesday. I decided to go down just before closing, talk to Sue in the office, in case I wanted to yell.

The C90 was looking lonely, over by the elevator. It's not good to let a motorcycle sit too long. I took the gate clicker from the Lincoln's sun visor and clipped it to the elastic netting over the bike's gas tank, then pushed the elevator call button (when not in use, it parked itself at the top level). Before it arrived, I decided to move the gold bearing aluminum case from the Lincoln's trunk down to the weapons vault on the workshop level, popped the trunk, grabbed the case, and got back to the elevator as the door slid open.

I entered the firing range, deciding to inventory the aluminum case. Why not before? It wasn't locked, I'm not prone to idle curiosity and had bigger fish to fry. The two to three hundred thousand dollars represented by the case was chump change compared to the sums I dealt with daily as principal of the Albert Brown Family Trust.

What prompted me, finally, to count the booty? Robert Daley and arithmetic. Daley had peppered his book, Treasure, with many interesting facts about gold I hadn't known before. Arithmetic? Gold, at the moment, was selling at around a twelve hundred an ounce. Walking from the elevator to the firing range I calculated two to three hundred K should come in between twelve and fifteen pounds. The case, surprisingly heavy for its size, felt like less than ten pounds.

I set it on the floor behind the firing range, in front of the vault door, released the catches. The contents were folded up inside a heavy plastic lawn and leaf bag. I lifted it out, unfolded and pulled up on the closed end, sliding out the contents, three parcels of tightly wrapped butcher paper, sealed across the final fold with a heavy, round adhesive patch, three inches across and decorated with a two inch equilateral triangle the color of gold.

"Word on the street," Office Sand's whiskey ravaged voice echoed across my brain pan, "is a hefty package of Golden Triangle heroin has gone AWOL."

I'd broken the first rule for success and happiness in Los Angeles: Believe none of what you hear, and half of what you see.

"Motherfucker," I said.

CHAPTER TWENTY-SEVEN

Could it be possible the three kilos of uncut China White in my possession were not the missing load Sand was seeking? In a city the size of Los Angeles, sure. But I couldn't afford to consider it. Getting caught with this quantity of this cursed drug would bury me long and deep in the worst prison system on the hemisphere. I must assume it was Sand's missing dope, must infer he suspected me of being in possession (before I suspected myself). I should prepare to be pulled over (on some lame pretext), and my vehicle searched, or even Sand showing up here with a search warrant and lots of back-up and drug sniffing dogs. Flushing it put Leni at risk of a bullet, and she was innocent in all this.

I wasn't going down to China Sea tonight, or any place, until I figured a stash for this shit. Probably just as well. At the moment, I wanted to slap Sue Hu so hard her house plants would die.

There was one nano cam in the firing range, but three in the weapons vault. I left the empty aluminum case on the floor next to the locked vault, shoved the three keys of scag back into the lawn and leaf bag, and took it across the hall to high performance heaven, using the computer module there to assure there would be no record of my actions for the next hour. The nanos couldn't be turned off, but the program inputting the data they supplied could be paused. I got them all up on the monitor, twenty eight little squares, and hit Control/ Quotation mark, then used the up arrow to go from fifteen to sixty minutes

My first impulse had been call Troll for advice, but fuck that. He had so many people bringing problems to him, he didn't need mine. The first night I stopped there, while we were catching each other up, his answering machine fielded at least fifteen calls, nearly every caller entreating him to pick up, it was real important. He did pick up on two of them, apologizing, "I've got to take care of this." One he promised to send a bondsman, in the morning. To the other he said, "What did I tell you about calling here, motherfucker? Do it again, and see what happens."

I put the lawn and leaf bag on the work bench, next to the box the Continental's drive shaft had come in, pushed the three packages tight into one corner of the bag, and used a mini razor knife on my key ring to make an L shaped cut, removing most of the black bag, leaving a couple inches of extra plastic around the heroin, then used the flat edge of the crate top to press the excess plastic tight against the steel bench top, and melted it with a hand held laser, designed for heating stubborn nuts and bolts without flame or sparking.

While the plastic cooled, I stuck a paper towel in the drain of the deep hand-washing sink, and ran about a foot of water in it, then brought the package over and held it under for half a minute, watching for bubbles. It was air-tight.

Went through the tunnel to the right foreleg of the Sphinx, stripped off my shorts and tank top, and took the package down to the bottom, leaving it under the two-foot square brass grill covering the pool drain. It was the best I could do on short notice.

When I got back to high performance heaven, the computer monitor showed sixteen minutes before the surveillance system resumed real time processing. I retrieved the aluminum case from the firing range, closed the remains of the lawn and leaf bag inside it, placed it on the concrete floor, and reduced it to a puddle of slag with the heat laser. After cooling the slag with water from the sink, I broke it loose from the concrete with a couple whacks of a lead hammer and dropped it in the trash, reclaiming my seat at the computer a minute before the nanos went live, positioning my hands over the control and quotation mark keys as time ran out, so the only evidence of a one hour gap in the saved data was a single digit in the time flag at the upper right corner. Again, the best I could do on short notice.

Stopped in the kitchen on the way to bed, picking up three ounces of JD and a schooner of Nautica.

How did I sleep? Pretty good.

CHAPTER TWENTY-EIGHT

In bed by 12:30, I woke at 7:00, out of a dream so deep I was left only with a vague sense of things rearranging, beyond reach of symbols or physical representation. The agreeable, faintly familiar emotional state I woke into evaporated so fast I jumped out of bed, as if kicked, turned back and saw my pillow, way out near the middle. Don't pull a hamstring over a Jack hangover, my conscience sneered. Then the house phone announced an incoming call, from a coin telephone on the fourth floor of the County Courthouse at First and Hill. I wanted to occupy my mind with something besides a dream I couldn't remember, broke character and picked up.

"Brown residence, good morning."

"Recognize my voice, Sergeant?"

I did, though I hadn't heard it in a couple decades. "Cap?"

"It's Deputy Chief, now."

"Congratulations."

"I'm sorry to keep calling you with bad news, Sergeant."

"Don't be, I appreciate it," I said. "Sand, again?"

"I'm afraid so."

"There's something seriously off about that guy."

"He broke under torture. It turned him vicious."

"You're calling from the court house, don't tell me he's got a search warrant."

"Search warrant, six detectives, couple dope dogs, and a big skip-loader in lieu of a tank. I got a DEA agent on the team, so he won't be packing in any evidence."

"Hang on a sec," I set the phone down, picked up the clicker and got the front gate on screen at the foot of the bed. I opened the gate, and picked the phone back up. "I'm back," I said, "wanted to open the gate, before that skip-loader gets here."

"You've got an hour or so, he just picked up the paperwork."

"What did he show for probable cause?"

"Unnamed C.I., a smart criminal lawyer can get the name for

you, wouldn't hurt you to have one there when piss for blood shows up."

"I'll get on it. Thanks, Cap."

Unless you do something rotten, Sergeant, I can't let you go down on my watch, not and call myself a man."

"I'll try to be good, Cap."

"You do that."

I broke the connection.

Despite, or maybe because of, my resolution last night, I had to call Troll. I didn't know anyone else I'd trust to hook me up with a lawyer on short notice. I punched in the number of his new wireless phone, at least I wouldn't have to explain myself to his answering machine.

CHAPTER TWENTY-NINE

When Troll arrived with the lawyer, detectives had been running dope dogs in grid patterns, all over the property, for an hour. Officer Sand served the warrant, then stayed close to me while the others fanned out to conduct the search.

I'd unlocked every door on the property with the clicker before the cops arrived. They hadn't yet approached any buildings.

We were in the kitchen, I was cooking breakfast, to demonstrate my lack of concern to Sand rather than desire to eat.

Troll strolled in, dressed in Levis, boots, and a sleeveless green sweat shirt bearing the legend: Reality is for people who can't handle drugs.

"This guy's the best lawyer in Tujunga," he said. "I had to go get him out of court in San Fernando. Ara Sarggossian, Mark Brown."

Sarggossian stood a couple inches higher than my 6' 3", but leaner, with a great beak of a nose, Groucho Marx eyebrows above piercing green eyes, and a hairline receding into a widow's peak.

We shook hands, his nearly big as mine. "I hope you haven't been conversing with this police officer, without me present," he said.

"He's been doing most of the talking," I said. "I've held up my end with uh-huh and is that so."

"That's a load off." Sarggossian had the face of a desert sheik, but his accent was pure Glendale. "Let's get a look at the warrant," he said, then, while flipping through it, "Is this a bad time to talk money?"

"Here's five K, as a retainer." I said, handing him fifty hundreds I'd folded together earlier. "Let me know when it gets short."

"Sure thing. I'll write you a receipt."

"Don't bother. Mr. Salvatore says you're a pretty all right guy"

"High praise indeed," Sarggossian smiled.

Officer Sand, lighting a cigarette off a stove burner, gave a derisive snort.

Troll let out an evil chuckle.

I almost smiled, but decided that would be laying it on a little thick.

Sand received a call on his belt radio, swept the three of us with an unfriendly glance and walked out.

"What a fucking asshole," Sarggossian said.

"He has some endearing qualities," I said.

"Are you fucking shitting me?" said Troll.

"Why yes, as a matter of fact, I am."

"Heh-heh," said Troll, "too chilly."

CHAPTER THIRTY

Employing the clicker from Hell, I had two angles on the bronze griffins at the pyramid's ingress point, and the law enforcement personnel assembled there, on the kitchen monitor before Officer Sand reached them. Troll and Ara Sarggossian joined me in front of the screen as Sand walked out to join the others.

One of the detectives told Sand, "This property's clean, sorry, bud." He didn't sound sorry.

"Okay," Sand replied, "Let's get started on the inside."

"No can do," the detective said. "I'm due in Van Nuys Court half an hour from now."

"Maclaren and me got depositions in forty minutes," another detective said.

"I can't stay," said another.

"Where are the dogs?" said Sand. "Where are the goddamn dogs!"

"Take it easy," the first detective said. "We had to let them go, suspected terrorist activity. Look, maybe we can get one of the patrol units up here to come over and give you a hand.

"Stick it up your ass," Sand spat, and stalked back inside.

CHAPTER THIRTY-ONE

The monitor was off, three of us gathered near the stove, munching on bacon and pumpernickel toast, when Officer Sand returned to the kitchen. He picked a slice of bacon off the grill and folded it into his mouth.

"No more of that," I said, "you're not a guest here. Besides, isn't that cannibalism?"

"Fuck you, Brown," Sand said around the bacon. "Your luck's not gonna hold, and when it turns I'll be on you like stink on shit."

I looked at Sarggossian. "Is he allowed to talk to me like that?"

"Sarggossian shrugged, "First Amendment."

"You know why he hates you," said Troll. I looked at him. "Because you were fighting Chuck, while he was spilling his guts to 'em."

I shook my head. "That's why he hates you. With me, it's something different."

"Like what?"

"I'm the dumb ass that carried him out of the POW camp, he couldn't walk."

"Broke legs?"

I shook my head. "Fucked up feet. Don't give me that look, it was carry him or blow him away."

"Fuck me in the neck," Troll said slowly. He looked at Sand. "Is this for real?'

"If he says so," Sand grunted. "I was delirious with fever, have no memory of the event."

"Yeah right," Troll snorted. "Ara," he said to the lawyer, "I'm swearing you to secrecy. If this ever gets out, your client will have people all over the Rock taking pot shots at him."

"As far as I'm concerned, it's all been privileged communication." Sarggossian said.

"Sand, you are one sick, twisted fuck," Troll said, and stopped. Sand was gone.

I clicked the monitor back on, and we watched him storm out, past the griffins. I keyed to a view of the outdoor parking area, and we watched him get into his unmarked cruiser and flog it up over the ridge.

"Don't go away mad, officer," Sarggossian said, "just go away."

"He doesn't care enough to get as pissed as he's acting." I said

"Why fake it?" asked the lawyer

"So people won't realize he's a soul-less zombie."

"Dead and stinking," Troll said, "but he won't lay down. Pathetic."

"The guy's never risen above patrol officer rank," Ara Sarggossian said, "nobody wants to partner with him, but he's packing as much as in the department as most Lieutenants and some Captains. Being a soul-less zombie must give one a leg up, as a bureaucrat."

"Leg up, my ass," said Troll. "The terms are practically inter-changeable."

CHAPTER THIRTY-TWO

Ara Sarggossian pulled the wad of Benjis out of his pocket, peeled off six and handed me the rest. "Six hundred for the house call," he said. "And I'm glad to have made your acquaintance."

"Likewise," I said. "If I need you again, in a hurry, will one large now buy me twenty-four hour access?"

"For sure," he said. "One time."

I peeled off ten bills and handed them over. "If I haven't needed you by this date next year, it's yours."

"Very generous.

"Maybe," I said. "Let's hope so."

"I'm gonna run Ara back to San Fernando," said Troll, "then shoot out to Valencia, talk to a Marauder. Anything changes on that front, call me."

"I will," I said. "And, man, thanks for doing this. Sand would have been pushing the envelope a lot harder without Ara's calming presence."

"Calming presence?" Sarggossian said, "I had him scared shitless."

"As scared as a soul-less zombie can get, and as angry," I said.

"Sand does display a disturbing flattening of emotional affect," Sarggossian said.

"He'd be a sociopath, if he had the energy."

"If his get up and go hadn't got up and went," Troll said, "Though he still excels at seriously fucking up the lives of citizens who irritate him."

"I could tell you stories," Sarggossian said, "heartbreaking."

"Don't tell me any stories," I said. "He's not worth hating, so don't get me started."

CHAPTER THIRTY-THREE

Annette arrived at three-thirty, driving the hybrid Honda van she'd had three years before, when her two kids were with her ex for a week, and she extended the hospitality of her La Tuna Canyon split level, while I waited for my buy to come together.

She'd explained she never would have a man stay over when her kids were there, and was nervous about it even when they had sleepovers, the canyon grapevine never slept. She didn't feel nervous at all about me. I wasn't hooked into the local gossip chain.

"I'm sure glad to hear that," I told her, and took Mr. Happy out of my pants.

"Jesus," she said. "I'm gonna have a hard time keeping quiet about this."

We didn't put our clothes on again until it was time for me to go, three days later.

I came out the pyramid's front portal, and waited between the griffins, while Annette made her way across the footing, flanked by her children, a girl, seven or eight, scale model of her mother, the boy, just hitting puberty, darker complected, Latino blood on the ex's side. The kids had the usual homework backpacks strapped over their shoulders, Annette, a large duffel.

"Thanks for coming," I said. "Good looking crew you've got there."

"Rory and Ava," she smiled. "Kids, this is Mister Brown."

I shook hands with them, and Ava asked, "Is this your house?"

"I'm the caretaker," I said.

"Like a janitor?" Rory said.

"Glorified janitor, I can invite people over, and the house pretty much cleans itself."

"That is so chill," he said, looking around.

"You have no idea, kiddo," Annette said, and ruffled his hair. "How long do you need us to stay?" she asked me.

"Couple days," I said. "I'll be in and out. When the place is empty, systems start going into snooze mode, after a few hours. With people here, it seems more alive, happier."

"I thought we'd camp in the Sphinx," she said, "if that's okay."

"Of course, wherever you like. The people who split a couple days ago left a bunch of food, consider it yours, and help yourself to whatever you want from the pyramid's kitchen."

"Wonderful," she said. "Would it be okay if the kids invite friends from school?"

"Don't have to ask," I said. "You're doing me a favor, being here. I won't be around much, or be any kind of company when I am. Make yourself at home, and don't ask permission. I trust your judgment."

"That's the nicest thing any man's ever said to me."

"You're young, yet," I said.

CHAPTER THIRTY-FOUR

I dressed for a motorcycle ride, tying off and double knotting my British Army boots, and pulling the bottoms of boot-cut black Levis over the laces. I've done plenty of riding in shorts and flip-flops, to show my respect for helmet laws and the ciphers who write them. When high speed freeway riding, I like some leather between my feet and poorly maintained road surface, and a Dunlop under my genitalia..

As happens when I'm trying to get out of the house, my phone rang. A normal cell phone would have shown UNKNOWN on the display, my wireless displayed Trac Phone, an (818) number, purchased with cash at Rite-Aid Drugs on Laurel Canyon Blvd., in North Hollywood, an hour earlier.

"If I'd known you were going to Rite-Aid," I answered, "I'd have had you pick me up a bottle of brandy."

It took fifteen seconds for a reply. The caller employed a voice scrambler that makes the user sound like lead croaker in a metal band. "You some kind of comedian? You can tell everybody you're so funny, you really killed your cousin."

"You believe you're talking to somebody who gives a shit? I've got three keys of horse sitting on the back of my toilet. Bet I can flush it before your ten dollar air-time card runs out."

Another pregnant pause, then, "Don't do that. Your cousin's a nice girl, don't make me kill her."

"I know she was alive yesterday afternoon," I said, "that doesn't tell me shit about now…"

After some brief static I heard Leni's voice. "Mark?"

"You okay, Len?"

"I'm fine. They're not abusing me, and (a roaring sound overrode her voice for about five seconds) I just can't leave, or even go outside."

"Are you near Van Nuys airport?"

"I can't…"

Metal voice came back on the line. "Okay, you know she's

175

alive, take care of my product." The call ended.

I was pocketing the phone when it rang again. "Hello, Julia."

"How are you, Mark?"

"Disappointed. You didn't tell me I was going to be raided by the police this morning."

"Oh, sorry. I've been flogging that horary figure about Leni's location, and haven't looked at your current transits. But I'm certain nothing came of it, or will come of it, so don't worry."

"How can you say that?"

"The Moon was void of course from about three this morning, until a little after noon."

"Whatever that means."

"It means, during that period, nothing happened, or could happen, but a bunch of talk."

"Are you shitting me?"

"Are we going to start this again?"

"No," I said. "Sorry, I lost my head."

"Now, that's impressive."

"Not as impressive as you telling me where Leni is. How about it?"

"Before I tell you, let me explain: It took me some hours of noodling to dig the answer out of this chart. Sometimes, the answer to a horary question jumps out at me as soon as I look at the chart, other times, I have to keep after it until it says uncle. The weirdest thing about horary is, if there are no strictures against judgment, the chart always addresses the question, though it may not be obvious before you've worked out the answer. I'll tell you about strictures against judgment some other time, and I won't waste your time explaining the procedures I employed to determine direction, distance, and other details that may identify her location. You might want to jot this down, here goes.

"Leni's present location is somewhere in Soledad Canyon, which lies a mile or two Southwest of Highway 14, the Antelope Valley Freeway, and runs parallel to it, from Canyon Country out to Acton.

"She's on private property, in the company of people employed by the property owner, who is unaware of her presence. The employees duties involve the care and feeding of livestock, large animals, possibly horses, cattle, or even camels. There are lots of horse properties out there, riding stables and the like. But the property Leni's at has no public interface and conducts no business engaging the public, no boarding of any outside livestock."

"No address?" I said.

"Very funny. It doesn't look like she'll be there very long, three days at most."

"Maybe I find her."

"It's possible. One way or another she'll be changing location in the very near future, and her life doesn't appear to be in danger."

"Let's hope the people holding her are aware of that."

"If I can dig any more tidbits out of the chart, I'll call you."

"Okay, and thanks."

CHAPTER THIRTY-FIVE

Rode down to the parking level, my thoughts racing, set in motion when Julia Hoffman placed Leni in Soledad Canyon. I'd retrieved Leni's phone little more than one exit South of the lower Soledad Canyon Rd. ramps to the 14.

The C90, happy to be out of the garage, tempted me to run out to Soledad, and look for Leni, but there wasn't enough light left in the day, and I couldn't afford to squander any time.

Putted down to Sunland, and went slow by China Sea. Sue Hu's Solara wasn't in the lot, so I turned down the side street and checked the back of the building. Nope. I cruised side streets on both sides of Foothill for a few minutes without spotting it, then backed the bike to the curb, across Foothill from the restaurant, pulling it up on center-stand.

I got comfortable on the Suzuki, my back against the sissy bar, one leg crossed over the tank, and called across the street on my wireless.

"China Sea."

"Sue Hu, please," I said.

"Sue is not in, can I have her call you?"

"Any idea when she'll be in?"

"I'm sorry, I don't. But she'll be calling for messages."

"Is this Rebecca?"

"Yes."

"It's Double-D."

"I thought so. She left a message for you."

"What is it?"

"Check your email."

"Do you know where she is?"

"No. She left a note, here at the store, saying she'd be unavailable for a couple days, she'd call in for messages, and if you called or came in tell you to check your email."

"Has she called in?" I asked.

"No, I thought she would by now. Should I be worried?"

"Are you worried?"

"She doesn't leave notes, as a rule, just calls and tells me what she wants, directly or on voice mail. I guess I'll worry until she calls."

"Was the note hand written?"

"Yes, it's her writing."

"When you haven't seen or talked to her for twenty-four hours," I said, "you can file a missing person report with the police."

"Do you think I should?"

"If she doesn't call, might be prudent."

"Will you try to find her?"

"I'll check my email," I said, "maybe send a reply."

"Could you put in it, for her to call me?"

"Sure, no problem."

Took Sunland Blvd. into The Valley, caught the 5 freeway, and blew down to Los Feliz Blvd., up Los Feliz into Hollywood, through the back door, stopped for gas at Hillhurst, then moved away from the pumps and pulled out my phone. She picked up on the first ring.

"Lisa Leopold."

"It's been two days," I said, "you haven't called, haven't written."

"You weren't supposed to scare Edward half out of his mind," she said. "You call that acting wimpy?"

"I acted plenty wimpy and you know it," I said, "until he let his alligator mouth overload his tadpole ass. So, his unconscious mind may know we fucked like bunnies, but his anxious little forebrain has no doubt you scorned my clumsy advances and breezed out of the sauna, virtue unsullied, glow on your face notwithstanding."

"Hang on, I'm in the supermarket...okay, that's better. I was glowing, I just thought it was from the steam."

"Of course you did, and so did Edward, I'm sure."

She laughed, "You're so bad."

"I try to be good," I said, "but that awful Mr. Happy makes me do bad things."

"The bastard. I could choke him out for you."

"You sure you want to encourage him?"

179

"Or maybe a good tongue lashing is what he needs."

"Are you still at the grocery?"

"In the parking lot."

"What store?"

"Gelsons, on Franklin."

"Start walking East, on Franklin. I'll pick you up, on my motorcycle."

"You have an extra helmet?"

"You bet."

"I'm walking."

I shot down Hillhurst to Franklin, started scanning the sidewalk on Franklin's North side, after crossing Western Ave., reached Gelsons without spotting her, and reversed direction, to check out the other sidewalk. I pulled over when I got back to Western, and called her phone. Straight to voice mail.

I got the message.

CHAPTER THIRTY-SIX

Took the 101 back to The Valley, up through Cahuenga Pass, named for a chief of the Tujunga tribe, past Universal City, known as Desilu Studios when I was in grammar school.

My inner hurt at Lisa tricking me, and at not being able to tell Julia Hoffman her hot, quick and over prediction didn't hold, was rendered trivial by Lisa's making no mention of Leni, as if she wasn't missing at all.

I caught the 170 from the 101 and wound it out. Ten minutes later, I walked through the public entrance of the LAPD Foothill Division and approached the information counter. A swell looking female officer gave me an inquiring look.

"I'd like to file a missing person report," I said.

If not forthright in the information I gave for the report, I told no lies, except by omission, seeking to convey the impression that the church, having fleeced Leni for close to three million in cash and property, followed her home to find I'd been drafted to look after my uncle's estate until Leni, as is said, came to her senses.

They stayed over a month, as non-paying guests, engaging in various ploys, designed to pry some money from the family trust. Once I convinced them no funds would be forthcoming, they decamped, Leni included. The following afternoon, the car Leni had driven was found abandoned in Ritchie Valens Park, keys in it. I'd had no contact from Leni, and was unable to get a response from her wireless phone.

The detective stopped writing and looked up. "Have you contacted the church?"

"No."

"Why not?"

"Don't want to make them nervous."

"You believe they're involved in illegal activity?"

"I'm open to the possibility."

She scribbled on a card. "Please call this number if there is any change in the situation. If I don't pick up, leave me a voice mail and I'll get right back to you."

"Okay, thank you."

When I came out of the cop-shop and straddled my bike, the Western sky was aglow with a type of late afternoon back drop common to the big states, from Texas to the Pacific, cirrus clouds painted pink to red between azure strips of sky.. It may have lacked the melodramatic grandeur of those L.A sunsets in the halcyon days of leaded gas, with their green and purple highlights, but was more beautiful in its simplicity.

I'd been startled by the depth of information accessible about individuals listed in Leni's call records, though I didn't do much digging. I wasn't planning on marrying any of those people.

That asshole, metal voice, had given me a good idea, a throw away phone. I found a Rite-Aid and bought one, not that I doubted the security of my wireless, but some calls you just don't want to make from your own phone.

After assuring myself the throw away was functional, I tucked it inside a small folding tool bag, under the motorcycle seat, then called Troll's phone from my own.

"I love this fucking phone," said Troll, in lieu of hello.

"Because it never has a weak signal?"

"That and you being the only one who's got the number. I aim to keep it that way."

"Can we get together and compare notes?" I said. "I'm out of ideas."

"Come to my place, we'll see if we can squeeze a little knowledge out of some sketchy bits of info."

"I'll pick up some fast food on the way," I said. "What can I get you?"

"Nothing, thanks," said Troll. "I'll be digging into some Eggplant Parmesan, in about twenty minutes."

"Whipped up by a fox in a string bikini, you rotten bastard?"

"Hell, no!" barked Troll. "This ain't no Ragu eggplant, it's the real deal. And if you had a drop or two of Italian blood running through your veins, you'd know it takes a tough man to make a tender Eggplant Parmesan."

"Save me some," I said.

"Better hurry."

CHAPTER THIRTY-SEVEN

The secret to safe motorcycle riding? You must simply assume drivers of other vehicles can't see you, and if they could they'd be trying to get you. On the other hand you're immune to gridlock, so their hatred is understandable, poor souls, sitting there holding their steering wheels, hour after hour, day after day.

I made Troll's in short order, catching the 118 East, which became 210 East, off at La Tuna.

Pulling the C90 onto its center stand in front of the Apache pick-up, I heard Troll's voice from behind, and looked to see him waving me over from atop the detached garage of his neighbor across the street, a venerable widow who pre-dated Troll in the neighborhood, and who had come more or less under his wing since her husband's passing, some years previous.

I crossed the street and looked up the small extension ladder, reaching a couple feet past the roof line on the side facing the house.

Troll sat astride the peak, coaxing a black glob of Henry's Roofing Cement out of a gallon can with a very large putty knife he used to press the gooey black goodness into cracks in the asphalt shingles.

"I thought I'd find you sweating over a hot stove," I said.

"You thought I was cooking the eggplant?"

"You're the only tough guy I know."

"If I could cook, I'd weigh five hundred pounds."

He scraped the big putty knife back and forth across the rough shingles a few times, to clean it, then used the handle to pound the top onto the can. "Just let these fall," he said, and pitched can and knife off the side, then slid to the ladder, using the heels of all four appendages as brakes. I jammed my foot against the ladder's bottom rung as he stepped on, and kept it there until he was halfway down, then retrieved the Henry's and the spreader, while he collapsed the ladder.

The aroma hit us as we walked in Troll's front door.

"Jesus", I said, "this is what The Godfather would have smelled like, if they'd released it in smell-o-vision."

"The scene where Pacino blew Sterling Hayden away, at Giuseppe's Good Eats.?"

"Nah, that would have needed a little cordite blended in. I was thinking about fat Clemenza's spaghetti sauce."

"Well, kiss my ass." The voice was familiar, as was the form stepping out of the kitchen. "Nobody told me it was old home week."

My eyes adjusted to the inside light. "Why, Fred Hardy," I said, "as I live and breathe."

"Surprised to see me...alive?"

"A little," I said, "though I for one always admired your absence of tact."

"I believe I've toned it down some, over the years," Hardy grinned as we shook hands, "but probably not enough so you'd notice."

"Hope not," I said. "So few things you can count on, these days."

"He's still plenty rude," said Troll, "but in a pleasant tone of voice."

"Intonations are important," I said.

"Tell me about it," said Hardy. A bell rang in the kitchen. "That's the dinner bell, you guys get comfortable and I'll bring you some nice eggplant Parmesan."

"I'll throw a cover over the poker table," Troll said, "we can eat there."

"Doesn't seem like Hardy's lost a thing," I said to Troll, while we adjusted a small blanket over the poker table. "I expected life would put more of an ass whipping on him."

"Same here. When he jumped bail on that bogus pot bust, I figured they'd gaffle him up inside a month. He had a big bond, unsecured, plus the pigs had a hard-on for him."

"Over what?"

"What do you think, his rude mouth."

"Course," I said. "Hell, I came close to punching him myself, once or twice."

"And he liked and respected you."

"How quick did they grab him?"

"Twelve years, and he gets pulled in on a routine traffic stop, in Ventura."

"They couldn't have slapped him with much time," I said, "or he wouldn't be in the kitchen."

"A year summary probation, go and sin no more."

"He skated," I said. "Very cool. How long's he been back here?"

"About a year and a half," Troll said. "I forgot you guys used to be neighbors, or I'd have said something. He turned into a not too bad astrologer while he was gone."

"Do tell," I said.

"About a week before I got raided, last year, he warned me it could happen, started jumping on my case about getting rid of any stolen or questionable property I had around, said for a three day period I should have no dope in the house. Started to piss me off, harping on it, but then I figured what the fuck, if he's wrong it's an inconvenience, but if he's right."

"A drastic change of lifestyle," I said.

"So I gave him everything I had of questionable pedigree, some chainsaws and other tools, couple Saturday night specials, then stashed about three pounds in the garage across the street. Forgot the half gram I'd left laying on my gem scope. Second day of the three day period, they come busting through the front door with a battering ram, took 'em a few whacks. Another bunch came in the back door, hollering and waving guns around, pretending to be real men. What a joke."

Fred Hardy came back from the kitchen, carrying a couple big plates, loaded with layers of sliced eggplant, melted cheeses and thick red sauce, smelled like heaven. He set the plates in front of us, and said, "Troll was giving me some mighty strange looks, for a couple weeks after that raid." He went back to the kitchen.

I tasted the eggplant. "Damn, the last time I had anything even close to this was seven or eight years ago, at a little place on Revere Beach, fifty bucks a plate." I looked at Troll. "Shame on you."

Troll drummed the fingers of his left hand on the table and looked peeved. "I can see I'm never gonna hear the end of this. Look here, asshole," he said, as Fred came back in with another plate of eggplant and a platter of garlic toast, "did I or did I not apologize?"

"You did indeed," Hardy said, seating himself. He took a bite and looked at me. "He did, he apologized. It's just, I'd have felt better if he'd done it before Sarggossian came up with the name of the real snitch."

I grinned at Troll. "Shamey shame."

"Fuck you guys," Troll growled. "Let's drop it, you're killing my appetite," he concluded, and started shoveling in the eggplant, chasing it with bites of garlic toast.

Fred Hardy smiled his approval and looked at me, tilting his head in Troll's direction. "He's a sensitive guy."

"I know," I said. "He told me so, himself."

Troll grunted his annoyance, and kept eating.

CHAPTER THIRTY-EIGHT

It was a meal without conversation. When we'd finished, I looked at Hardy, "You didn't cook like that when we were neighbors."

"Like you'd have noticed?" Fred scoffed. "The only thing you paid attention to were my old lady's tits."

"That's bullshit, I noticed her ass, too"

"And quite an ass it was," said Troll.

"Was being the operative word," added Fred.

"She let herself go?"

"No way," Fred replied. "She worked that bod hard, stayed in shape. But she worried about her ass, worried so much it stopped being sexy, still firm and tight, but it lost the vulnerability that made me want to slide nine inches of rock hard love into it."

"Split up?" I asked

"Long time ago," Fred nodded. "She tried to make me stop using drugs."

"The cunt," I said.

"It was no contest," Fred shrugged, "I'm all about sex, drugs and rock n roll."

"And in a pinch," said Troll, "you can jack off and whistle a little country and western, long as you've got the drugs."

"There it is," said Fred.

CHAPTER THIRTY-NINE

"How did you become an astrologer?" I asked Fred Hardy.

"I'd always been interested in it, used to shoplift American Astrologer, as a kid, when I couldn't get up nerve to go for the tittie mags. Don't recall ever reading it, but I figured, from about eighteen on, anything denigrated by the scientific community was worth a look and might be gold. For me to actually buckle down and learn the basics took an act of desperation. Life had me in a pickle, and I was too tired for running back and forth. All of what I considered my hard won knowledge had turned to useless mush in my brain. I couldn't afford the services of an Astrologer, so I shoplifted the books I needed. When I could erect my own birth chart, figure the major planetary periods affecting it at the time, and read what they meant, it perfectly described what I was going through, indicated it would end in eighteen months, and would be easier to deal with if I gave myself permission to be confused. That saved my life.

"I started buying my astrological texts, in used book shops and on line, and began doing charts on everybody I knew whose birth data I could get."

"Ever hear of hoorey astrology?" I said.

"Horary," Fred corrected. "I started getting into it about six months ago, pretty trippy stuff."

"It can be used to find lost things?"

"Yeah. I misplaced my wallet a couple months ago, found it with a Horary chart. How did you hear about it?"

"My astrologer."

"I'll be dipped in doo-doo," Fred shook his head. "You're the last person I'd have figured to have an astrologer."

"Same here," Troll said. "How come you never mentioned it?"

"Just met her a few days ago, she was my uncle's astrologer, daughter of his next door neighbors, at his old house. When she was in college, he offered to buy her a car, for researching astrology, let him know if it had any validity. That's how she got into it. Seven years later she went to work for him. He said his net worth began doubling every year, from that point."

"Then he died," Troll told Fred. "and left our close personal friend here, in charge of all those ducats."

"Fred smiled. "I knew there was something I liked about you."

I smiled back. "Get in line, motherfucker," .

Advising Fred Hardy a chef of his talent shouldn't do dishes, I undertook clearing the table. After finishing up in the kitchen, I cracked a bottle of Michelob, took a leak in the bathroom, and continued through to the bedroom, where I found them fingering rigs full of Dr. Troll's Verdugo Hills Diet.

"Shoot out at the O. D. corral," I said.

Fred Hardy looked up. "Whenever I have a good meal, like that," he said, "it makes me want to shoot up. But then, everything makes me want to shoot up."

"Best get to it." I said.

Troll caught my eye and nodded to a loaded gel cap atop the headboard. I popped it in my mouth and chased it with the Michelob I'd brought from the kitchen.

Fred Hardy tossed his empty rig at the trash can, and huffed and puffed to accommodate his galloping heartbeat. "Jesus (puff puff) Christ. You (puff puff) ate that (puff) shit (puff puff) on top my eggplant? (puff puff)."

"I apologize, Freddie," I said. "Don't know what I could have been thinking, I'm such a Philistine."

"And (puff puff) an uncircumcised one at that (puff)."

"Damn. She told."

"(Puff puff) Don't they always?"

CHAPTER FORTY

Troll frowned. "No chance she heard about Leni's phone?"

"Remote. I don't tell her things, she tells me."

Troll shot a look at Fred. "Sounds like you."

"What's the woman's name?" Fred asked.

"Julia Hoffman."

"Your uncle didn't come out half-stepping."

"Not in front of me."

"Julia Hoffman authored the best text on Horary Astrology since Barbara Watters. She dragged Horary, kicking and screaming, out of the seventeenth century into the twenty-first."

"So, she's famous?"

"Not to the public, but within the competitive ranks of top-flight American astrologers, she's accorded a respect bordering on veneration. You won't see her book on any best seller lists, though."

"Why not?"

"Shit. How to explain. Okay, it's like this: Unless you can look at a Horary chart, determine the houses ruling its question, the planets ruling those house cusps, and their position and condition in the chart, at a glance, her book is too deep for you to swim in. Anyone who tries to utilize it, without having cast a few dozen Horary figures, will misinterpret much of what she says, mistakenly applying it to natal figures, becoming a less competent astrologer. It damn near happened to me."

"The old saw about a little knowledge is a dangerous thing," I said.

"You got it, Leroy."

"So," I said, "if Julia Hoffman says Leni's in Soledad Canyon?"

"I'll be real surprised if she turns up someplace else," Fred said.

"Here's the thing, though," I said, "when that asshole metal voice put Leni on the phone, she got drowned out for a few

190

seconds by a roaring sound, like one of those small jets that take off from Van Nuys airport. Any airports out that way?"

"Just Agua Dulce," Troll said. "But it's way over on the other side of the 14, from Soledad, and I don't know if it gets any jet traffic."

"Could it have been a lion?" Fred Hardy asked.

"Mountain lion? Nah, they scream, it was nothing like that."

No, no, I mean a real lion, like from Africa."

"Have them running around that canyon?"

"I was out there a few weeks ago," Hardy said, "taking video footage of some weird rock formations they've got. I pulled my car over on a wide shoulder of the road that had a good angle on the rocks.

"There was a chain-link fence, running right along the roadside, about ten feet high. I'm trying to figure out how to shoot my rocks through the fence, when I realize I've got a full grown lion standing about twelve feet away from me, so motionless I didn't notice him. He moseys over to the edge of the canyon, sends some signal down, and a whole grip of lions down there start roaring like hell, reminded me of jet engines."

"It could have been," I said, thinking back. "Good looking out, Fred."

My phone made noise, and I checked the display, another Trac phone, purchased within the hour, in Northridge, of earthquake fame. "It's your dime, slick," I said into the phone.

"That's right, funny man. Now, I'm gonna tell you how you get your cousin back, so pay attention."

"I'm all ears, slick."

CHAPTER FORTY-ONE

I took the C90 home, and picked out some lighter, looser clothing and footwear, took a quick shower, and checked out the pool on the bed's big flat screen.

Half a dozen kids were splashing around the shallow end, watched over by Annette and a couple other yummy mommies, on chaise lounges.

I needed to retrieve the heroin from the pool drain for my midnight meeting with metal voice. If he was Mutt, as I suspected, I needed it a little sooner.

Left the pool view on screen, used my wireless to get the phone number of China Sea in Channel Islands, and called the number on my throw away.

"China Sea."

"How late you open?" I said in a high pitched voice.

"We close at ten."

"Thank you."

Metal voice's instructions were for me to bring his dope to him at an apartment on Sepulveda, near Burbank Blvd., at midnight. He wanted me in the area, and would call me with the address when he arrived at the apartment. I would bring the package to the apartment, help him cut it and bag it, then he'd tell me where to pick up Leni.

I told Troll the gist of the call, substituting in a cash ransom, to not burden him with knowing I'd be transporting three keys of scag, thus not have to suspect him if I got popped.

When I left his place, he and Fred Hardy were discussing going to where Fred had seen the lion, Hardy appeared hot to go, Troll, less than enthusiastic.

I glanced at my watch, ten before eight. I figured the Lincoln could get me to Mutt's place of business inside an hour, then I would follow him back to the apartment and eyeball the situation before walking in with the dope.

I looked over at the flat screen, the pool area was vacant.

Things were looking up.

I gave it another twenty minutes before putting on my black trunks and crossing the bridge to the pool. The area was well lit, and would be for another hour or so. I slipped in under the diving platform and surfaced with the package half a minute later, to find Annette standing by the low board.

"Hey," I said.

"Hi," she smiled. "I wanted to be sure it was you."

"Anyone but me, Troll, or Leni would have been doing the funky chicken before they got anywhere near here." I put the package on the edge of the pool, pulled myself out and, catching Annette's eye, said, "You don't want to know."

"Oh. Well, be careful. I'm such a worry wart."

"If you haven't heard from me by the time you take your kids to school, might be best to head back to your place after you drop them off. But I'll most likely be back before sunup.

CHAPTER FORTY-TWO

I reached China Sea at Channel Islands before 9:30, and parked the Lincoln among cars near the supermarket anchoring the shopping center, giving myself a clear shot of the seafood place. The last seafood lover didn't get out the door until quarter after ten. An old Subaru station wagon coming from behind the supermarket ten minutes later slipped under my attention, but caught a beam from an arriving shopper's headlight, long enough for me to recognize Mutt as the driver. I let him get out of the lot, onto the Southbound side of Channel Islands Blvd. and fired up the Lincoln.

Following Mutt back to The Valley was like putting on more break in miles, hanging a quarter mile behind in the right lane. We crawled up the Burbank exit of the 405 at 11:53, and I stayed with him, South on Sepulveda for a block and a half. He turned right into a complex offering furnished apartments, I continued to the next cross street, turned right and parked.

I put my phone on vibrate and fast walked back to the complex Mutt turned into, spotted the Subaru three doors in, walked back out and straight across Sepulveda, taking a seat at the bus stop.

The backs of the apartments had small patios with waist high stucco walls, the glass sliders behind them backed with light colored drapes. Lights were on in the unit Mutt parked in front of, and in the unit to its left. The two apartments between Mutt's and the driveway entrance were dark. A shadow moved across Mutt's drapes, and I got a glimpse of his face as he pulled one end of the fabric aside and peered into the night.

Several shadows showed against the drapes of the apartment to the left of Mutt's, all male and moving about restlessly, too many for a no bedroom apartment. I decided Mutt was going to have to meet me somewhere else, and left the bus stop, walking South on Sepulveda. I started crossing back over to the street I'd parked on, and the phone vibrated in my pocket. "About time, slick," I answered.

"Don't cut loose of that cash," Troll's voice came back, "I got 'em."

"What?"

"Leni, and Sue Hu. I just dropped Sue at her place, taking Leni home now."

"Annette and her kids are in the Sphinx."

"Lori told me. That's good, cause I can't hang, and I don't think Leni really wants to be alone, right now."

"I'm on the way."

"Stop by my place, if you want."

"I will."

I pulled the Lincoln across the street, into a building's parking entry, to turn around, and stopped cold staring at a familiar vehicle, curb parked next to me. I left parking lights on, and got out for a closer look, the trash on the passenger side floor told me all I needed to know. I pulled my shirt over my hand and tried the door, unlocked.

I skipped back to my car and raised the rear shocks, then reached under the left rear fender and tore the plastic package loose from the top of the water tank, holding it with my shirt and rubbing it against my pant legs as I hurried back to Officer Sand's unmarked cruiser and shoved it under the passenger seat, hit the door lock with my elbow and slammed the door with my hip.

A minute later, I caught the left turn arrow at Burbank, and shot up the Northbound 405 at a velocity that would have got me pulled over in half a tick, if I'd given a shit.

I was crossing the 118 East connector when my phone vibrated again. I stuck it in its slot on the console and pulled down my sun visor. "Hello."

It was metal voice. "Okay, funny man, here's the address." I knew the address. "You can pull into the parking spot for apartment three, and we'll finish our business."

"Sounds good," I said. "But do me one favor."

"What favor?"

"Hold your breath until I get there, ass wipe." I lifted the visor, breaking the connection.

CHAPTER FORTY-THREE

Troll's street was quiet and dark, the infrequent streetlights on energy saving mode, his porch unlit. I parked the Lincoln behind his pick-up and walked onto the darkened porch. The open door seemed but a deeper shadow on the wall, then soft chuckling sounds drifted out as I came near. I slowed to ¾ time, took a couple steps inside and looked into the bedroom. The big oak dresser's top was cleared of firearms, and Troll stood before it, dumping scoops of Vita-Blend from a two gallon container onto a small mountain of powdered crystal in a giant Tupperware bowl, shuffling the two substances together with a pair of oversized playing cards, and cackling like a vendetta driven brujo invoking a deliciously noxious curse, or other such hindrance..

"Knock it off," I said. "You're having too much fun."

"Guess I am," he said, looking my way. "Button that door, while I catch hold of myself..."

I threw the barrel bolt, then went back and looked on while Troll weighed out pounds   (packaged in clear blue plastic), half pounds (clear yellow) and quarters (clear green). He performed the physical motions necessary to bagging dope with an economy of movement that seemed to me unnatural, as if the process had been subject to the machinations of an efficiency expert. Yet every motion and gesture seemed to proceed from a place where time was of no account.

"You're about a dope bagging motherfucker," I said.

He cocked an eye at me. "Don't act surprised. You knew I was a motherfucker, you knew I bagged dope."

"Guess I never thought about you, or anybody, being that good at it."

"Just takes years and years of practice. I hit my ceiling on this activity long time ago. Now, I bag dope whenever I've got some serious thinking to do. It keeps my body from fucking with my head, while I'm trying to think, plus I never run out of bagged up dope and start eyeballing issues, giving away the farm."

"Any leftover eggplant in the fridge?"

"You're in luck, Hardy was so hacked off I wouldn't go to Soledad with him, he forgot to take some when he split. You could zap us a couple plates, while I finish here."

"Then you'll tell me all about it."

"Yeah, but you've had the good news. The rest of what I have to tell you isn't likely to make your day, and I'm not sure I'm reading it right."

CHAPTER FORTY-FOUR

After we'd finished our plates of steaming eggplant and wiped up the excess sauce with hunks of garlic toast, I looked at Troll across the poker table. "Freddie may be a sonofabitch, but he sure can cook."

"Gets him a lot of slack with me, that and him having the nuts to stay on my case about that raid."

"Before or after."

Troll thought a moment. "Guess I'd have to say both."

"Still, he couldn't talk you into going out to Soledad."

"I was set to go to Soledad tonight before either of you showed, I just wasn't taking Fred with me. The situation looked a little delicate to risk bringing his mouth along."

"You went to Valencia," I said.

Troll nodded, "Talked to the Marauders' prez, pretty good dude. He put me on the phone with Misdemeanor Mike. I told him I'd gotten wind he was asking around about a friend of mine, said I might be able to put you in touch. He didn't want to talk on the phone, asked me to come see him, after dark."

"In Soledad Canyon."

"Yeah, Tippi Hedrin's place."

"The actress?"

"Actress and lover of very large felines. She took Michael Jackson's two tigers, when they got too big for him, back in the day."

"Tigers and lions, running around loose?" I said

"Pretty much. I think they make them go inside to eat, and they feed them good, self-preservation."

"Misdemeanor invite you to commune with nature?"

"No, he had me meet him a couple miles down canyon, at the fire engine bone yard, fire trucks for days, row after row."

"He had a key for the yard, we talked while he did a walk through, with a big mag-light. Dude seems to be connected like a motherfucker, but doesn't make any big deal about it. We hit it off from the gate, know all kinds of people in common, like the same folks, hate the same folks."

"Such as Officer Sand?"

"Mike refers to him as Officer Whaleshit."

"How's he know Sue Hu?" I said.

"One of his brothers steered her to him, she was having permit problems with her restaurant."

"Fits," I said.

"See if this fits. For the last thirty years there's been a persistent rumor, kind of an urban legend, the biggest heroin importer on the West coast is a woman. Mike says he's starting to believe it, and thinks Sue Hu could be the mystery woman."

"He say why?"

"Couple weeks ago, he took this chick, Tuesday, to lunch at China Sea. Sue gave them red carpet treatment, takes him aside after lunch and starts pumping him for information about Tippi's big pussy refuge. Mike's like what's with the third degree. Sue tells him she's got a lady friend who heard about the place, it's called Shangri-La or Shamballa, something like that. This friend is very well to do, and expressed an interest making a donation, or possibly providing ongoing support for the work being done there. Mike tells her he can put her in touch with the people, Sue says what her friend would like to do is spend day or two there, see things first hand before she makes a decision. Mike says he'll set it up, when do they want to do it? Soon as possible, Sue tells him.

"Mike asks her, who's the rich friend. Turns out he's met her."

"Oh don't tell me," I said, "let me guess."

"You got it," Troll nodded. "Mike did some consulting work for your uncle, when he was building the place, making sure inspections went smoothly, got introduced to Leni one of the times he was up there."

"So, after the people from the church pulled up stakes, Leni drove out to Soledad Canyon," I said.

"Right. Sue had met Mike there earlier in the day. While they were waiting for Leni to show, she enlisted him in her plan to help Leni. So Leni could help the lions and tigers."

"Sue Hu," I said, "always eager to help."

"You took the words right out of Misdemeanor Mike's mouth."

"I bet it was a dandy plan."

"If you can sympathize with the plight of an innocent heiress cheated out of her inheritance by a greedy, grasping, drug pushing relative, if you can get behind helping the poor thing reclaim her rightful property, at the same time visiting a terrible vengeance on the slime ball who tried to leave her penniless, then it was a fine plan, fine and dandy."

"I knew it," I said.

"Mike had a little trouble buying an altruistic Sue Hu, though. That's why he spent the afternoon trying to check you out, up here and down in Sunland. Talked to somebody who remembered you wholesaling H.A. product on the Westside, told him you were a rock solid businessman, who wouldn't say shit to the pigs if you had a mouthful."

"How does this make Sue the Heroin lady."

"He was a little vague on that, said it was just speculation on his part, so far, and he didn't feel he ought to be running his mouth about it. He did suggest I run it by you, if I had the chance."

"Implies you might not. Have the chance."

"Yep. How about it?"

"When we were burning up the Glendale freeway in the Lincoln, day before yesterday."

Troll's eyes narrowed. "What?"

"We were carrying three keys of uncut China White in the trunk."

Troll's eyes bugged out of his head, but he said nothing, it was worse than if he'd started hollering.

"I thought it was little gold bars," I said, lamely.

CHAPTER FORTY-FIVE

I recounted every detail of my recent encounter with Sue Hu beginning, as I pointed out, with him giving her my email address. "She's got to be the slickest liar that ever drew breath," I concluded. Even when I finally looked in the case, I expected to find gold, not something ten times the value of gold.."

"Ten times the price, not the value," Troll said. "Without the protection provided by state and federal legislators, it wouldn't command one tenth the price of gold.".

"And Sue Hu would be working at Red Lobster."

"Or Panda Express. Does she have any burning reason to hate you."

"After her man, Jackson, was killed, she wanted me to step into his shoes. I told her the war was at endgame, and she needed to get out of the country with her round-eye kid, got her on an airlift to Thailand, carrying Jackson's back pay."

"A woman scorned?"

"I did the best I could, for her, under the circumstances, for Jackson, really, but I didn't stress that to her. She seemed appreciative. Besides, Jackson was third generation Marine officer, and they were married by the battalion sky pilot. The advantages she gained as widow of a highly decorated officer would have lost some juice if she acquired an enlisted boyfriend."

Troll twirled a tuft of his beard and said, "She probably arrived in Thailand with enough cash and prestige to gain easy access to the poppy farming fraternity."

"And enough savvy to set up her own import apparatus," I said. "But, I'm having a hard time with Leni buying three mil worth of church, then ditching them to take up with Madam Morphine at the house of big cats."

"Seemed a little off the wall to me, too," said Troll. "When I bounced it off Mike, he said she wasn't leaving the church, only changing congregations, to Glendale."

"Why the change?" I asked.

"The supervising executive of Glendale's chapel and book store volunteered to put control of the Albert Brown Family Trust solely and permanently in Leni's hands, without involving the church or any of its membership."

"I return for what?"

"The honor of Leni's name on their membership roster. Oh, and I called Sarggossian, after I dropped Leni off, to see if he'd had any luck on Sand's confidential informant, Mrs. Andrew Jackson Jr."

"Which must make the supervising executive of the Glendale chapel and bookstore Andrew Jackson III," I said.

"Old Hickory is spinning in his grave," said Troll

"To say nothing of Andrew Jackson Jr."

"I asked Mike how he'd feel about a short vacation in Vegas." said Troll.

"And?"

"He said, with Officer Sand running amok in the situation, how soon could he leave. I gave him three grand and told him to check in with me when he gets there, which (he glanced at his watch) should be in two or three hours. He told me which cabin Sue and Leni were in, called the guy at the gate, and told him I was coming to stage a daring rescue, and to get the lions roaring up a storm while I hustled them out of there."

"I've gotta meet this guy," I said.

"He's our kind of people," said Troll, "no question."

"When he checks in," I said, "tell him to move to Luxor, after noon. The trust holds a big block of their stock. I'll see that he's comped to a suite and given house money to play with."

"Good. I tried to give Leni and Sue the idea, without coming right out and saying so, that Misdemeanor Mike has gone to join his ancestors. He agreed to play along, said he has to let his family and the people at Neptune's Net know where he is, but he'll tell them to keep it close."

"Think they'll call in the heat?"

"I'd bet on Sue Hu. I had a hard time getting a fix on Leni, not even sure she knew how they were gonna take you out of your position at the trust. You dump the junk?" I said.

He smiled. "Could be sweet. Worst case, he finds it first and some hapless citizen catches a whole bunch of time."

CHAPTER FORTY-SIX

I called Annette.

"Hello."

"Sorry to wake you," I said.

"No prob, I was just drowsing. Things okay?"

"Thanks to Troll," I said. "How's Leni?"

"Exhausted. She fell asleep on the couch, here in the Sphinx. I threw a quilt over her and let her sleep."

"You're great," I said. "Can you stay another day "

"Sure, Leni's nice."

"Cool. I've got a couple things I have to check on, see you after a while."

I took the freeways back to Burbank and Sepulveda. Officer Sand's unmarked cruiser was gone. I pulled through the parking area Mutt's Subaru had occupied. It was gone.

I got back onto Burbank and tooled slowly across Sepulveda Dam Basin, mulling things over. By all the timing, Sue Hu was Metal Voice. She couldn't call me at midnight because she was in Troll's car. The time lapse between Troll's call informing me he'd dropped her off at her place and metal voice's last call pretty much cinched it.

Officer Sand was too much on my mind, since I'd realized he was the little schlub I carried out of the POW camp. I would never have connected the infamous Officer Sand with the half-starved and scared shitless little weasel I packed half a klick to the LZ, dumped into a lifting copter, then forgot as I turned to deal with the flip-flop wearing sons-of-bitches who were hot after us. If I'd even heard his name it left me next time I peed.

When we were riding to Ritchie Valens Park I found his too familiar manner offensive, but chalked it up to bureaucratic arrogance and let it ride. When I reached into the car to pick up the LAPD card he slid across the seat, we must have been at the exact angle and distance as when I'd first seen him, but more importantly he had exact facial expression, one of shying away from too bright a light. For me, it was like one of those dreams where things you thought were real start to change, and not in a good way. I wondered if he felt me flash. Probably not, he's a soul-less zombie.

It seemed he'd remembered me very well, and I him not at all. I'd first heard his name from a regimental Captain I reported to during my third tour of duty, who resigned his commission after Watergate and joined LAPD on a fast track. His contempt for Sand was unvarnished when he called from a North Hollywood pay phone to warn me of the impending raid, all those years ago. "He's a rogue cop, who should be off the force and doing time, but the Chief's in love with his mother. Believe that shit?"

"Should have turned down the Annapolis appointment, Cap. Your life would have been different."

"Don't bust my balls, Sergeant."

"Sorry, Cap. I appreciate you risking your career, like this."

"You'll never tell them, so the risk is slight.".

I drove through a Jack In The Box, on Reseda, and got two tacos and a Coke. Jack's tacos remain, to my mind, the perfect L.A. food, and have endured time's march, staunch as Fred Hardy's rudeness."

CHAPTER FORTY-SEVEN

It was a little after 3:00 am, a period of relative quiet separating the last call drunk drivers, scooped up between two and three, and the Mexicans starting off to work at four-thirty. I traveled at the speed limit, obeying all laws, happily devouring my tacos and wondering how to best act when I saw Leni.

I barely recognized the street I grew up on. The trees had grown enormous, forming a tunnel over the street, neatly shaped.

The plant life in Al's old neighborhood, on the other side of Roscoe, had sustained no such growth frenzy, and looked more or less as I remembered. I parked beside the house, near the mouth of the service alley, a spot I'd employed as a teen, parking my van there and sleeping it off, when I was too plowed to show up at home. I shut off the Lincoln, rolled the driver's window down a few inches, closed my eyes and tilted the seat a few degrees. Dozed.

"Nice car."

I cocked an eye open. Julia Hoffman's face was level with the gap in my window, her eyes surveying the interior."

"Guess I was the favorite nephew," I said

"I could have told you that."

"You live with your parents?" I asked.

"I'm their next door neighbor."

"Oh. Makes sense," I said

"It does to me. I've loved this house since I was a little girl."

I smiled. "It's just like the one you grew up in."

It's got the same floor plan," she said. "That's all they share in common. I take it Leni's no longer missing."

"She was asleep in the Sphinx, an hour ago. How long I can expect her to stay?" I shrugged.

"Let's talk inside," she said. "I'll make some coffee."

I followed her through the pre-dawn darkness, down the alley, past the front of the big detached garage, and through the gate just beyond. She led me along the familiar rose bush lined walkway, down the side of the house opposite where I'd parked. The three step stoop to the side door was illuminated by a fluorescent coil inside a carriage lamp. When she passed into the circle of light, I noticed she was wearing a sleeveless tee shirt from Gold's Gym and raggedy old cutoffs. She had world class legs, I was suddenly glad Lisa dumped me.

We went through the laundry room to the kitchen, where nothing had changed in thirty years. I slid into the giant red leatherette booth Al salvaged from some restaurant building he'd bought and razed in the distant past, then re-upholstered every ten years or so.

Julia Hoffman went to an espresso machine, mounted on the underside of the dish cabinet next to the sink. She ground some beans, filling the room with a fine fragrance, tapped the grinds into a couple little filter cups and locked them into the machine. I began flipping through the mini-jukebox, mounted in a mirrored bay window beside the booth, dropped in a quarter from the ever-present mugful, and punched in Dylan's Ballad of Frankie Lee and Judas Priest, Elvis' Surrender and Tom Petty's Breakdown. Am I not subtle?

We regarded each other across the booth, sipped the excellent coffee and nibbled narrow slices of cheese danish.

"Leni returned of her own accord?" she said.

"Not exactly," I said, and told her about Troll and Misdemeanor Mike.

When I finished she said, "Jesus, that's some friend you've got there."

"He's remained the most interesting person I know, for a long time," I said.

"And no one was hurt?"

"So far, only their vanity."

"What are you going to do about Leni?"

"Act fat, dumb and happy she's back."

"Think she'll buy it?"

'I won't have to fake being happy she's back," I said, "the other two can ride in on its coattails."

She smiled. "Very bad boy."

"I didn't ask for the job," I said, "but I damn sure took it, and I'm too proud to bitch."

"What about Sue Hu?"
I shook my head. "I don't think she's too proud to bitch."
She chucked a little piece of Danish at me. "Smart ass."

CHAPTER FORTY-EIGHT

I picked the piece of Danish off the table and popped it in my mouth. "Thank you." I took out my phone. "I've got an email from Sue I haven't looked at, want to take a peek?"

"You don't want to look first?"

"If I can't trust my astrologer, who can I trust?"

"Exactamundo," she said, and slid around the curve of the booth until we were shoulder to bicep.

The email read: Double D, I am so sorry. I had no idea what those two greedy fools re-invested their urchin profits on, until I got back from V to my office, last night. You are only person I know accustomed to handling this sort of thing, hear Jeff's motorcycle pull up outside. Please keep safe, must send before he comes in.

"She wants you to keep safe," said Julia, "how sweet."

"She's instructing me to keep the three keys of heroin she just dumped on me safe, while she and Officer Sand get a search warrant together."

"Well, she's got some nerve."

"Fair amount of gall, too." I said.

"Lucky for you," said Julia, "they didn't have an astrologer telling them to wait until Moon left the void before moving against you."

"Sand wouldn't listen to an astrologer," I said, "he's a soul-less zombie."

She looked up with a worried expression. "What are you going to do, now?"

"I don't know," I said, and she looked less worried. I bent down and kissed her lips, "but I'm giving serious consideration to jumping your bones."

She curled an arm around my neck and kissed me back. "You don't know how happy I am to hear you say that."

"Does this mean we're astrologically compatible."

"Suppose we let you find that out for yourself."

She led me into the master bedroom suite, an addition to the original house, with twin baths, walk-in closets, and a circular stairway to a rooftop sun deck.

She kissed me again, "I'll be back in a couple minutes," and went into one of the bathrooms.

I kicked off my flops and stepped out of my pants, hanging them on a foot post of the king size cannonball bed. I began pulling my tee-shirt over my head.

"Holy shit!" I got the tee-shirt off and saw Julia Hoffman, stepping out of the bathroom in some diaphanous bit of fluff, hand still on the doorknob, paused in mid stride, staring at Mr. Happy with an expression difficult to describe, but falling between greed and terror. "What do you expect me to do with that?"

I smiled. "Make it bigger."

She did.

ABOUT THE AUTHOR

Born in Lynn, Mass. Came home crying first three days of first grade, because a trio of third graders was beating me up, after school. Mom told Dad. Dad took me down in the cellar, hung a heavy bag and taught me how to punch, told me not to mess with them together, but follow until they split up and take them one at a time. I thought he was out of his mind. But I did it, I was six and used to obeying my dad. It worked great. Two days later, my mother was getting phone calls from irate moms about her little bully attacking their boys. Moved to Los Angeles and discovered reading. Got in trouble for reading Les Miserables in class, hiding it behind my open textbook.

Left college after one semester, when advised by guidance counselor (who was also English Comp. professor) that there was nothing else I could learn about writing in school. Events from that point to the present I am only at liberty to reveal under the cloak of fiction.

www.ingramcontent.com/pod-product-compliance
Lightning Source LLC
Chambersburg PA
CBHW051248250626
47155CB00009B/3215